FATE OF BLOOD

VITARIAN CHRONICLES VOLUME 1

S. L. WATSON

S. L. Watson

slwatsonauthor.com

ISBN 978-1-954440-00-5 (print) ISBN 978-1-954440-01-2 (hardcover) ISBN 978-1-954440-04-3 (ebook)

Cover Design by Rena Violet

*For my Family. You are my rock, my compass, and my inspiration.
I love you infinity times infinities forever!*

CHAPTER 1

*T*he door chimed as I pushed into the Craft Haus. Familiar faces filled the tables and sofas with laughter and chitchat. A group of hipsters exiting the craft room drew the attention of the front-of-house customers as they exclaimed over their fresh-made soaps.

"Daddy, I want to learn to make soap," said a young girl to her father as I walked past their table.

The Craft Haus was a local hot spot, a one-stop shop for eating, drinking, and learning to make your own homemade beauty products.

"Hey, sweetie," said my mother as she wiped down the long stainless-steel craft table.

"Hi, Mom. Looks like you had a fun class tonight."

"Yeah, it was a great group." She tossed the rag she was using into the laundry bin. "All very eager to learn. Will you grab me the dish soap?"

She filled the dishwasher that was for craft supplies only. "The café's been busy today. I'm sorry I have to take off early, but Molly's going to stay late and help you close up."

"No worries, Mom. I got this." I sealed the lid on the

container of dried lavender buds and placed them in the craft cupboard, on top of the dried rose petals.

"I appreciate you coming in early for your shift," my mom said as we closed the craft room and walked into the office next door. "My friend Creagan dropped by unexpectedly. He's only in town for a couple more hours, and we're going to meet up before I have Bunco tonight with the girls." She untied her apron and hung it on the office coatrack.

"Sounds busy," I said.

She straightened her blouse and let her hair loose from the clip holding it tight atop her head. Her raven waves spilled free over her slender shoulders. "It's my night to host," she said as she smoothed her hair into a long side ponytail, securing it with a silver clip, "so I need to make sure I'm home in time. Calista's getting to the house early to help get things set up."

"Creagan's been popping into town more often lately," I said inquisitively as I opened my employee locker and pulled out the pair of maroon work clogs I kept at the café. I slid my feet out of my flats and into the clogs.

My mom performed the same task, only she removed her clogs, sliding them under her desk, and pulled her black boots on and zipped up their sides. "I suppose he has. He's had some personal things going on and needs a friend to talk to." She glanced at the clock hanging on the wall above the desk. "I should probably get going. Do you need anything before I head out?"

"No, thanks. I'm good, but hold on." I grabbed a tissue from a box sitting on her desk. "You have some mica coloring on your cheek." I carefully wiped the purple craft powder from her skin.

Her sapphire eyes shone with amusement. "Thanks, sweetie." She wrapped her arms around me and squeezed.

"Oh," I said, "I made some mini quiches and stuffed dates

for tonight. They're wrapped in the fridge, along with plenty of Chardonnay I brought up from the cellar."

She smiled. "How did I get to be the luckiest mom on all of the planets?" She kissed my forehead before releasing me. "I love you. Promise you'll call me if you need anything." She slid her purse over her shoulder and grabbed her sweater.

"I will, Mom, and I love you too." I fiddled with the hem of my top.

"And, Mom?"

She paused at the door and turned to look at me.

"How many other planets have moms, anyways?"

She winked and walked out.

She says the quirkiest things sometimes.

I hurried and put my bag and cardigan in the locker, then grabbed an apron hanging on the coatrack on my way out of the office.

Lively chatter mingled with the soft instrumental music playing over the café's sound system. Molly whirled past me as she bustled from table to table, her purple ponytail bouncing atop her head. Last week it was blue.

"Everly, thank goodness you're here. Ty is buried in orders, and two new tables just walked in. Can you take those, please?"

"I'm on it, Molls." I wrapped and tied my apron around my waist as I did a quick scan of the room. A group of teenagers huddled in the small sofa area at the front of the café, giggling as they watched something playing on one of their tablets. Excited vibrations swam over their group, filling the room with youthful optimism.

A few tables over, the sheriff sat in uniform with his daughter, his vibrations and aura tangled and constricted, betraying the positive exterior he exhibited for his daughter's sake.

My breath caught when my eyes landed on a man sitting

3

alone at one of the tables near the wall. Our eyes met, and the air charged with intense energy. His vibrations felt … different. My stomach tightened and my cheeks warmed as we maintained eye contact. I quickly turned away to catch my breath and pretended to survey the rest of the room, although everyone else had become a blur. When I looked back in his direction, his attention was on his menu.

"Earth to Everly," Molly's voice buzzed in my ear. "Are you going to get those new tables?"

"Oh, yeah. Sorry. I got distracted." I hurried and grabbed a notepad and pen from behind the counter, then hustled to the new customers.

"Hi, Sheriff Baze, and hello, Piper. How are you two this evening?"

The young girl stopped her doodling on paper and smiled up at me. "My daddy's going to let me take one of your soap-making classes," Piper said in her chipper voice.

The sheriff smiled fondly at his daughter, who had inherited his unique eye condition. Each had one blue and one brown eye, with each iris containing specks of the other eye color sprinkled within. Their unusual eye color stood out all the more against their shining dark hair and caramel skin.

"Well," the sheriff responded, "I suppose that'd be okay, as long as it's safe?" He looked at me questioningly.

"Oh, it's safe, Sheriff. We only use all-natural and organic products. And we have a class designed just for the youngsters." I leaned down to match Piper's level. "We put special surprises inside the soap," I revealed with a touch of dramatic flair, and winked at Piper.

Her eyes grew wide, and she clapped with excitement.

"Ooh, can I, Daddy? Can I?" Piper asked as she bounced in her chair.

The sheriff laughed, and his vibrations relaxed a bit. "It looks like you just got yourself a new student," he said.

"Yay! Thank you, Daddy!" Piper picked up her crayon and continued her doodling.

"I'll bring you a schedule of upcoming classes and the paperwork you'll need to sign Piper up. She's going to love it! So, what can I get you two tonight?"

As I jotted down the sheriff's order, I sneaked a quick glance toward the stranger sitting alone. His long, muscular form leaned back casually as he gazed toward the large front windows, observing the group of teens. His energy radiated around him, giving his skin a faint glow. He turned his head and looked directly at me, and my entire body flushed with heat.

The sheriff's voice cut through my daze. "And I would like a pot of your Headache Remedy tea."

"Okay, you got it, Sheriff. I'll go get that started."

My heartbeat sped as I approached the next table.

"He's so hot!" Molly whispered in my ear as she passed, carrying a tray full of rattling mugs and a steaming teapot.

I shot her a glare and turned back toward the man sitting alone. *Hot* was an understatement.

I mean, seriously, is he even human with those blue-green eyes and that golden hair?

His energy exerted confidence, but I could tell by his expression and posture that it wasn't a cocky confidence, just that of someone completely comfortable in his own skin.

He'd combed his hair back, revealing strong bone structure and a stare that made my legs wobbly. His honeyed five-o'clock shadow had the same golden hue as his hair and added an edge to his look.

I resisted the urge to reach out and gently touch the arm he had draped over the vacant chair next to him.

He watched me with a devilish grin, and I realized I'd been standing there a little too long without saying anything.

"Um … hi. My name's Everly. Can I start you off with something to drink?"

"I'd love a pot of Wake Me Up."

A sexy voice, too. Not too deep or high-pitched, but just the right tone to wake something up in me.

I caught myself staring at his lips, and a knowing expression lit up his face.

My mouth pulled up into a nervous smile. "Sure, I'll be right back with that." I fumbled as I reached for his menu, and it slipped down to the floor, skimming past my shiny maroon clogs.

The tips of my ears burned with embarrassment as he picked up the menu and handed it back to me.

"Thanks." I took the menu and sped away behind the employee counter.

"Wow!" exclaimed Molly. "I've never seen you so fidgety around a guy before."

"I'm not fidgety, Molls," I said as I fanned my face with a menu to cool the stinging.

"He must be new in town. I've never seen him around before," she said, ignoring my rebuttal.

"Molly—please stop staring at him. He's going to notice. Oh, and could you grab me a class schedule and registration packet? Sheriff Baze is going to sign Piper up for a class."

"Oh, that's great. It's good to see them getting out after … what happened," Molly whispered as she handed me the paperwork.

"Yeah, it is. Shame that—"

"What are you two gossiping about?" Ty craned his head over the kitchen bar. His copper skin glistened from the heat of the grill.

"Hey, Ty, and we're not gossiping, just making observations. Can I get a slice of the daily quiche?"

"Your wish is my command, my lady," he said with a bow

of his head, his straight, dark hair bending forward over his trademark bandanna.

"You're such a dork," Molly and I said simultaneously, and the three of us laughed.

"Okay, you guys. Let's get back to work."

I delivered the stranger's tea order. "It needs to steep for at least five minutes," I instructed. The teacup rattled atop the glass plate as my shaky hand set it on the table, next to his teapot.

Molly's right, he does make me fidgety.

I got an odd sensation in his presence, like he knew what I was feeling, and I wasn't used to being on the opposite end of that spectrum. I was tempted to let my guard down and use my ability to fully get a sense of his inner emotions, but that would selfishly violate his privacy.

It's just my nerves. That's all.

"Thank you," he said, looking at me quizzically. I'd been staring again for longer than appropriate. He was probably wondering if something was wrong with me.

"You're welcome. Is there anything else I can get you?"

"No, thanks. Just the tea."

"Okay, then. Enjoy your tea, and I'll check back on you in a bit." I smiled and walked away, feeling like an idiot.

I noticed him watching me as I delivered the sheriff's order. I glanced away and focused on the task at hand.

"One slice of daily quiche with a special treat for our newest soap maker, and for the sheriff, one pot of Headache Remedy with your favorite lavender-and-honey scone. You two enjoy, and I hope to see you in class real soon, Piper."

She nodded eagerly while she ate her cookie, crumbs falling from her mouth and garnishing the top of her quiche.

Such a sweet girl.

I looked forward to teaching her how to blend herbs into the perfectly scented soap.

The night continued to bring in a steady stream of customers. I tried to keep my attention from the stranger as I moved from table to table, his unique energy a constant presence in the café. With every movement, my body wanted to turn toward his table, but Molly had already eagerly refilled his teapot. I noticed him watching me more than once, but not in a creepy way. His vibrations indicated a curiosity, a curiosity I also felt toward him.

I wondered again if it was possible, but no, it couldn't be. I'd met no one else with my ability, or any unusual abilities, for that matter. Without thinking, I set the tray of dirty dishes down and moved toward his table. I was almost there when the door chimed and a familiar face walked in.

"Jasper! What are you doing here?"

"Hey, Evs." He lifted me off the ground into a hug and gently set me back down. "What? Can't I come and visit my best friend?"

"Of course, but I thought you still had finals in Portland."

"I finished early. I'm on my way home to my parents, but I wanted to see you first."

I looked up into his big amber eyes, and my whole body relaxed in his presence. "It's great that you're finally home. I've missed you."

"Now that's the welcome I was expecting," he teased with a grin, and there it was, that flash in his eyes, the same look he'd had before he left for a summer term at Portland State University. I'd hoped it was temporary, but now I worried it wasn't.

"Hey, Jasper." Ty popped out from the kitchen. "What's up, man?" He waved Jasper over.

"Go on." I nudged Jasper with my hip. "I've got tables to bus."

Jasper squeezed my arm before heading off to catch up with Ty.

When I looked back toward the stranger, cash sat on his table, and he was gone. My stomach tightened and a frown formed. I looked out of the front windows and glimpsed him dashing through the parking lot. He stopped at the guardrail that overlooked the river, and a man approached him.

Wait a minute. Is that Creagan he's talking to? I thought he was meeting my mom.

I moved closer to the window for a better look.

Do they know each other? Maybe Creagan was running late and thought he was meeting my mom here at the café.

I squinted. The two men chatted rapidly, Creagan casting glances over his shoulder.

Strange. I shook my head. *Maybe the stranger had just stopped Creagan to ask for directions to some place.*

"Excuse me, miss?" a customer called out.

I turned to attend to the customer, and when I looked back, Creagan and the man were nowhere in sight.

How odd. If Creagan thought he was meeting my mom here, wouldn't he have come in?

I'd have to ask my mom about it later.

I picked up the tray of dishes I'd set down and took them to the kitchen. Jasper and Ty stood near the walk-in cooler, talking excitedly about a video game they both loved.

"Okay, man. I'll catch up with you later," I heard Ty say as Jasper headed in my direction.

"I better get home. My parents want to see me before they leave on their trip. I'll see you tomorrow?" he asked.

"Yeah, I'm off tomorrow. Come by in the morning, and I'll make breakfast."

"Deal!" Jasper kissed the top of my head and left the kitchen.

The rest of the night flew by, and before I knew it, it was closing time.

Molly and Ty helped clean the café to a shine, and the

9

three of us were just heading for the door when the phone rang.

"You two go on. I'll lock up. It's probably just my mom calling to see how the night went."

I ran to get the phone before the automated voice mail answered. "Craft Haus Café. How may I help you?"

"Everly!" the voice demanded.

My senses went on immediate alert.

"This is Everly. Who am I speaking to?"

"Everly—" a man said in a frantic whisper and paused. Ruffling sounds came from the other end, and then the voice spoke again. "This is Creagan. I need to see you. It's urgent. Can I meet you at the café?"

I hadn't realized it was Creagan's voice at first. He normally sounded calm and soft-spoken, but now his tone carried grit and tension—like he was desperate.

Mom must have told him I was here when they met up earlier, but that didn't explain why he would need to see me. Why hadn't he come in earlier, when I saw him talking with the stranger?

"I don't know," I responded. "I'm just closing up the café and heading out. You can tell me now over the phone." I glanced nervously at the front door. I'd left it unlocked when I ran to answer the phone. A creepiness crawled up the back of my neck.

"It must be in person. I don't mean to frighten you, but you'll understand once you know what I need to tell you."

I hesitated to respond, but Creagan was a friend of my mother's, and I'd sensed nothing mistrustful of him over the years.

"How soon can you be here?" I asked him.

"I'm five minutes away."

"Okay, I was just locking up. I'll wait for you out front."

There was no answer on the other end, and the call disconnected.

I locked up the café and got in my car, which was parked in the space right out front of the entrance. I locked my car doors, then started the engine and kept it idling as I waited. The tone of Creagan's voice unsettled me. I sensed he was genuinely afraid of something or someone. Maybe that was what he wanted to tell me. But why would he come to me? We barely knew each other outside of the occasional chitchat when he visited my mom.

Five minutes passed, and no sign of him. I glanced out of my windshield and side windows to see if anyone was heading in my direction. The sky was dark and lit only by the stars and a few streetlights, so it was hard to see too far into the distance, but no pedestrians were within visible range, and no vehicles drove in my direction. I waited another ten minutes, then put the car in gear and backed out of my parking spot. Just to be safe, I drove around the block in case he was running behind. Unsure of whether he was driving or walking, I had already waited for a sufficient amount of time. With a dreadful feeling in my gut, I made my way home, a nagging sense of unease lingering in the air.

CHAPTER 2

$\mathscr{B}$right lights were aglow in the windows on all three floors of our house as I pulled into the drive, and several vehicles were parked in the front gravel lot, which didn't surprise me. Bunco night could sometimes last until the early hours of the morning with my mom's eccentric group of friends. I drove around to the back of the house and parked in my normal spot, closest to the guest house, which I'd turned into my own apartment after high school graduation.

Leaning against my car, I couldn't help but replay the odd phone call with Creagan in my mind.

There was fear in his voice, I'm sure of it, but why? What could he have been afraid of that involved telling me something so urgent?

I considered talking to my mom about it tonight, but then a flickering light coming from one of the third-floor windows caught my attention, and I saw shadows dancing from within the room.

I'd wait until tomorrow. I didn't want to interrupt her good time.

Creagan's strange behavior must have a reasonable explanation.

I walked through the outdoor herb garden and closed my eyes, breathing in the herbal scents. Echoes of laughter escaped the house and mingled with the chirping of the hiding crickets and tree frogs. A light wind blew and rustled a nearby lavender bush. I reached out and picked a stem covered in plump purple buds, then rolled it between the palms of my hands. The freshly crushed buds released an intoxicating scent.

Sensing an unfamiliar energy, I paused in my tracks. It wasn't coming from the house. I peered out at the dark forest of Douglas fir trees surrounding our property. Something angry was lurking in their shadows. I scanned the woods, but it was too dark to see anything out there. The creeping sensation I had back at the café returned, and the back of my neck prickled with goose bumps. I let down my guard just slightly and allowed my "sixth sense," as I liked to call it, to activate. Closing my eyes, I focused on what direction the vibrations came from. It wasn't an animal—the make of the energy felt connected to a person. I focused harder on tracking the energy back to its source, but it was fading deeper into the woods. I took a few steps toward the trees and considered following it, but then I heard the back porch door creak open.

"Hey, Evs," called a familiar voice. "Come in here and help us win some of our cash back from your mom, will ya?"

My guard snapped back into place as I turned toward the silhouette leaning out of the partially opened door.

"Ha! I know better than to bet against Mom when she's on a roll. You guys are on your own tonight. I'm exhausted and gonna call it a night."

"Okay, hon." She smiled. "Get some rest."

"Thanks, Selkie. Will you tell my mom that I'm home and calling it a night?"

"You got it, Evs. See you later, sweetie."

I turned back toward the forest as my guard slipped back down. A wave of sensations completely engulfed me as I opened myself up to *feeling* everything. Emotions of love and friendship and a touch of envy vibrated from the house, but nothing came from the woods. Whatever had been lurking there before was gone now.

I pulled my phone out and dialed Jasper's number as I headed toward my apartment.

Jasper's voice answered. "Hey, Ev. What's up?"

"Are you busy?"

I heard clicking on the other end of the line. "Nope, just surfing the net and plotting out my next Warcraft move. Why?"

"Can you come over? Something kind of weird happened tonight."

"Of course. But what's going on?" Jasper must have set his phone down and switched to speaker mode, because his voice faded in and out with his movements.

I stopped on my deck and looked out at the woods, searching again for anything out of the ordinary. "Now, don't freak out, but I sensed someone lurking around out in the woods when I got home tonight. Whoever it was is gone now, or far enough away that I can't sense their presence anymore, but I'm a little uneasy, and I was hoping you'd come check the area with me."

Keys jingled over the speaker. "Is your mom home?" Jasper's tone had gone from casual to serious.

"Yeah, but it's her girls' night, and I don't want to worry them all, since whoever it was seems to have moved on."

"I'm on my way. I'll be there in five."

"Thanks, Jasp."

I slid the key into the doorknob to unlock my apartment door and paused, feeling for any vibrations just to be sure before I went inside. The experience with Creagan and then the presence in the woods had put me on edge. I shook my head. I was probably just tired and overreacting.

I flipped on the lights and tossed my bag onto the small kitchen island counter top, next to my unfinished crossword puzzle. The temperature wasn't cold, but my bones trembled with a chill. I clicked the thermostat up a couple of degrees and grabbed the hooded sweater I'd left hanging over one of the bar stools. I pulled the sweater down over my head and readjusted my ponytail.

Jasper's Ninja motorcycle crunched over the gravel as he parked out front. I opened the utility drawer in the kitchen and found two small flashlights and clicked the buttons to make sure they both had some life, then hurried back outside.

Jasper was already off his bike and scanning the woods with a baseball bat strapped to his back. "What direction did you sense the energy coming from?"

"I'm not exactly sure. Someone interrupted me while I was trying to figure it out, and then it disappeared. I don't sense anything now, but I'd feel better having a look around. Here." I tossed him a flashlight and started walking toward the woods.

Jasper moved to block my path, his tall frame hovering over me. "Oh, no you don't. I'm going to look around by myself. You should go inside the house with your mom."

I met Jasper's stern expression with my own. "That's totally out of the question. No way am I letting you go out there alone, and besides, I'm the one with the ability. Someone could sneak up on you without you knowing."

Jasper narrowed his eyes. "Why are you so stubborn?"

"Why are you so overprotective?" I countered.

He released a sigh. "Okay, but stay behind me."

"Seriously, Jasp. Have you forgotten that we hold the same-level black belt?"

His scowl deepened, and his posture remained fixed in place.

"All right, fine," I acquiesced. "Let's just get moving."

Jasper turned, and we both crept toward the woods. I was thankful I'd put the sweater on, since the temperature seemed to have dropped a few degrees already.

Jasper pointed, indicating which direction he wanted to go. His dark hair and clothing blended with the night shadows as he led the way into the forest.

The tree-tops created a canopy of darkness, making it impossible to see what was in front of us.

Something soft and sticky clung to my forehead, and I reached up to peel the spiderweb I had just walked through from my skin.

I carefully clicked on my flashlight inside my sweater pocket to muffle any noise as we wove between trees. Jasper left his flashlight unused in his pocket. Instead, he pulled his baseball bat from his backpack and held it poised to swing.

The scratch of claws on bark caught my attention, and I turned, pointing my flashlight to see a raccoon scurrying up a tree. It stopped for a moment and observed us. The light of my flashlight reflected in its pitch-black eyes before it disappeared somewhere into the branches.

Jasper cinched up to my side. "Do you sense anything?"

"No. It's just us and the night creatures. It must have just been someone passing through. Maybe one of the neighbors was upset and walking it off through the woods."

Jasper looked at me with a dubious expression. "Yeah, maybe, but I'm staying over tonight just to be safe."

The wind rustled through the leaves, causing me to shiver and adding a stutter to my words. "I … I'd like that. It's been a … a weird night."

"Come on. Let's get you back to some warmth." Jasper wrapped his arm around me, and I got a whiff of spice and wood from his leather jacket as we ran arm in arm back to my apartment.

We flew up the balcony steps, taking two at a time, and pushed through my front door. "Ahh … It feels so good in here." My jaw jittered as I pulled a fleece blanket out of the small, round cream-colored storage ottoman and hopped onto the matching sofa, tucking the blanket over me. The soft fleece quickly warmed my skin.

Glasses clinked from the kitchen as Jasper rummaged through the cupboard and pulled out two mugs. He heaped cocoa powder into each mug without measuring, as usual. I'd given up on asking him to use the measuring scoop years ago.

The kitchen and living room made up one large space in the apartment's open floor plan, each distinguished by its furniture and fixtures.

Jasper moved around with comfort and familiarity, pulling out the cinnamon and whipped cream. He'd shed his leather jacket when we came in, and his bronze skin stood out against his dark-cocoa hair and snug black T-shirt and black cargo pants. He looked at me out of the corner of his eye, and his mouth lifted in a smile when he saw me watching him.

"So, tell me what happened earlier that got you weirded out," he said over the running kitchen faucet as he filled the kettle.

My eyes drifted to a framed picture of the two of us, taken on the beach, that was propped on my wooden bookcase. Jasper was laughing about something just as the image was captured and had a big cheesy smile on his face.

"Well, you know my mom's friend Creagan, who visits from out of town sometimes?"

Jasper nodded, leaning against the kitchen island. "Yeah, what about him?" he said, tilting the whipped cream toward his mouth and filling it with cream.

"I got this really strange phone call from him tonight, when I was closing the café. He said he had something urgent to tell me and insisted on meeting right away. I waited for him, but then he never showed. It was totally weird, and his voice sounded … I don't know … afraid?"

Jasper's brow furrowed. "That is strange. I wonder what it was all about." He pulled the whistling kettle from the stove and filled our mugs, spraying them with whipped cream and sprinkling the tops with cinnamon.

"I have no idea," I replied, pulling my ponytail free and transforming it into a loose bun. The tightness in my scalp relaxed immediately.

"It's not like we were that close. He and my mom usually spend their time together away from the house when he visits. In fact, she left the café early today to meet him while he was passing through. I'm going to talk to her about it tomorrow."

Jasper sat down next to me and said, "That's a good idea. I think you should mention the presence in the woods, too. Even if it was just a neighbor, she should know." He took a big mouthful of whipped cream from his mug, giving himself a creamy mustache. "How do I look? Irresistible?" He wiggled his eyebrows, and his amber eyes twinkled with mischief.

"More like a doofus. How about me?" I dipped my lips in the frothy whipped cream and smiled as the melting cream slid down my chin.

Jasper reached over and scooped the dripping cream from my chin, then ate it off his finger. "You look like a sugar-coated goddess."

I rolled my eyes. "Like I said, doofus." I gulped down my cocoa. "Well, I'm beat." I set my mug down next to the lamp on the end table. "I'll go get you a pillow and blanket."

"Hey, now. Wouldn't you feel safer with this big hunk of muscle snuggled up next to you?"

"In your dreams." I ruffled the top of his dark, wavy hair. And there it was, that look again. The unspoken look that said he wanted *more*.

More of something I'm not sure I'm ready for.

"Oh, ouch." Jasper dramatically placed his hand over his heart.

I averted my attention to picking up my empty mug and hoped he wouldn't voice the words that had been on the tip of his tongue so many times recently.

He stood up and smiled awkwardly. "I'll go grab the blanket and pillow, Ev."

"Thanks for staying." I lifted the throw pillows from the sofa and tossed them next to the ottoman to make more room for Jasper.

"Of course," he replied, then turned down the hall toward the linen closet.

A silent tension hung in the air as we both moved quietly, completing our tasks. Jasper settled onto the sofa, while I flipped the lights off. His fingers brushed my arm when I leaned near to switch off the end-table lamp. "Night, Ev. I'm here if you need a warm body to snuggle up to." He laughed, and I pulled his blanket over his head.

"Night, Jasp," I said, sternly.

I closed my bedroom door and pulled out the sketchbook and colored pencils I kept in my nightstand drawer. My hand started moving across the page, and after a few minutes, a pair of blue-green eyes stared back at me from the paper.

Would I ever see those eyes again?

I tossed the sketchbook aside and opened my journal, adding today's entry.

I stared at my last words:

What was Creagan trying to tell me, and why did he sound so afraid?

CHAPTER 3

*J*asper headed out after an early breakfast of eggs and coffee, and I was just finishing up my workout when a loud knocking on my front door startled me. I fell forward out of my Crow Pose, and grabbed my workout towel off the floor, then quickly dabbed a bead of sweat from my forehead before it dripped in my eye. The knocking grew more persistent as I made my way to the door.

"Okay, okay, I'm coming."

I opened the front door to Selkie's fist, swinging midair for another attack on the door.

"Whoa—whoa, put 'em down, slugger." I held my hands up in a boxer's block for show.

The expression on Selkie's face told me she didn't find my joke amusing.

"Oh, Everly. You need to come to the house immediately. Something … has happened, and your mother needs you."

"What do you mean? What's happened?" I remembered the presence I'd sensed last night in the woods, and a dizzy rush of panic flew through me.

I should have told my mom last night about Creagan and the energy I sensed in the woods.

Without waiting for Selkie's reply, I sprinted toward the house as fast as I could. Despite the sharp rocks digging into my bare feet, I pushed through the pain and sped up. My heart hammered in my chest, and I almost missed the top stair leading up to the back porch. I flung the back door open and rushed through the kitchen.

"Mom!"

"In here," Calista's voice replied from the living room.

Calista held my mother in her arms. Her body rocked with sobs. I didn't know what had happened, but my heart broke seeing my mother in such a state of despair.

"Mom ... Calista ... what's happened?"

I carefully sat down on the sofa next to my mother, afraid to cause even the slightest motion in the cushion, and gently placed my hand on her shaking back. The heartache coming off her slammed me in the pit of my stomach so hard I nearly doubled over in tears. My bones ached with her pain. I swiftly pulled my guard back up and swallowed down the emotions that weren't my own as my fear quickened. The sea-green walls spun around me. I squeezed the cushion under my leg to steady my balance and looked up at the canvas on the wall, focusing on one image to quell the spinning. I held my gaze on the unusual flower that appeared in most of my mother's paintings until all of its vibrant colors remained in place.

"Ev, are you okay?" Calista asked.

I shuddered, trying to compose myself. "Yes. What happened?"

Calista rubbed my mother's back and wiped a rolling tear from her own cheek. She glanced nervously at Selkie, who had just come back into the room with a hot cloth that she pressed to the back of my mom's neck.

"Something terrible. Your mother's friend …" She paused as if considering whether she should continue and looked again at Selkie, who nodded. "Your mother's friend Creagan" —her arms tightened protectively around my mother's limp form—"was found dead early this morning."

My chest tightened at her revelation.

I sensed something amiss last night. If I'd just said something right away instead of waiting. But how could I have known something like this would happen?

Hearing Calista's words sent my mother into another fit of shaking sobs.

"Oh, Mom. I'm so sorry." I felt helpless seeing her in this state.

I slid onto my knees on the floor and laid my head on her back, unsure of what else to do.

I knew she and Creagan had been close, and I often wondered if their relationship went beyond friendship throughout the years. But he'd never spent much time here at the house. Suddenly, that fact seemed odd, considering how close they must have really been and how often he'd visited over the years.

If they were romantically involved, why would they have kept their relationship such a secret from me?

I thought of Creagan's phone call.

Could that have been what he needed to tell me so urgently? No, that couldn't have been it. It had to have been something more important.

"Everly." My mom breathed heavily.

"I'm here, Mom." I lifted my head from her back as she pushed herself upright out of Calista's arms.

She rubbed at her eyes with the backs of her hands, causing the swelling skin to turn an irritated red.

"Here, Cacsha, honey." Selkie passed my mother a handful of tissues.

She pressed the tissues to her eyes and then swiped at her cheeks and nose.

"I'm sorry, sweetie." She cupped a hand to my cheek. Her sapphire-blue eyes were dark with a grief that knew no bounds.

"Oh, Mom." I placed my hand over hers and held it tight as I repositioned myself next to her on the sofa. "You have nothing to be sorry for."

She shook her head, and strands of jet-black hair fell over her face. "Yes, I do. It's all my fault." She choked as more tears tried to break free. "I'm so sorry."

I moved her head to my shoulder and smoothed back her hair. "Shh … Shh … I think maybe you should lie down and get some rest."

Calista and Selkie both stood. "Come on, Cacsha, honey." They each wrapped an arm around my mom as I guided her up. "Let's get you upstairs and in a hot bath."

"Here." Selkie handed me the wet cloth she had pressed to my mom's neck. "Why don't you make your mom a cup of tea while we take her upstairs?"

I nodded as my mom's two best friends supported her up the stairs, my chest tight with what I knew.

I eased back down onto the sofa and dropped my face into my palms.

I can't believe this is happening.

"You okay?" Calista asked, coming back down the stairs.

The weight of my head was heavy as I lifted it from the darkness of my cupped palms. "Honestly, I don't know. How about you?"

"It's been a long night." She sighed and ran her fingers through her chestnut curls. Her complexion was a shade paler than usual.

"Do you know what my mom was talking about when she said it's her fault?"

Calista curled her legs up onto the sofa. "I don't know, Ev. She's exhausted and distraught. None of us has slept all night. I think she just needs some sleep."

"When did you find out about Creagan?"

Calista twisted her hair up with a band she pulled from her pocket. "It was early this morning, right after most of the girls left. We were just calling it a night, or morning, I guess, when your mom got the call."

I glanced at the top of the stairs, my gut churning. "Will you come in the kitchen with me while I make the tea? There's something I need to tell you, and it's eating me up," I whispered, even though I knew the running bathwater upstairs would drown out my words.

Calista frowned but followed me into the kitchen and filled the kettle while I gathered the herbs. "What is it, Ev?"

I told her about the call from Creagan and the presence in the woods. Calista and Selkie were the only people besides my mom and Jasper who knew about my ability.

"I should have mentioned it last night, but after Jasper and I inspected the area, everything seemed fine. And the call with Creagan was strange, but I didn't think it was this serious."

My gaze shifted towards my feet. I had completely forgotten that I wasn't wearing any shoes or socks. I ignored the cold tingle spreading across my toes. "If I'd said something last night, maybe I could have prevented this from happening. Maybe my mom could have reached Creagan and … I don't know … changed something. How am I supposed to tell her now?"

"Look at me." Calista lifted my chin so that our eyes met. "You did nothing wrong, and you can't think like that. Okay?" She pulled me into a hug. "And your mom will tell you the same thing."

~

T carried the tea upstairs and knocked softly on my mom's door. Selkie opened up and held her fingers to her lips.

"She's finally fallen asleep," she whispered.

"Do you mind if we trade places? I'd like to sit with her awhile." I carefully set the tea down on the bedside table.

"Of course. I'll be downstairs if you need me." Selkie quietly left the room.

I sat in the vacant chair next to my mom's bed. Even while asleep, her expression remained distressed. I gently lifted her damp hair from her neck and laid it over her pillow.

She tossed and mumbled. "We can't tell her, Creagan." She shook her head in her sleep. "She'll never forgive me."

"It's okay, Mom. You're just dreaming." I smoothed her forehead.

She rolled over onto her side. "You're in danger, Creagan. You shouldn't come here anymore."

What is she talking about?

Her pillow shifted when she rolled over, and something stuck out from underneath. It looked like a picture.

I carefully slid the photo out from under the pillow and examined it. My mom and Creagan held a baby together between them. My mom was smiling, happier than I'd ever seen, and Creagan was looking down at her and the baby with a look of pride. A rock plummeted into my stomach. The baby in the picture was me.

Oh my God.

I took the picture and left the room. My chest tightened up. I leaned against the wall outside and took a deep breath.

It's just a picture. She's known Creagan a long time. It doesn't

26

mean anything. But why is she sleeping with it under her pillow if it doesn't have meaning?

I crept up to the third-floor room where we kept the photo albums.

What the ...?

Candles covered the hardwood floor, all arranged in different formations, making up some kind of symbols.

What was going on up here last night?

I remembered the dancing shadows I'd seen from outside when I got home.

I maneuvered around the candles to reach the bookcase. I took down all the photo albums from the shelf and carefully looked through each one. Over the years, I had gone through the albums countless times. Since I had never come across any pictures of Creagan before, I wasn't shocked to find none this time, either. However, what did surprise me was the absence of complete images of my mom's face in any of the photos from my younger years.

She was always looking to the side or bending down toward me. It was like she had intentionally avoided direct eye contact with the camera.

How did I never notice this before?

I put the albums back and crept back into my mom's room. She was still asleep. Guiltily, I opened her closet and closed the door behind me, leaving just a crack, then pulled the chain to the light. I quietly shifted the clothes on hangers and examined the area behind them. A cloud of dust tickled my nose as I pulled down shoe-boxes from a shelf. I quickly covered my mouth to mask my sneeze. I meticulously examined every box within my reach, but to my disappointment, not a single one contained any pictures.

I stood on my tiptoes and slid the shoe-boxes back onto the top shelf, then felt an odd shift in the floorboard underneath my feet. Kneeling down, I folded the small rug back and examined the boards. Someone had cut a patch of boards differently from the rest, leaving an open gap around the edges. Using my fingers, I felt around until one jiggled out of place. I carefully lifted the board and the two others on either side.

I sucked in a breath and rocked back on my heels.

I can't believe this.

A small box sat hidden beneath the floor panels. I lifted it out and slowly released my breath, hesitant to lift the lid.

I shouldn't be doing this. These are my mother's private things.

I ignored the guilty voice echoing in my mind and lifted the lid. Pictures and other small items filled the box.

My hand flew to my mouth to mask the gasp that escaped. I flipped through dozens of photos of my mother, Creagan, and me. I was a baby in most of them and a toddler in others. Every image represented that of a family. I took one picture of the three of us and slid it into my back pocket. I was just about to replace the lid when another photo stood out. Inside a tightly sealed bag with the photo was a lock of black hair tied with a delicate blue bow. The child in the picture was a small boy, maybe a couple of years old. He stood alone in a garden and stared straight into the camera with solemn eyes the color of liquid silver.

The creak of footsteps moaned outside, and I stuffed the bag and its contents back inside the box, and tucked it beneath the floorboards. I flipped the rug back in place and pulled the cord to the light. I barely reached the chair before Selkie popped her head through the bedroom door and waved me over. "We made some lunch and thought you might be hungry."

"Sure, thanks. I'll be right down."

I waited until I was sure Selkie had gone all the way back downstairs, and I went back to my mom's side. I pulled out the picture I'd taken from underneath her pillow and studied it one last time.

The couple in this picture appeared not only as two people in love but as two proud parents.

This just can't be. My mom never knew my dad. He was an anonymous donor at the in vitro clinic she went to. At least, that's what she told me. But if that were true, why would she have hidden all the pictures with Creagan?

I looked harder at the picture. Both she and Creagan looked almost exactly the same then as they did now, neither appearing to have aged over the last nineteen years. I pulled out the photo I'd taken from the box, where I was a few years old, and examined their faces. Their images were identical in that one as well. I sat back down in the chair. My head grew heavy with confusion, and I slipped the first picture back under the pillow and went downstairs.

I picked at the lunch Calista and Selkie had made. My stomach had too many knots to tolerate any food.

"You okay, Ev? You've been really quiet since you came down."

"I'm actually not that hungry. Do you two mind if I head back home and change?"

The two women exchanged worried glances. "Of course, sweetie. We're not going anywhere."

$\sim$

*W*hen I got back to my apartment, I closed the door and slid to the floor.

Is it possible that my mom lied about how I was conceived and not knowing who my father was? Could that be what Creagan wanted to talk about?

I pushed myself back up and went to find my phone. I sent Jasper a message:

Something happened.

I need to talk to you.

I hurriedly changed out of my workout clothes, snatched up my phone, and made my way back to the house.

Calista and Selkie stayed through most of the day, cleaning up after last night's party and taking turns carrying up a variety of foods to my mom's room, most of it coming back uneaten.

Gloom hovered around us as we leaned against the kitchen counter while Selkie mixed one of her tonics. "Here, why don't you try getting your mom to take a few sips of this? It'll help her sleep through the night."

The drink had a strong medicinal odor, and I definitely caught an unmistakable whiff of valerian. Not the most pleasant smell, but it would help you fall and stay asleep.

My mom was sitting up when I entered her room. Her bedside lamp was on the low setting, casting a soft glow of light throughout the room. She quickly stuffed something under the blanket when she saw me coming in.

Her eyelids were still puffy, and her cheeks were chafed pink.

"Hi, honey." She tried to form a semblance of a smile.

I reached out my hand, careful not to splash the contents in the cup. "Selkie mixed up this tonic for you. She said it'll help you sleep through the night."

She looked at the liquid cautiously and said, "Smells like she's doubled the valerian since the last one she brought up." But she took the cup and drained its contents.

I set the empty cup on her nightstand, then went to her private bathroom and ran a cloth under hot water. I carried it back to her bed and tapped the pillow with my hand. She slid her body down until her head was propped on the pillow, and I gently laid the hot cloth across her eyes.

I felt tempted to ask about the picture under her pillow,

but even though I was burning with curiosity, I knew it wasn't the right moment. I switched off the lamp and stayed watching over her until her breath had the slow and steady rhythm of someone in a deep sleep.

Instead of going back downstairs, I headed up to the third floor. Since I first saw them, I hadn't stopped thinking about the candles I found and the shapes they were arranged in. I opened the door to the room they'd been in and felt a stab of disappointment. The floor was now clean, and no sign of the candles remained. *Strange. I didn't see anyone come up here.* I pulled the door closed, wishing I'd come back up sooner.

"Okay, I'll be right there," Selkie was saying to someone on the phone as I came down the stairs.

She looked up with a worn expression and said, "Snafu with one of my catering events. I need to go, but I'll be back. I'll stop in and check on things at the café on my way, okay?" she said as she pulled on her fern-green jacket and grabbed her bag from the coatrack.

"Thanks, Selk. Do you need some help?"

"I'll be fine, but thanks." She smiled encouragingly.

I grabbed an afghan from the back of a chair and followed Selkie out onto the porch. "I hope everything works out with your event. Ty and Molly are closing tonight, so things should be good, but I appreciate you checking in."

She waved and got in her car, and I watched her back up and turn out onto the road.

The sun had set, and the stars shone bright above the sky, oblivious to the happenings of life below them. I sat on the front porch steps and pulled the afghan tighter around my shoulders to ward off the cool breeze. The wisteria planted near the front of the house swayed in the wind, and the air filled with its sweet scent. Light spilled out from behind me as the front door creaked open. I didn't need to turn around to know whose energy I felt. Calista quietly sat down beside me and stared up at the stars.

"It smells nice out here," she said.

"Yeah."

"Your mom's a survivor. She's going to be okay."

"I've never seen her so upset. She and Creagan have been friends for years, but he never spent much time here. I didn't understand how much he really meant to her before today."

I waited, hoping Calista might divulge some information, but she remained silent as she gazed up at the sky. If she knew anything more about the relationship between my mom and Creagan, she kept her knowledge to herself.

Several minutes passed in quiet, and I felt a deep sense of longing vibrating from Calista as she stared up at the sky. It was as though she were missing something or someone terribly. I slipped my guard back in place to be careful not to violate her private feelings, but I wondered at what she missed that made her feel that way. I leaned my head on the thick wooden porch column. My eyelids drooped heavily, and I had nearly dozed off when Calista's voice roused me from my own quiet thoughts.

"Do you ever wonder what else is out there?"

"Out where?" I asked.

"Out there." She nodded up at the sky.

"You mean, like other life? I don't know. I guess. You?"

"All the time. It would be a lonely universe if Earth was the only planet with evolved life." She shook her head and stood. "Ignore my tired ramblings. I'm gonna go check on your mom."

"I'll go. You get some rest." I pulled the afghan off and swung it up and around Calista's back. She wrapped her soft hands around mine as she accepted the blanket from me. The porch light reflected in her chestnut eyes as she touched her forehead to mine.

32

"Love you, Evs," she said.

"Love you too."

Calista yawned as she followed me back into the house. "I'm gonna just crash here on the sofa. Wake me up if you need me."

"I will. I promise." I gave her a hug. "Oh, what was with all those candles on the floor upstairs?"

Her drooping eyelids lifted open. "What candles?"

"When I was upstairs earlier, I went to the third floor to look for something and found a bunch of candles on the floor, laid out in different shapes, but they're gone now."

"Oh, it was just a silly game us girls were playing last night. That's all."

The line between her eyes made me pause.

"Ah. Maybe you can show me sometime. Looked interesting."

"Sure, sweetie." She crawled onto the sofa and snuggled into the cushions.

I turned off the lamp and headed upstairs.

Before entering my mom's room, I flipped off the hallway light, then tiptoed across the floor to her bed and climbed in next to her.

"Everly," my mom's voice echoed in the dark room.

"It's me, Mom." I pulled the covers over my shoulders and nestled closer to her, wrapping my arm around her back. Her body relaxed, and the room fell back into silence.

CHAPTER 4

My mom sat at her dressing table, her somber expression a still canvas in the mirror.

The brush glided through her hair, and soft waves flowed down past her shoulders as I pulled the brush through from root to end. I swooped one side of her hair back and pinned it in place using the brooch she requested.

"This is lovely, Mom." I admired the prisms of color dancing across the jeweled flower.

A strained smile reflected back at me. "Thank you, sweetie. It was a gift from Creagan. I'm wearing it today in honor of him."

I looked away from the mirror. "I'm sorry."

She swiveled in her chair. "You have nothing to be sorry for. You and the girls have been walking on eggshells, taking care of me these last few days. I'm so grateful for the three of you." She smiled, and this time it was less strained.

I glanced at her closet. "Mom ..." I started, but someone interrupted me with a knock at the door.

"You two ready in there?" Calista called from the other side.

The smile faded from my mother's face, replaced by a solemn expression. "I suppose we have to be." She glanced back at the mirror and gently touched the brooch in her hair. "Come on, it's time."

~

*T*he casket creaked in protest as it was lowered into its final resting place. The man inside lay quiet and oblivious as he became enveloped in his dark, cavernous cell of soil walls. Silent tears slid down the cheeks of those who watched their beloved leave the land of the living.

The attendees were few, and most of them were strangers to me. I stood aside and watched as they circled the fresh rectangular cavern cut into the ground, each taking a handful of soil and letting it slip through their fingers down onto the coffin.

My mother stood at the head of her friend's grave and addressed the small crowd. "Creagan Aeros Caldwell was a true and fearless leader. He was a loyal and trusted friend to many. A selfless and devoted father, he would do anything to keep his loved ones safe, even if it meant sacrificing his own life. He will forever remain in our memories as a great man, and I will miss him every day for the rest of my life."

I wondered at the meaning of her words and how he had given his life.

And who was Creagan a devoted father to? He never visited with children in tow. With all the traveling he did, I just assumed he was single and childless. And if he was my father—my heart jumped at the thought—well, devoted wouldn't be the word I'd choose.

After everyone had their turn at offering their farewell, I approached the grave and drove my hand deep into the mound of freshly dug earth. I stretched my arm out and slowly let loose the tiny particles. The insides of my fingers tickled as the soil sprinkled out into the depths of the hollowed-out grave. The small particles of rock mixed with the soil pinged off the top of the coffin, *tick-tick*, as they reached their target. I ignored the ache growing in my knees from being pressed against the cold, hard ground.

"What were you trying to tell me, Creagan? And why did you sound so afraid?" I whispered.

I shivered as a cool gust of the early morning breeze whipped my long ponytail around and across my face. I gathered the thick, black hair obscuring my view and secured it neatly behind my head. While searching for my mother in the crowd, a chilling sensation of being observed compelled me to shift my attention towards a different person. My eyes locked with his. He stood just a few feet away, at the edge of the tent covering the grave site and vacated chairs. My breath caught as I recognized those blue-green eyes.

Why would he be here?

A pulsing thread of energy flowed from him to me, and as I channeled into it, I could feel a heated message of warning. I didn't know exactly what the warning was, only that there was one. I let my guard down completely to focus on the thread of energy he was sending me, but at that moment, a hand rested on my shoulder.

I jumped.

"Everly, are you okay, sweetheart?"

I tore my eyes from the stranger and turned to my mother, who now stood by my side. "Yes, I think so."

Even in the day's gloom, she was a stunning sight in her feminine black pant-suit. She didn't look a day over thirty. I thought of the picture with her and Creagan, and how neither appeared to have aged over the years.

How can that be? There should be some wrinkles, some fine

*lines, something that's changed over nineteen years, but her skin is
as creamy and smooth now as it was then in the picture.*

"Are you sure you're okay, honey? You look like you've
seen a ghost." She studied me with her sapphire-blue eyes,
the same color as mine, and a dimple of concern formed.

"Do you know who that man over there is?" I turned to
point in the direction he was standing, but found an empty
space.

My mother followed my gaze. "I'm afraid I don't know
who you mean, darling. What did this man look like?"

"How strange. He was just standing right there." I pointed,
indicating the spot I meant, and looked around. He was gone,
like he'd just vanished.

"I guess it doesn't matter now, but he was in the café the
other night for the first time, and now he shows up here. I
wonder how he knew Creagan."

A loud squawk caught my attention. I turned to find a
flock of geese scurrying past as they headed into a nearby
pond.

My mother watched the geese with a thoughtful expression. Her eyes darkened with clouds as she turned back to
face me. She wrapped my hand in hers. "Honey, there's
something we need to talk about later, when we're alone."

My stomach tightened when I thought of what she might
be referring to.

Two figures approached and drew both our attentions.

"Hey, you two," Calista called out as she and Selkie
walked toward us. The two women were in stark contrast to
one another in appearance. Where Selkie was petite with fine
strawberry hair, Calista was taller than average with unruly
chestnut curls.

Calista and Selkie had been my mother's closest friends
and my surrogate aunts for as long as I could remember,
since I had no other aunts or uncles or grandparents for that

matter. It'd always just been me and my mom, and her close group of friends, who took it upon themselves to fill the familial positions of our vacant family tree.

Calista moved to stand next to my mom in her sleek black dress and wrapped her arm around my mom's waist. "Cacsha, how are you holding up?"

My mom glanced at us all. "I'm just so thankful I have the three of you."

"How about you, sweetie?" Selkie asked, taking my hand in hers and giving it a soft squeeze.

"I'm okay. I feel bad about what happened to Creagan, but I didn't really know him that well."

A meaningful glance passed between Calista and my mother, hinting at something unspoken. They quickly looked away from each other.

"Do you mind if we borrow your mom for a few minutes?" Calista asked.

"Sure. I think I'll take a walk."

"Stay close, okay?" my mom added, a frown forming.

"Mom, I'll be fine, but I won't go too far."

"Good." She kissed my forehead, and the three women walked toward a small group of people heading in our direction.

While the crowd mingled, I wandered up a hill toward a cluster of trees just far enough away to be out of sight, but not too far that my mom would worry.

~

I sat on the ground in front of an ancient oak tree and leaned my back against the thick bark of its massive trunk. Prickles of cool moisture dripped down from the leaves and dotted my skin. I drew in a deep breath of the dewy autumn air and lifted my face to the ray of sunshine sneaking through the clouds and branches. My skin relished the energizing warmth of the yellow glow.

The season was still in its early transition from late summer to early fall, and remnants of late summer still lingered. It was a magical time of year: a time for change and introspection. Since it was still early in the new season, much of the foliage hadn't begun its transformation yet. Some of the surrounding trees were just beginning to show a hint of crimson creeping in at the tips of their leaves, and others a bit of toasted orange with splotches of yellow taking over what was once a vibrant green.

This moment of privacy was a reprieve from all the surging vibrations of emotions coming from those who said their goodbyes to Creagan.

Settling into the belly of the oak tree, I thought about Creagan's call. His voice had sounded desperate. Surely, whatever he'd had to tell me couldn't have been what he was afraid of. It had to have been something more imminent.

I remembered the presence in the woods.

Could it have had anything to do with Creagan? But how and why would someone who had dealings with Creagan be lurking outside our home?

"Hello, Everly." A nearby voice startled me from my thoughts and brought me back to the present.

I flinched and smacked my elbow hard against a bony knob protruding from the tree trunk. I stood, rubbing my throbbing elbow, and turned to find a man standing close behind me, too close for my comfort.

Raven-colored hair accented silver eyes, and an ominous vibe oozed from him. The more I looked at him, the more otherworldly he seemed. His skin and hair shone with a faint glimmer. I would have considered him attractive if he wasn't staring at me like I was some kind of species in a specimen jar.

Surprised that I hadn't sensed him nearing me, I backed away a few steps while replying, "Hello … Have we met before?"

"No, we haven't. But you could say I'm an acquaintance of your father."

My skin prickled. If I had never known my father, then I didn't know how this man, who appeared to be around my age, could have any idea who my father could be.

"I'm sorry," I responded. "You must have me confused with someone else."

Not wanting to give away any personal details, I played along with the ruse and added, "I've never seen you with my dad before."

He looked at me with a sly smile and said, "My name is Darion."

I got the impression that he was gauging my reaction to see if his name held some kind of familiarity for me. It didn't.

The cold edge of his stare sent shivers down the back of my spine. He took a step toward me and reached out his hand. As he came closer, my body burned to get away. This guy was creepy, and he was intentionally shielding himself from me; I could *feel* it. He wanted me to feel it; I could see it in his eyes. Fear snaked its way into my mind. I was completely out of sight from everyone at the funeral. This spot had felt so peaceful just minutes ago, and now it seemed like the trees pressed in on me, closing the open space. Time for me to go.

"It was nice to meet you, Darion, but I need to get back." I pretended not to notice his outstretched hand as I turned to leave.

Then another man appeared by my side.

It was the guy from earlier, who'd been watching me at Creagan's grave. I hadn't noticed him approach us, but he now stood so close to me that our sides nearly touched. I became acutely aware of an awakening in my body that I'd never felt before. He was vibrating a mix of emotions that I instantly picked up: fury and wrath toward the one who called himself Darion, and a feeling of protectiveness toward me that I found perplexing. I couldn't imagine why he would feel protective of a complete stranger, but I was glad to have him at my side at this moment. There was another emotion that he seemed to restrain within himself, but he quickly guarded it from me. I could actually *feel* him block me out. It was like having a door suddenly slammed in my face.

My skin chilled. It was becoming apparent that somehow these two men knew something that was very personal and different about me, and I suspected that there was also something very different about the both of them.

The clouds rolled directly over us, and the cemetery suddenly felt even darker and cooler than a moment before.

The two men continued to watch each other, and neither seemed willing to look away. Both tall and nearly equal in height and build, they made an equal match. Their familiarity and distrust of one another was apparent. They were both fierce and intent on standing their ground, like two warriors in a standoff, about to begin battle. I didn't have to tap into my ability to sense the power struggle happening between them, which oddly felt connected to me.

Darion broke the silence. "Arden," he said sharply, "what an unexpected surprise to see you here. I was just introducing myself to this lovely young lady."

"Yes, thank you," I interjected. "And how were you acquainted with Creagan?"

He regarded me. His reply took long enough to make the silence awkward.

"Let's just say …" He paused briefly, as he seemed to weigh his words. "We share something in common with the recently deceased."

41

I don't like the way Mr. Cryptic said the word, we.

Darion turned to Arden and said something quickly in a language I didn't understand, but I understood the meaning behind it, and it was clearly threatening.

Goose bumps spread across my flesh.

Arden acted unaffected by Darion's words when he responded smoothly, "It's time for you to leave, Darion."

Darion turned his attention back to me. For a moment, he just looked at me without speaking, as though he were trying to find some answer to a question. "Until we meet again, my dear Everly." And with that, he turned and walked away into the thickening forest of trees.

He actually left. I had half expected the two to draw hidden swords or daggers and begin battling right in front of me. When he was out of sight, I turned to Arden. "Who are you? What was that all about? And how do you and Mr. Creepoid know me?"

His eyes blazed green, the blue barely visible. He turned from where he watched Darion disappear. "I'm sorry, Everly, but this isn't the time or place for explanations. Speak to your mother. She has the answers you're looking for. We'll meet again soon." And then he turned and left in the same direction as Darion.

CHAPTER 5

$\mathcal{J}$t had been a long day. I commonly felt drained after being in the presence of several people at once. Larger crowds were even more tiring. My own emotional stability could become vulnerable by letting my guard down around so many. When I felt too much of what other people were feeling, I could get sucked into that emotion and become overtaken by it myself.

By the time we arrived home from the funeral proceedings, my mother looked the way we both felt: exhausted. Her eyes—normally bright with life and happiness—were now sunken and rimmed with dark circles. She stood with her shoulders hunched, and my heart tightened with a painful ache seeing her this way.

"Mom, why don't you sit down and rest? I'll go put on a pot of water for tea."

"That's very sweet of you. Today was a hard day."

I spotted her favorite knitted afghan, a gift from Calista, hanging on the back of a chair, and wrapped it over her shoulders. "I love you, Mom."

"I love you too, honey." She squeezed my hands in hers. Her fingers were ice cold, and their touch gave me a slight chill.

I thought of the creeping chill I'd had back in the woods at the graveyard.

Who were those guys? And why were they at Creagan's funeral?

Mom curled up on the sofa, cocooning herself in the afghan.

Maybe this isn't the right time to question her. I'll wait and make the tea first.

The dusk light poured in through the open kitchen blinds. It provided just enough light that I didn't need to turn on the overhead.

Rummaging through the cabinet where we kept the fresh dried herbs and spices from the garden, I shuffled aside jars of rose hips, peppermint, and lemongrass in search of a specific set of ingredients.

"Aha! There you are."

I plucked out the English lavender nestled between jars of nettle and rosemary. I found the chamomile flowers and vanilla beans, and set them on the counter next to the lavender. This brew would require some of my own baby's breath honey, some I had just harvested this summer.

I reached atop the fridge for the jar; it was a stretch even on my tiptoes. As I was an average five foot four inches, sometimes reaching for things high up could be a pain. Using my fingertips, I shimmied the jar toward the edge of the fridge until it slid into my grasp.

I filled the kettle with water and set the burner on high. While the water worked up to a boil, I blended together just the right amount of lavender buds with the chamomile flowers and added the fresh zest of vanilla bean. This tea blend was a customer favorite at the café, great for relaxing the nerves and calming the mind. It also helped with headaches. I added a dollop of the sweet, earthy honey to each of the mugs and waited for the kettle to whistle. The water gurgled as the temperature rose. The sound lulled me into a meditative trance.

I thought back to the encounter at the funeral. The whole scenario seemed so surreal now that a part of me just wanted to chalk the entire experience up to a random run-in with a couple of disturbed dudes, and I probably would have, but I couldn't shake the last thing Arden had said to me—that my mother had the answers I was looking for.

What answers can she have that Arden, a complete stranger, has anything to do with?

The kettle whistled as angry steam hissed from its spout. I poured the steaming water over the tea infusers and set the stove timer for five minutes to let the ingredients steep. My mind raced with a torrent of questions, with one burning at the surface for an answer:

What secrets are you hiding from me, Mom?

Until these last few days, I would never have doubted my mother's honesty.

There has to be some kind of misunderstanding.

The timer beeped, and I removed the infusers. As I inhaled the intoxicating aroma, the tension around my eyes melted away and a sense of lightness washed over me. I carried the mugs into the living room and handed one to my mom. Steam billowed off the top of the liquid as she took a careful sip.

"Mom, I know you're exhausted, but there's something I need to talk to you about."

"Sure, honey. What is it?" She patted the spot next to her on the sofa.

I sat down and took a deep breath, trying to calm my

jittery nerves. "Well—" I began and released the breath I had taken, but then a familiar series of knocks on the front door interrupted me.

Jasper's knock was always the same: knock five times in quick succession and pause, and then knock two more quick knocks. It reminded me of the theme song to the Super Mario video game that the two of us had spent too many hours playing over the years.

I opened the door to a teasing grin. "Hey, babes."

"Jasper! You know I hate it when you call me that." Jasper was my best friend, but even best friends had limits.

"I know, I know," he said, holding up his hands with palms out in defense. "I'm sorry. I promise it's the last time."

"Yeah, you say that every time." I moved aside, letting him walk past me.

"Hey, Ms. C.," he said, ignoring my annoyance and leaning down to plant a kiss on my mom's cheek.

My mom's fondness for Jasper was easy to see, and she wasn't tepid about sharing her high hopes of us becoming more than friends someday. My lack of a dating life had become something of concern for her, and any boy I'd introduced her to in the past hadn't lived up to her Jasper comparisonitis.

"Jasper, it's good to see you." She patted his hand.

"You too, Ms. C. I'm so sorry to hear about your friend. Is there anything I can do for you?"

"That's sweet, but no, thank you. Just having you here with my Evy is enough, and now that you are here, I think I'm going to excuse myself for the night." She folded the afghan and set it back on the chair.

"Honey, can we finish our talk in the morning?"

"Of course, Mom. You should get some rest and maybe soak in a hot bath. I could run one for you." I swallowed back my disappointment. Now that I'd built up the courage, waiting until tomorrow would feel like an eternity.

"That's okay. You two catch up. I'll see you in the morning." She hugged us both before heading upstairs to her room.

"I'm sorry for what your mom's going through." Jasper wrapped me in his long arms. "How are you holding up?"

"I'm okay. Things have been strange ever since that night that Creagan called me. But first, tell me what you're doing here. Aren't you supposed to be in Portland, getting ready for your fall-term classes?"

He fiddled with his cuff. "I've decided to take the term off and move back home for a couple of months."

"Jasper—please tell me you're not missing an entire term because you're worried about me."

The corners of his mouth turned up in a grin. "I'm not missing an entire term because I'm worried about you."

"Seriously. This isn't a joke. You worry about me too much, and I don't want you falling behind because of me."

Jasper looked up the stairs and then nodded for me to follow him into the kitchen. He leaned down so that our faces were closer and whispered. "Listen, I know this is serious. It's one term. Not a big deal. I'm not leaving you alone after what you found in your mom's room."

He pulled the fridge door open, scanning its contents. "Have you asked your mom about the pictures yet?"

I leaned back against the counter and slid the photo out of my pocket and sighed. "I was just about to bring it up before you knocked, but I'm glad you're here. Something really odd happened today at the funeral. Let's go out back to my place, and I'll fill you in."

～

*W*e followed the path through the garden that led to the guest house. I breathed in whiffs of rosemary and thyme as we passed the greenhouse, where we grew our own ingredients for the Craft Haus Café.

"Hold on," Jasper said, and pulled me into the greenhouse.

All around us were different types of herbs and colorful flowers that we could eat.

Jasper bent down and picked two *Monarda* flowers from a nearby pot of edible flowers and handed one to me. We used *Monarda* in our recipes to treat a variety of symptoms, from stomachache and headache to throat and mouth irritations. It was also delicious, freshly picked and added to a dish as a garnish.

"Cheers," we both said as we ate the bright purple flowers.

My mouth filled with minty flavors of spearmint and peppermint, followed by a hint of peppered oregano.

"Mmm ... I love those," Jasper said. His golden-amber eyes glowed under the florescent heating lights hanging overhead.

"I know you do. We have to plant extra seedlings to keep our stock up with all your grazing." I tickled his sides.

Jasper bent over laughing. His wavy curls mingled with mine as he bent his head down and touched his forehead to mine. "I'd be happy to work off my free product with labor," he joked.

He took a step closer, then wrapped one arm around my waist and wiggled his dark eyebrows.

I reached up and tucked a lock of his hair behind his ear, then slowly trailed my hand down his chest. His grip tightened. I stopped my hand at his abdomen. His breathing paused, and for a moment, I forgot we were just two best friends joking around.

"Evy ..." Jasper's free hand slipped softly up my jaw and

cheek until his fingers spread through my hair. His lips were so close to mine that our breath became one. It would be so easy to let go with Jasper. He knew about my ability and had always been there for me.

A loud crackle of thunder boomed overhead, and rain pinged off the glass greenhouse.

"Jasper, you're a hopeless flirt," I teased, tickling him some more to make light of the passing moment between us.

"Definitely, guilty." He winked. "Evy—" he said more seriously while slipping his hand over mine.

I knew what he wanted to say. It was in his eyes and had been many times over the last year. I never used my ability on Jasper. I'd used it for him many times to tell if a girl liked him—not that he needed me for that. Girls were always hanging on his every move.

Jasper's feelings had changed toward me recently, from best friend to something more. He hadn't voiced them yet—maybe out of the same fear I had over losing what we had—but the transformation was clear in his gestures and his looks.

I loved Jasper, but I just didn't know if that love meant more than friendship to me.

"Come on," I said, pulling him out into the rain. We ran to my apartment, both dripping wet by the time we got inside.

I grabbed two towels from the linen closet, and we dried off while I told Jasper everything from the moment I had first seen Arden in the café.

But I omitted the giddy feelings I'd experienced. There was a time when I would have shared those with Jasper, but knowing how he felt about me changed things. My stomach tightened with the realization of that knowledge and losing a confidant. Until this moment, I hadn't realized how the new dynamic between us had affected our relationship.

"I got the impression that they both knew about my ability. I could feel them guarding their emotions from me," I said, breathless. "And what do you think that comment Arden made about my mother having the answers was all about?"

Jasper's eyes darkened with a shade of anger, dark pupils dominating the golden bronze of his irises.

Not exactly the reaction I'd been expecting, but he'd always been overly protective.

He leaned forward on the sofa, placing his elbows on his knees. "You're sure it was Creagan you saw talking to that guy Arden outside the café?"

I reached out and motioned for his wet towel, then tossed both his and mine over a kitchen barstool. "Yeah, I'm positive. Their interaction appeared brief, so I couldn't say if it looked like they knew each other or not. And I wonder what Creagan was even doing there."

Jasper scooted toward the edge of the sofa, knotting his fingers together over and over. "Do you think it could have been that Darion dude or Arden in the woods that night?"

I stopped pacing and sat down next to Jasper. "I don't think it was Arden. When he was at the café, I got a good read on his vibrations, and they felt nothing like what I sensed coming from the woods. Darion was totally creepy, but I can't be sure if it was him either. Ugh!" I leaned back into the cushions. "Why is all this crazy stuff happening?"

Jasper furrowed his brow. "Hey, come here." He pulled me over to lean against him and rubbed my shoulders. "It's going to be okay."

I relaxed into his hands. "I hope you're right. I need to talk to my mom, but honestly, I'm terrified of what she might say. Why would she hide those pictures under the floor? I need answers, and I've waited long enough."

I hadn't told Jasper yet about my other discovery with the

pictures. He might think I was losing it if I told him I didn't think my mom had aged in nineteen years.

I'm starting to think I might be losing it.

"Do you want me to stay here with you tonight?"

"No, no. I'll be fine. Bedsides, you'll just be right up the road."

Jasper lifted his hands from my shoulders, and I shifted back to the other side of the sofa. "Promise you'll call if anything comes up."

"Promise," I said, squeezing the top of his thigh.

Jasper stood up abruptly. "Well, I guess I should go so you can talk to your mom."

I wondered at his sudden nervousness.

We walked to the back of the house, where he'd parked his Ninja motorcycle next to my car. He paused and had that look in his eyes again, like he wanted to tell me something.

"Ev … there's something important I need to talk to you about, but not now. I'll meet you at the café tomorrow, after your shift."

"Yeah, okay. I'll see you then."

I knew this time would come eventually.

Jasper got on his bike, and we stood quietly for a moment.

"Tell your parents hi from me," I said.

"I will. They're out of town on a trip, but should be home in a couple of weeks." He strapped his helmet on and the Ninja roared to life.

He rolled the bike backward with his legs and called out, "I'll be up late if you need to call after you talk to your mom."

I smiled and mouthed, "Thanks."

He lifted his feet back on the pegs, and his bike propelled forward. I stood watching until his brake lights faded into the purpling night as he made his way down the driveway to the road, and then I turned toward the main house.

Quietness pervaded the house as I walked through the

kitchen to the living room. The lamps still shone, but there was no sign of my mom anywhere on the main floor.

Maybe she's still upstairs.

The second floor appeared dark from the bottom of the staircase, and the old floorboards creaked in protest as I made my way up.

"Mom, are you up here?"

She didn't reply.

Her bedroom door was partially open, and light crept out.

Pushing it the rest of the way, I peeked into the room and found it empty.

Quickly I checked the two other second-floor rooms, doubling as a guest room and office space, with no luck. The additional upstairs bathroom was vacant as well. *Strange.* Where the hell was she?

I ran up to the third floor, used for crafting and storage of books and family albums, and where I found the candles from my mom's girls' night, but it was empty and dark.

Cold ran over my skin. I didn't like this at all. My fingers tightly gripped the banister, the smooth wood pressing against my palm. Just as I was about to retreat down the stairs, a glimmer of light escaped from the small storage space in the third-floor attic, hidden beneath the roof's peak. I crept toward the door and slowly turned the knob. A handful of boxes sat open in the middle of the cramped space in the attic, appearing to have been rummaged through after someone had pulled them down from a stack. Old books and papers lay spread across the floor.

What was she doing up here?

Trying to make sense of it, I flicked through the papers and books, but nothing made sense. In fact, fewer things made sense every hour.

With nothing to go on, I hurried back to the living room and peeked out of the window.

Her car was gone.

This wasn't right. I pulled my phone from my back pocket and checked for any missed messages from her, but my screen was blank. My heartbeat picked up.

She shouldn't be driving anywhere alone right now.

I paced the floor, trying to think of why she would have left the house.

Where have you gone, Mom? And what are you looking for?

I dashed to the kitchen and checked the cork-board attached magnetically to the side of the fridge, where we sometimes left each other notes.

With a sigh of relief, I unpinned the note she must have written before she left: *Went to office at the café. Love you, honey. See you in the morning. Love, Mom.*

My hand trembled as I thought through everything that had happened lately. She was safe in her office, but I decided the discussion couldn't wait. I locked up the house, went back to my apartment, and grabbed my bag and keys.

$\approx$

I parked my blue hybrid next to my mom's dark gray 4Runner and hurried into the café. The scents of lavender and other herbal aromatics immediately greeted me.

The café was closed today for the funeral proceedings. Molly and Ty had closed the night before, and the tables, lounging chairs, and sofas stood clean and organized. An assortment of homemade spice and tea blends, herbal oils, jars of honey, bath salts, soap bars, and my signature jams filled the shelves, creating a colorful and inviting display. But even the familiar sight didn't settle my nerves.

A glow of light spilled out from under the office door. I took a few apprehensive steps down the hall and stopped.

My breath quickened and my hands felt clammy as I reached for the doorknob. I inhaled deeply and pushed it open.

"Mom, what are you doing?"

On the floor, she was on her knees, hunched over the built-in floor safe. Her eyes widened in surprise as she looked up, quickly closing the safe and twisting the lock back into place.

"Everly, honey, you scared the daylights out of me. What are you doing here?" She tossed the corner of the throw rug back over the safe and rolled the plant stand over the top, brushing fresh tears from her puffy eyes as she stood and walked toward me.

"Oh, Mom, are you okay?" I wrapped my arms around her, my gaze snagging on the plant stand. What had she just locked away in the safe so quickly?

I pulled back and smoothed the stray strands of hair from her wet cheeks. "I thought you were taking a hot bath and going to bed. I came back to the house to see if you were still awake to talk, and found your note. Why did you come here tonight?"

She cleared her throat and backed away. Taking my hand in hers, she led me to the small cobalt-blue sofa we kept in the office for breaks.

"I'm sorry if I worried you. I had some things to tie up here, and I knew I wouldn't be able to sleep, so I came to get some work done." She used her free hand to reach for a tissue from the box on the coffee table and blotted her eyes and nose. "I thought you were spending some time with Jasper."

"I was." I smiled out of habit, trying to calm my nerves. "But there are some things I need to talk to you about. It's important, and that's why I drove straight here after I found your note."

She shifted, her throat bobbing. "Yes, I think it's time we

had a talk. I have some important things I need to share with you, too. But you first."

The weary look on her face almost made me change my mind about questioning her, but then I thought of the photos and remembered what Arden had said, so I proceeded with everything that had happened.

She listened carefully without interrupting, only looking down briefly when I told her how I'd found the photo under her pillow and the box filled with more under her closet floor.

"I'm sorry I snooped through your things, Mom, but I was just so blindsided when I found the photo with Creagan. I had to know if there were more."

She took a deep breath and closed her eyes. When she opened them, she said, "It's okay, Everly. I understand why you wanted to look. And you had every right."

Her hands shook nervously atop mine.

I chewed at the bottom of my lip and tried to calm the tingling sensation moving through my body. It wasn't just her nervousness my body was responding to, but my own.

Her aura was a mix of blue, purple, and gray hues that blended into a dark mass. Her fear wasn't just evident in the colors swarming around her, it was ablaze in her eyes. Until these last few days, I'd believed that my mother and I had no secrets between us.

"Everly," she began tentatively, and reached over to take my other hand.

I couldn't stop the tremble that took hold of me, my ability intensifying with the touch. I resisted the urge to pull my guard into place, dulling the transfer of emotions.

I want to know everything.

With my guard down and our physical contact, her fear became my own. I swallowed hard as a knot formed in the pit of my stomach and bile bubbled up my esophagus. It wasn't just the connection that caused me to feel an overwhelming sickness; it was also knowing that whatever she was about to say had her terrified.

I pulled my hands free and bent over my knees, taking a few deep breaths.

"Oh, honey, I'm so sorry. I don't know what I was thinking. I just assumed you would have your ..." Her face paled as she realized I knew the true depth of her feelings.

A whimper gurgled from my throat.

"Just breathe, sweetie."

She jumped up and went to a small table holding a pitcher of water and filled one of the empty glasses.

"Here, honey, take a drink of water and eat this." She handed me the glass and a piece of dried ginger.

I chewed the ginger and took a few careful sips of water.

"Mom, I'm better now. Please finish what you were going to say."

She nodded, sitting back down.

"Everly, you are my entire world, and I love you more than anything. I hoped you could live a happy life here without ever needing to know what I'm about to tell you. I didn't want you to grow up feeling any more different than you already have."

I don't like the sound of this.

I couldn't help but notice how her fist clenched the tissue in her hand. She was really scared.

A lump stuck in my throat. Did I really want to know something that made her this afraid to tell me? My words came out dry and cracked. "It's okay, Mom. Please, tell me everything."

Her brow tightened. "The ability you have is unique because you were born on this planet." She paused, taking a deep breath and watching me steadily. "But you were conceived on another."

A nervous laugh left my lips. "Is this some kind of joke? You can't be serious. What do you mean, conceived on another?"

She looked down, waves of guilt pricking at her. *She is very serious.*

My head pulsed, and my throat constricted, causing my words to sound choked. "What are you talking about? How can that even be possible?" My body went cold to the core. Streaks of color disoriented my vision.

The floor spun. I shook my head and kneaded my temples. "I don't understand. What exactly are you saying?"

She took another deep breath and continued. "We came here from a planet in another galaxy shortly after your conception. I traveled the dangerous journey here to protect you. I made an enemy of someone very powerful on our planet who would have done anything to harm you and punish me. I was forced to make a difficult choice."

Unable to sit any longer, I got up and moved toward the table with the pitcher and refilled my water. I wasn't thirsty, but I needed a quiet second to clear my thoughts.

I looked around the office where I'd spent so much time over the years, as a child playing, while my mom built her business, until I grew into an integral partner, helping grow and sustain the day-to-day runnings. It all seemed so surreal now—a facade of a life that wasn't real.

My eyes drifted to a framed picture of Jasper and me on the desk.

"What about the pictures with Creagan?"

My mom wrung her hands, hesitant to answer.

"Everly, there are so many things you still don't know or understand."

"Well! Help me understand. Who is Creagan really?"

She looked away toward the spot on the floor where the safe lay hidden beneath its coverings. "I did what was necessary to ensure the survival of my child. I knew we could never return to my home, because of the circumstances, so I decided it would be better for you not to know the truth and to live as normally here as possible. I didn't want you to feel the loss of a home we could never return to." She looked at me, her eyes boring into mine, pleading for understanding.

I ignored my urge to protect her and halt my questioning. "Who is Creagan, Mom?"

She sighed, and her shoulders slumped.

"Creagan was the love of my life, and he was your father."

I stumbled backward onto the table. I had suspected the possibility when I found the pictures, but I couldn't allow myself to believe that she would lie about something so important.

I turned and placed my hands flat on the table to stop their trembling and steady my balance.

He wanted to tell me the truth. That's what was so urgent and must have been why he was so afraid.

"All of these years," I said through gritted teeth, "Creagan's been visiting you." My chest burned, and my heart felt as though it were being pricked repeatedly with a sharp blade.

I stared down at my knuckles as their tops turned white from the pressure of my hands being pushed against the wooden table. "Why would you both lie and hide the truth?"

"I know you feel betrayed, but Creagan should never have come to this planet. It was dangerous for him and the both of us. He was supposed to stay on Aenoas-Vita to keep us protected from our enemy. We failed you in our weakness to stay away from each other, and now you are in more danger because of it."

"Aenoas-Vita. That's where you're from?" I asked flatly.

"It's where we are both from. The name of our planet means 'ever-living life.'"

"Why?" I didn't know why it was the first question that came out, but it was all I could think of.

My mom rubbed her temples. "There is much to teach you about our people, honey. It's called by that name because we do not age like the humans of Earth do. Time moves at a slower pace on Aenoas-Vita, and we can live hundreds of years on our planet, and sometimes longer."

I thought of all the pictures where she was always looking away, hiding her face instead of facing the camera, and then the hidden ones with Creagan, where they both looked exactly the same now as they did when I was a baby.

I understand now. She doesn't want tangible proof of her agelessness.

A heaviness settled into my chest. I turned back to face my mom with the cold realization that I didn't truly know her at all.

She sat hunched on the edge of the sofa, her shoulders hanging forward. Dark circles of exhaustion encased her eyes. Meeting my cold stare, she wore a pained expression, her eyes filled with a mix of hurt and regret.

I pulled my guard up tight and hardened my emotions. I wouldn't allow myself to feel sympathy for her. Not after what she'd kept from me.

"He wanted to tell me, didn't he? That's why he asked to meet me."

Her face flushed, and her eyes shone with fresh tears. "Yes, he wanted to tell you. He knew his travels here had been discovered, and he wanted you to know the truth before …" she trailed off.

"He was afraid when he called me. I could hear the fear in his voice. He knew someone was after him, and he wanted me to know he was my father."

My mom covered her face with her hands and nodded

into them. "I refused him when he asked to tell you sooner, and I'll regret my choice for the rest of my life."

Ignoring the feeling of numbness creeping through me, I continued my questions. "Are there others here from this other planet?" The images of Darion and Arden immediately entered my mind.

"Yes," she replied, "there are others, and some that have been here for many years."

My fingernails dug into my palms as I balled my hands into tight fists to keep from lashing out and throwing something across the room.

"Who's this enemy that wants to hurt us?"

My mom's expression darkened as she sat quietly for a moment. "Her name is Siobhan." She paused and rubbed her legs nervously. "And she is your father's wife."

"My father's ... wha ... wife?" I squeezed my eyes shut and wished what I'd heard wasn't true. When I opened my eyes and looked at my mom, it was like I was seeing a stranger. "How is this all happening?" I shook my head. "You were having an affair with a married man. Is that why you had to leave your planet?"

She stood up and took a few cautious steps toward me. "Everly, there is so much more to it than that."

"Did she kill him?"

"I believe she had something to do with his death. Your father suspected Siobhan had discovered he'd been traveling here secretly over the years. He feared she'd placed a Tracker on him to find our whereabouts. She's always been a malicious being and very possessive of him, even before they were married."

My eyes widened. "You knew him before he was married?"

She halted her steps. "Sweetie, there's so much history

that you don't know. I want to tell you everything." She reached for me.

I moved away from her grasp. "My father was murdered?" My stomach tightened with an ache for the loss of the parent I'd never known and the betrayal of the one standing in front of me. The queasiness from earlier returned.

I stumbled toward the door. My body shook with sorrow and anger for all the things she'd been keeping from me, including my father, who I may have had the chance to know but never would now.

"I'm so sorry, Ev. I was afraid that you would hate me for lying." She attempted to follow me.

"No! Stay away from me. I can't even stand to look at you right now."

Colors swirled all around me in a dizzying halo.

I couldn't hold back the rage any longer, and the angry words I'd tried to keep in flowed freely.

"I will never forgive you for lying to me all of these years and keeping me from knowing my father when, all the while, you enjoyed his company on your little visits. You're the reason he's dead. You and your hidden box of secrets."

I stormed out of the office, slamming the door behind me. A glass picture frame fell from the wall in the hall and shattered on the floor.

"Everly! Please wait," my mother called after me, but I ran to my car without looking back.

I drove slowly down the road, unsure of what to do next.

After a few blocks, I stopped in the middle of the deserted street and rested my head on the steering wheel. Hot tears stung my cheeks. My life felt as shattered as the glass from the broken frame. I didn't even know who I was anymore: human, alien, normal, freak. I lifted my head to check my rear-view mirror and wipe the tears from my eyes and nearly jumped out of my skin. A dark figure stood in the middle of the road behind my car, staring directly at me. My heart hammered against my chest. I turned to look back over my seat, through the back window, but the figure had vanished. I checked my mirror again and saw nothing but an empty, dark road.

"Okay, now I'm seeing things. Get it together, Everly."

I inhaled a long breath and slowly released it. The thumping of my heart gradually returned to a normal beat. I checked the mirror again—nothing but a dark, vacant road behind and ahead of me. I put the engine back in gear and drove with no destination in mind.

CHAPTER 6

*W*ithout really thinking about where I was going, I pulled up to Jasper's parents' place. I checked the time, almost ten at night. It was late, and the house was pretty dark, but I knew Jasper would still be up, especially since his parents were out of town.

I got out of my car and ran to the door. Heavy rain started pouring during my drive, and I didn't have a jacket on. My cotton T-shirt was soaked through by the time I opened the screen door and knocked. Shivers from the chilly, wet wind rippled over me.

Jasper opened the door completely shirtless and wearing only gym shorts. His tan skin glistened in the glare of the porch light. His body was perfectly sculpted and muscular, without being too extreme. He looked like *he* was the one from another planet.

I don't know what came over me, but there was an undeniable electricity between us. The next thing I knew, our bodies were intertwined and our lips locked in a passionate kiss. My guard slipped and his intense passion vibrated, igniting my own. His lips matched mine perfectly, and his tongue expertly guided mine in a way that made my entire body tingle. As he lifted me up, my legs instinctively wrapped around his waist, and we moved seamlessly into the house, our lips locked in an unbreakable embrace. It felt good to be pressed up against him so tightly. A comforting feeling of safety settled within me. I yearned for the sensation to spread through my entire body.

Jasper released a soft groan as he pressed me against a wall.

I pulled my head away from his. "Jasp," I breathed heavily, "I don't know if I ever told you, but I'm … uh …" Before I could finish, his lips traveled down my neck.

"It's okay. I know, Evy. I'll take care of you."

Somewhere between the living room and Jasper's bedroom, my shirt came off, and I was down to my bra. My body pulsed with pleasure as Jasper kissed the tender cleavage of my breast.

His heartbeat rapidly matched mine as our bodies welded together.

Suddenly, he pulled his head back. "Wait. I know this isn't you. Something is wrong. What is it?"

"Jasper, please. I don't want to talk about it. Just kiss me." I tightened my grip on him and bit at his bottom lip.

He loosened his hold on my hips, and my legs settled down to the floor.

The desire burning in his golden-amber eyes and flooding from his aura didn't match his actions. His breath came heavily as he said, "I'm sorry. I can't believe I'm going to do this, but as much as I've wanted this for so long, it can't happen yet. Not like this." His hands slipped away from my waist, and he walked into the living room and grabbed his zip-up hoodie off a chair. He brought it back and wrapped it around me.

"I might not have your ability, but I can tell you're upset. Talk to me," he said, his voice smooth and comforting.

I looked up into my best friend's eyes. "I …" And then the tears that I'd been fighting broke free. My cheeks warmed with the hot spring of salty liquid. Once I started, I couldn't stop.

Jasper pulled me to him and lifted me into his arms, carrying me to his room.

He whispered in my hair. "It's okay. I've got you."

I tightened my arms around his neck and buried my face in his chest.

He gently placed me on the edge of his bed.

I tried latching the zipper on the sweater and zipping it up, but my hands were too shaky.

Jasper bent down on the floor and zipped the sweater closed with steady fingers. He got up and went to his dresser. His reflection watched me in the large square mirror hanging on the wall as he moved around. There was a hint of something in his golden eyes—something he yearned to say. He ran his hand through his dark waves, and then the look was gone, as though he'd pushed it away to the recesses of his mind.

Without looking away from the mirror, he reached into his drawer and grabbed a T-shirt from the top of a neatly folded stack. He turned as he slipped it over his head, threading his arms through the sleeves in one solid motion.

He sat down next to me on his bed, folding one of his long bronze legs into a triangle as he turned to face me.

"Are you ready to tell me what's bothering you?"

I stared at the framed sheet music hanging on the wall, a signed copy of "Surfing with the Alien" by Joe Satriani. I'd emptied my savings account to buy it on-line as a birthday present for Jasper. It was so ironic that I couldn't help but almost laugh.

"Well?" Jasper said.

I readjusted my legs into a cross-legged position and tucked my hands tightly under them to keep them from shaking. "After you left tonight, I went to the house to talk to my mom. She was gone but left a note that she had gone to the café, so I drove down there to finally get some answers."

I pulled my ponytail loose and let my hair fall over my shoulders, nervously twisting the black mass over my right shoulder.

Jasper watched my action and knew I was stalling.

"What did she tell you?" His voice was calm, but his eyes were eager for answers.

I released a long sigh. "She told me that Creagan was my father." I wiped at my eyes with Jasper's sweater. "And that he was married to another woman." I wasn't ready to tell Jasper the rest of it—that my mom and I were actually from another planet and she didn't age. Just thinking it to myself sounded crazy, much less saying it out loud to another person, even my best friend, who I trusted more than anything and who already knew that I was *unusual*.

"Oh—I'm sorry. Did she tell you anything else?"

"That's not even the half of it, but I don't want to talk about it right now." I started to get up.

"Where do you think you're going?" Jasper wrapped his arms around me and slid me closer to him. We lost our balance and fell back on his pillows.

We lay on our backs, staring quietly at the ceiling, until Jasper rolled to his side, propped on his elbow.

"Ev."

"Yeah."

"There's something I need to tell you."

I closed my eyes, blocking out everything within the deep-blue walls of Jasper's room.

Please, not now. I'm not ready for this.

I bolted up. "I need to go home. What happened between us was a mistake, and I'm sorry."

I regretted my words immediately. The stricken expression on Jasper's face made my stomach twist with guilt. I had loved Jasper for years as my best friend, and now my feelings for him were tangled in a mass of confusion.

"That may be, but you're upset, and I don't want you to leave. Stay the night with me," he said decisively. "I won't put the moves on you, I promise," he added with a grin, trying to lighten the mood.

"I'm sorry. I shouldn't have said that. My mind is in a terrible place right now, and I just need to go home and be alone for a while."

"Okay, I get it." He stood up. "But I'm following behind you to make sure you get home safe."

My irritation flared. "You're being ridiculous. I'm perfectly capable of driving home, five minutes away," I emphasized, "without a chaperone."

His features turned sharp as he narrowed his eyes and stood over me. "Either way, I'm following you home."

"Fine! Whatever. Let's just go."

I stormed out of his room and walked angrily down the hallway, grabbing my shirt as I went.

~

Jasper's single motorcycle light stayed close behind me all the way to my apartment.

He pulled up and waited for me to get out of my car, flipping up the visor on his helmet as I closed my car door and walked toward him. He was a silhouette of darkness sitting atop his black motorbike and wearing his black riding gear and helmet.

"Satisfied?" I asked in a sarcastic tone.

"Come here."

His eyes glowed against his dark attire. "Do you want me to stay?"

Fog filled the air as I huffed in exasperation. "I'll be fine. I need some time to myself to figure out how to move forward with my mom."

He reached out, and I took his gloved hand. "Call me tomorrow."

"I will. I promise."

I slid my hand from his and ran up to my door. I twisted back to wave him goodbye, but he'd already turned his bike around and was speeding down the driveway back to the road.

I'd have to deal with our relationship soon.

My entire body weighed heavily with exhaustion, and my bones still had a chill from the rain. I didn't bother turning on any lights as I walked through my apartment to the bathroom. I filled the clawfoot tub with hot water and poured in a scoop of lavender-scented bath salts. The water stung my skin as I sank below its surface, letting my head rest at the bottom, listening to the sounds of my heartbeat echo deep in my ears. I lifted my head, then leaned back against the top of the tub and breathed in the heady steam. Immersed in the salted water, I remained still until its temperature transitioned from stinging to tepid, and I could no longer feel the chill in my bones.

I pulled the plug and grabbed the towel I'd hung nearby, tucking it snugly around my body. The water gurgled and chugged down the drain as I moved my fingers across the misted mirror. I stood back and watched the words *Who Am I?* drip down the mirror as steam turned to condensation.

I wiped the mirror clear with a hand towel and tried to recall Creagan's image as I examined my reflection to find a resemblance. He'd been a handsome man—tall with a lean, fit build. His hair had been dark brown, and his eyes were a shade of steel-gray encased in a silver-blue ring. I remembered asking him once, when I was a little girl, why his eyes were funny, and he had laughed and said the eye fairy couldn't decide on a color for him and gave him two instead of one. His explanation had made perfect sense to my five-year-old brain.

My sapphire-blue eyes stared back at me from the mirror as I ran a brush through my wet raven hair, both traits of my mother's. But maybe I had inherited my high cheek-bones from Creagan, or his laugh. I tried to remember how his laugh had sounded, but the memory was too distant, like an echo in the breeze or a word on the tip of my tongue. It was there, but out of reach. It hurt to know he'd stayed away from me intentionally, instead of spending time getting to know me while he had the opportunity. My eyes burned as I resisted the urge to cry.

How could they have lied to me for so long? Why didn't they just tell me the truth? Did they think I couldn't handle it?

None of it made any sense. I walked to my room and yanked the sheets back from my freshly made bed. Tossing my towel to the floor, I climbed under the sheets and pulled the blankets up tight under my chin, then forced myself to sleep.

Unanswered questions haunted my dreams, gnawing into my subconscious until my eyes refused to stay shut. I stared into the darkness.

This is pointless.

Sighing in frustration, I threw the blankets back and pulled myself upright to the edge of the bed. My body yearned for more sleep, but I ignored its protest as I moved sluggishly through the dark room to the window. The sky was on the cusp of turning from night to day. Cracks of light were just fracturing the darkened sky.

With a flick of the light switch, a bright intrusion filled the room, causing my eyes to squint. My hair hung like a matted mess atop my head. As I ran my hand through the mass, I could feel the snarls and tangles caused by my incessant tossing and turning on my pillow. I stared at my rumpled blankets, wishing I could just hide under them and forget the world and all its lies, but my desire for answers outweighed the temptation to hide from them.

"Huh." I sighed and pulled open the double doors to my closet. Choosing an outfit felt like a burden. My arm responded on autopilot and fished out a pair of blue skinny jeans and a soft gray sweater.

I'd need some caffeine before I made my way to the house. The exhaustion of every disclosure my mom had made last night felt like a crushing boulder sitting heavily on my chest. And still there was more untold. She'd just scratched the surface of her well of secrets. Of this, I was certain.

I slid back the vertical blinds from my living-room and kitchen windows and stood still for a moment to watch as the sun bestowed the land below with its energizing glow. A sunrise never lost its magic or enigma. It was a gift to witness each time.

The coffee pot hissed as it completed percolating. I filled a mug and topped it with a splash of coconut milk. I practically chugged down the entire pot, hoping to relieve just the slightest bit of the heavy fog clouding my mind.

As angry as I was with my mom, I was ready to hear the rest of her story. Better sooner than later.

And maybe then some of this will make sense.

The sky had brightened significantly since I'd first awoken. I made my way to the main house as I pondered which questions to ask first: *Where is the planet we came from? Why didn't Creagan leave Siobhan if he loved my mother? Why did he keep returning to Siobhan? Does everyone from our planet have powers like mine? Is there anyone else in our lives who is also secretly from our planet?*

I thought of Calista and Selkie.

Selkie had always had an aversion to photos, but Calista relished in taking selfies. And now that I thought about it, they both also had incredibly youthful skin, which I'd always attributed to exceptional self-care and good genes.

Have they been lying to me too?

The thought stopped me in my tracks. A memory of Calista's odd musings on the porch the other night came to mind.

Was she hinting at more in her questions?

And the comments that my mom always made about the *other planets.*

Have they been hinting all this time, and I've been missing all the signs?

I remembered the single photo of the boy sealed in the plastic bag. Another question for the building list.

I reached the back door. The knob refused to turn when I twisted it. Not wanting to walk all the way back to the apartment for my keys, I went over to the birdhouse hanging in a nearby tree and found the spare key we kept hidden under a small floorboard inside.

I recalled when my mom had suggested the idea of leaving one board loose to hide the key beneath when we built the bird-house.

Apparently, she's got an affinity for hiding things under floors.

It was quiet as I entered the kitchen, and the only light was the sun peeking through the wooden blinds reflecting off the caramel-painted walls.

This would normally be the time I'd find my mom stretched on her yoga mat. Sundays were her day off to decompress and cultivate herbs and new product recipes for the café and classes.

The living room showed no hint of being occupied this morning. I suddenly realized that the house was lacking in the aromas of coffee and herbs. Not the norm.

I checked the cork-board, and the only note was the one from last night, and nothing new. I made a sweep of the rest of the house, and everything was exactly as it was the night before.

Did she not come home?

I tried to remember if I'd seen her car when I drove in from Jasper's, but I'd been too tired and hadn't noticed.

I ducked my head out the window. It wasn't there now.

Retrieving my phone from my pocket, I eagerly searched for a new message or voicemail from her, but was disappointed to find none.

Something didn't feel right. She never stayed out without letting me know. Despite our fight, I was actually surprised now that she hadn't attempted to call after I stormed out.

Is she just trying to give me my space?

My hands shook as I dialed her number and waited for her to answer. After three unanswered calls and an unreturned text, worry settled deeper into my bones. Maybe I was being paranoid after what had happened to Creagan, but I left the house with an ominous feeling.

As I entered the parking lot outside the café, I noticed my mom's car—it remained parked in the same spot as the previous night. I exhaled a deep breath, and my shoulders relaxed with relief.

She probably just fell asleep on the sofa.

After locking my car, I headed towards the entrance. I came to a sudden halt. The café door sat unlocked and ajar. My senses went on alert as I stepped inside. Furniture littered the floor, and a few jars lay smashed on counters. I let my guard down and scanned the building for other vibrations.

"Mom ... are you here?"

I maneuvered around the overturned chairs as caution morphed into panic.

What happened in here?

"Ack—" I yelped as my foot slipped in a glob of spilled honey on the floor, and I grabbed hold of the condiment shelf to steady my balance.

Several broken jars lay on the floor with their contents oozing into puddles. I continuously checked for any other emotional signatures in the air, but felt none.

I carefully hopped over the wreckage on the floor. The building was quiet, except for my breathing and the sticky noise my shoe made as it stuck to the floor with each step.

The beating of my heart filled my ears as I crouched down and peeked behind the employee counter. The open window that looked through to the kitchen was dark. I avoided looking through it for now and kept sliding along the hall wall toward the office.

Pinpricks needled at my scalp, and my forehead broke out in a sheen of sweat. I was almost there when my feet crunched over the broken glass from the fallen picture frame. I cursed silently at the noise.

My chest tightened when I spotted a trail of tiny blood drops leading out of the office.

Screw it.

I sprung away from the wall and rushed into the office, looking around in a panic.

Empty.

My temples pulsed as I spun every which way, scanning for any sign of my mom.

"Oh—my—God!" Fear spread through me.

Blood smeared the floor—a lot of blood.

I ran out of the office and tore through the café, no longer caring if someone still lay in wait.

I checked every space more carefully: the kitchen and walk-in cooler, stockroom, craft room, and bathroom.

"MOM … Mom … where are you?"

A crumpling realization sank in: she wasn't anywhere in the building.

I snagged my cell phone out and dialed 911.

The operator answered, and I practically screamed at her. "There's blood … My mom's missing … Her car's out front … Someone broke in … Please send someone to help. PLEASE HURRY!"

"Take a deep breath, ma'am, and give me your address."

I did, and she said, "An officer is on his way, ma'am. Please try to stay calm."

I hung up. *Calm, my ass!*

Maybe it's not her blood. Oh, God—please don't let it be hers.

I ran to the bathroom as a wave of nausea became too much to bear, and threw up into the toilet. My body broke out in a sweat with the uncontrollable beat of my pulse. I splashed some cold water on my face and rinsed out my mouth. The back of my throat stung with the bitter, acidic taste of bile.

Returning to the office, I carefully scanned the surroundings, hoping to spot something that had escaped my attention during my initial search. I avoided looking at the blood; there was so much of it. I spotted a crumpled-up sticky note under the desk chair. I bent down and picked it up, then smoothed out the wrinkled paper. As I read the note, a jolt of terror stabbed me. I found scribbled words in my mom's handwriting:

Help Dar

A bloody fingerprint smudged one corner of the note. The blood had completely dried. I read the unfinished message over and over, all the while feeling more scared for my mother each time. I stared at the two words, trying to decipher what she could have meant that second word to be. It could have been the start of *Darling*, but I couldn't imagine she'd have wasted time writing an endearment when she must have known she was in danger. She was too smart for that; she would have used the opportunity to leave a clue behind to help me find her. She capitalized the letter D. That must have meant something. Maybe it stood for the name of something, a place somewhere, or the name of someone. A name immediately came to mind: *Darion!* The second I thought the name, I knew I had it right.

The sound of a siren alerted me to the arrival of the police. I tucked the note into my pants pocket and hurried to the front door.

Sheriff Baze strode inside and, without beating around the bush, said, "Everly, take me to where you found the blood, and tell me everything from the beginning."

I recounted my steps for the sheriff from when I first arrived until I discovered the blood on the office floor. I left out everything from the previous day.

Somehow, I don't think mentioning the part about being from another planet will go over too well.

I also omitted telling him about the note I found and my suspicion about Darion for now. There was one person I needed to talk to first.

"We will do everything we can to find your mother," said the sheriff, his dark brow furrowed.

While the police taped off the crime scene, I called our employees to let them know what had happened and that we'd be closed until further notice and that we would compensate them for any lost wages. I guiltily let Ty and Molly know through text message, since I knew both would have a torrent of questions and neither would let me off the phone easily, and there was no time to waste.

I left the café and went to see the only person I could think of who I suspected might have some answers and be able to offer some help.

≈

*A*fter a few knocks, Calista called out from inside, "I'll be right there." She cracked the door out of breath. Even dressed in yoga pants and a T-shirt, she was a stunning sight to look at.

As soon as I saw the face of the woman who had always been like a second mother to me, and my mother's dearest friend, I broke down in tears.

"Oh, sweetie, come here and tell me what's wrong." Calista wrapped me in her arms and guided me inside and onto her soft mocha leather sofa.

"Something happened at the café last night or this morning. I'm not sure when, but my mom's missing," I got out between sobs. I could hear the panic rising in my voice.

Calista's eyes grew wide and she stifled a gasp.

"Take a deep breath, Ev, and tell me what happened at the café and why you think your mom is missing."

The tightness in my lungs made it nearly impossible to manage inhaling. I looked around the room to find something to anchor my emotions to and landed on the statue of the Hindu deity Durga that Calista had brought back from her trip to India. The ten-armed, demon-slaying goddess sat atop her lion, armed and ready to defend the universe. I studied the stony features of the goddess and willed myself to be strong.

I forced my chest to fill with air and tried my best to speak calmly. I explained to Calista how my mother and I had had an argument the previous night and the scene I'd found this morning in the café. Nausea rose all over again at the flashback. I took the bloody note from my pocket and held it out for her to see.

Calista's calm exterior melted away at the sight of the bloodied note. Her skin paled as the panic growing within her aura matched my own.

It seeped into mine, like two parts forging together as one. I tried snapping my guard back up, but nothing happened. My eyes squeezed shut tight, trying to block out the overwhelming sensations as my body rocked back and forth. The room closed in on me, and I struggled to remain conscious.

A new fear snaked through my veins.

Why can't I control my power?

"Oh, dear." Calista reached out and took my hands in hers. "Breathe, Everly. You're okay. Just breathe."

My body stopped rocking as a calming energy passed through me.

Calista's long, slender hands were warm and smooth, and smelled of cocoa butter.

My head drifted forward, and I felt woozy, as if someone had sedated me.

As the powerful emotions loosened their grip on my body and mind, a realization hit me.

Calista's using magic on me.

The energy surrounding her changed. It became thick and pulsed with invisible sparks.

Despite feeling my muscles relax and experiencing relief from not being able to shield myself from siphoning her emotions, a tightness gripped my lungs as I realized another person I cared about had hidden secrets from me.

I tore my hands free from hers and bowed my head into my palms. The feeling of sedation lifted as soon as I broke skin contact with Calista, but my thoughts remained hazy, like trying to see through thick fog. I wished I could go back to sleep and wake up to find that the last couple of days had all been a terrible, messed-up dream. But I knew there was no waking up from this new reality.

My head shot up, and I narrowed my eyes at her. "Selkie?"

Her pained expression confirmed the answer before she spoke.

Calista cast her gaze down. "I'm sorry, Everly." When she looked back up, regret and apologies filled her eyes.

My stomach twisted as though someone had torn through my flesh and yanked on my insides, gripping, intending to destroy.

Nearly everyone I love has been lying to me for my entire life.

"How much did your mother tell you?"

There was no reason to withhold further information. Calista knew where my mother came from, because she also came from the same faraway place.

I glanced again at the Durga goddess.

Pick your battles wisely, as the goddess did.

I wouldn't make the same mistake with Calista as I had with my mother. I cast my anger aside and reiterated everything my mom had told me, while Calista listened with close attention.

Folding her hands together under her chin, she said, "This is really bad. I was afraid of something like this happening."

I tried massaging the ache from my temples, to no avail. Everything seemed to crumble around me, even my ability to control my power.

"I'm sorry that you feel so betrayed," said Calista, "but I swore an oath to both of your parents to keep their secret and to help keep you safe."

"Creagan knew we weren't safe," I said, trying to hold back the sharp edge in my tone. "He wanted to tell me the truth, but my mom refused, and now he's dead and she's missing."

Calista's brow wrinkled. "What are you talking about?"

"Don't you remember the phone call I told you about? When Creagan called me because he urgently needed to see me and tell me something important. He wanted to tell me the truth. My mom confessed as much. She had refused him, so he was going to tell me without her. I was so angry with her last night, Calista. The last thing I said to her was that I would never forgive her. What if those are the last words she'll ever hear from me?"

Calista's expression softened. "Don't think like that. Your mother knows how much you love her and that you only said those things out of hurt and anger."

"I hope you're right," I replied, hardening myself against the graying blues of pity swirling around Calista.

I need to figure out what's wrong with my ability and how to get it back under control before I'm rendered useless.

Shaking off the weighty cloud of emotions, I said, "There's something else I forgot to mention."

I told her about Arden showing up at the café and then seeing him outside that same night with Creagan. I described the incident at the funeral when both Arden and Darion had appeared, and my theory that Darion may have had something to do with my mother's disappearance.

"And … there was something about Darion that almost seemed familiar, but I have no recollection of ever seeing him anywhere before. One thing was for sure, though: his aura was dark. He played at being friendly, but there was something hostile and dangerous in his mannerisms."

My hands squeezed into tight balls of fists. "Do you think Darion had something to do with my mom's disappearance?"

Calista tucked a fallen curl behind her ear. "If Darion is on this planet, we're all in danger and will need to act quickly and carefully if we stand a chance of saving Cacsha."

My stomach lurched. All in danger? What on earth did that mean? But I steeled myself.

She was being direct and honest, which was exactly what I needed. No more lies.

"But why? Why would he want to hurt my mom? He doesn't even know us." My nails cut into my skin as I squeezed my fists tighter in frustration.

Calista stayed quiet for a moment.

Then she sighed, as if coming to some unspoken resignation.

"Darion is what you call a Tracker on our planet. Siobhan must have sent him here to trace your father's whereabouts. If he took your mother, I can only presume it was at Siobhan's behest. To what end, I don't know." Calista stared off with a hint of defeat in her eyes.

"Siobhan must hate my mother. It could have been her at the café, or maybe she was with Darion and they attacked her together." The thought of my mother alone and defenseless against two monsters made me sick. "But she wrote 'Help Dar.' What else could that mean … except that she was trying to tell us that Darion was the one who attacked her?"

"If I know one thing about Siobhan," Calista said in a scathing tone, the defeat in her eyes replaced with fevered hate, "it's that she would consider it beneath her to come to this planet. Many of our kind view Earth as a toxic wasteland and fear the dangers of the pollutants. I would be surprised if Siobhan is here. She would most likely send others to do her bidding, but if we've learned anything from the recent events, it's that she should not be underestimated."

A thought occurred to me. "Does Siobhan know about me?"

Calista's eyes locked on mine, shining with fury. "Siobhan has always known about you. Your mother's pregnancy was the weapon she used to exile Cacsha from our planet. It's a long story, and one that you should know in time. Creagan, Siobhan, and your mother have much history."

My throat clenched as I struggled to ask my next question. I couldn't even bear to think it. "Do … do you think my mom's still alive?"

I'll never forgive myself if …

Calista stood up and walked quietly around the room, momentarily consumed with her own thoughts. Her bold and gregarious personality gave the impression that she lived a life of luxury to those who didn't know her well, when in fact Calista was a minimalist. She preferred open and airy spaces devoid of clutter. She chose her items carefully and only added things that spoke volumes. Her passion for the study of theology and historical relics was evident throughout her home.

I gazed up at one of her most treasured items hanging front and center on her living room wall, and hot tears burned in my eyes at seeing the familiar brush strokes. My mother had painted a majestic landscape. The hues on the canvas sparkled and glittered with life and the words, 'abundance lives in the heart,' floated above the scenery.

I swiped away the fresh tears and refocused my attention on Calista. She paused at her yoga mat, rolling it up as she continued to move in silence. It was as though by performing simple tasks; it allowed her mind to sort through all the facts. She propped the rolled mat against the wall and walked back toward me.

"Let me see that note again."

I held out the partial note my mom had managed to leave behind.

Calista carefully placed the paper in her palm, then took a seat next to me. "I haven't used this type of magic in a long time," she said as she positioned her free hand on top of the bloody fingerprint.

She began reciting some kind of chant, and a spark of energy swirled around the piece of paper. The air became thick and dewy, as it had before, when Calista used her magic on me.

Each person's aura represented their own unique emotional signature, so to speak. I wondered if it was the same with our magic.

She stopped chanting, and the air returned to normal. "Your mother is alive, but she's weak. We need to contact the others to warn them and gather our strength. I'm afraid our cloaking spell, which we cast many years ago, has weakened and we'll need to recast it."

"How can you tell if she's alive?" I asked skeptically. "And who else is there besides Selkie?"

"To answer your first question, it's one of my abilities. As for the second, I promise to tell you more later, but right now, we need to move. There's no time to waste. Darion could already know our locations."

I jumped up. My body pumped with a rush of adrenaline. "Can you use your ability to locate where they took my mom?"

"I'm afraid not. I tried when I sought her lifeline, but she's being guarded by powerful magic, stronger than my own. My magic is not what it used to be, having lived on Earth these years."

Calista stood. "I need to change and grab a couple of important items we'll need."

"Calista, wait—"

I remembered something that seemed insignificant before, but now I wondered ...

"At the cemetery, Darion said he and I shared something in common with Creagan. What do you think he meant by that?"

Something flashed within her eyes, and she reined in her emotions. "Honey, I can only guess that he must've been referring to our home planet, Aenoas-Vita."

Her answer was only a half-truth.

Normally, I would refrain from using my ability on people close to me, but considering recent events, I didn't feel particularly trusting. And given the way Calista had guarded her emotions as she answered, I knew she was holding back on more.

I'll let it go for now.

I didn't want to give away the fact that I could sense when someone was intentionally shielding their emotions from me. It'd become apparent that people weren't aware of this little facet of my ability, so instead of calling her out, I followed suit.

"Hmm … you're probably right."

∼

 alista carried a small wooden chest with her as we locked up her house and headed for her car.

"What's that for?" I asked.

She glanced sideways at me. "Some tools to help strengthen our magic." She popped her trunk, and ducked the top half of her body inside, while she situated the box beneath a blanket. She slammed the trunk closed. "Let's go."

We flew down Columbia River Highway in Calista's red Mustang convertible. She turned right on Wikstrom Road and drove for about a quarter mile before making a sharp left turn down a private dirt drive that led to a small house painted in a vibrant teal. Two newly updated bay windows decorated either side of the enclosed porch.

Selkie had filled her front yard with exotic plants of all kinds, giving it the appearance of a mini rain forest. Tall Tetrapanax stood in each corner, their enormous, thick leaves spreading wide. Huge banana trees bordered a forest of bamboo that Selkie had strategically planted so that you could walk through the thick bamboo maze and enjoy the natural shade it offered during a hot summer or listen to the rain run down its stalks on a stormy day.

Calista didn't bother driving around to the back of the house, where there was extra parking. She stopped the car next to a path that led straight to the front porch. From inside the car, we could see that the front door was partially ajar.

"Something's wrong." Calista reached for me.

"I sense it too." I gripped the door handle.

We slid out of the car and left our doors cracked open to reduce excess noise and hurried to the entrance as quietly as we could. We stopped at the door, and Calista used her foot to widen the opening. Furniture and broken items were strewn about the room and floor.

My throat constricted at the familiar scene. *Not Selkie too.*

Calista stayed ahead of me, with her hand extended out in front of her. A bright bluish-white glow emanated from within the skin of her hand. She motioned for me to follow her as we crept silently around the overturned furniture.

"Selkie!" Calista called out as we spotted her crumpled body on the floor.

We rushed to her side. She held a blood-covered hand to her neck, and she was barely conscious.

I whipped my phone out of my pocket, about to dial for an ambulance, when Calista said, "No. Go get something to stop the bleeding."

Not asking questions, I hurried to find some towels. I quickly reached the linen closet and piled my arms full. I ran to the medicine cabinet and grabbed bandages and antiseptics, then hurried back.

Calista had propped Selkie up against the wall. I knelt down to locate where the blood was coming from and gasped when Selkie removed her hand from her neck.

"Oh my God, Selkie. What did this to you?" Two gaping holes had opened on the side of her neck, the flesh torn back and blood seeping from the gashes.

"You mean *who*?" she muttered, her voice raspy and dry. Without moving her head, she shifted her hazel eyes to look at Calista. "Take me to Felix. Quickly—"

Selkie's hair clung to her neck, matted and sticky with blood.

I willed my hands to stop shaking as I gently pulled the goopy hair away from her skin and dumped some antiseptic on the bleeding wounds. The holes were bleeding too heavily for the small bandages, so I tied a towel around her neck as tightly as I could without cutting off her windpipe.

With each of us supporting her on either side, we carried her out of the house and set her in the back seat of the Mustang.

Calista got the car turned around, and instead of heading back towards the hospital on the highway, she turned in the opposite direction and headed farther up the mountain.

"Calista, where are you going? Shouldn't we be taking Selkie to the hospital?"

"There's nothing a human hospital can do to help her. I'll explain later."

The trees blurred as Calista took the corners at max speed. I worried we might fly off the cliff and into the dark pit of the forest at each turn, yet Calista maintained complete control of her vehicle. I had questions I wanted to ask about what Selkie had said attacked her, but I didn't want to distract Calista's attention from the road, and I needed to hold on to Selkie safely so she didn't bang her head against anything.

Calista's speed slowed, and she turned onto an unmarked drive leading farther up into the forest. As we climbed to a higher elevation, the bumpy road narrowed and the woods became darker and denser. I had no idea where we were going. We crawled up the hill, swerving slightly here and there to avoid large potholes in the gravel road. Whoever lived up here definitely did not keep the road maintained, and I had the feeling it was to discourage visitors. After what seemed like endless twists and turns, we finally arrived at a cabin nestled in a small clearing in the woods.

"Who lives here?" I asked.

"Someone who can help us." Calista had barely shifted the gear into park before she flung her door open and dashed out of the car.

I wasn't sure how someone living in a remote cabin in the woods could be more beneficial than a trained doctor in the emergency room, but what did I know anymore?

Together, we lifted Selkie out of the back seat. She'd lost consciousness on the drive, so moving her was more of a challenge.

We began to carry her, but as soon as we moved toward the cabin, we hit an invisible wall. Its force blasted us backward, causing us to nearly drop Selkie. I released my mental guard and immediately *sensed* a powerful energy force that seemed to encompass both the cabin and the woods surrounding it. Whatever the energy source was, it acted as some kind of protective shield that kept us from walking through it.

"Crap! I forgot," cursed Calista.

She placed her hand on the invisible wall and spoke in the

same strange language as earlier. I *felt* the energy give way, and we rushed Selkie up the few steps to the front door as quickly as we could move. Selkie wasn't a large person, but my arms ached from the weight of her unconscious body.

The door wasn't locked because most people would never have made it this far onto the property.

We entered a dimly lit room. The only light came from what few rays of sunlight sneaked through the trees and streamed through the bare windows that made up an entire wall in the main room.

"FELIX!" Calista called out. "Get your healing ass out here! Selkie's dying!"

A man suddenly appeared at our side and was removing Selkie from our grasp.

Before I could process, he'd carried Selkie to the dusty couch in the living room. Long champagne hair flowed behind his tall, slender form as he practically glided across the floor. He radiated energy stronger than anything I'd ever felt before. He lifted Selkie's shirt and placed his hand flat on her chest. Her skin glowed, and then it faded.

"We're losing her," he stated.

He untied the towel from around her neck and hissed some words in that other language. It sounded like he was cursing from the tone of his voice.

He looked back at us with glowing eyes and said with authority, "She needs a transfusion immediately." Throwing a quick glance my way, he added, "There is no time for delicacy."

He left the room and returned within a second, holding a sharp blade. Without hesitating, he held the blade to his palm and made a wide slit. Blood immediately flowed. He positioned his hand over Selkie's mouth, and I winced as blood flowed from his body into hers.

Felix and Calista each took a turn giving Selkie blood in

this manner while Felix continued to hold his free hand pressed to Selkie's chest. He repeated a chant over and over until finally her skin maintained a continued glow. He stopped the chant and lifted his hand. His expression softened.

"She will survive," he said. "But she'll need rest for quite some time before she will have the energy to tell us her story."

He lifted Selkie from the couch, then carried her into a nearby room and tenderly laid her on the bed. His soft and graceful steps barely made a sound as he crossed the room to retrieve a blanket and some medicinal-looking amber bottles.

He and Calista applied a green salve to Selkie's wounds and then their own self-inflicted ones. Not knowing what to do, I walked back into the living room.

The rustic room was spacious, and the furniture sparse. A fire blazed in a grand fireplace built into the center of an east-facing stone wall, warming the space. The outer border of the fireplace had a mantel of thick wood, with ancient-looking symbols carved into both the wood and stones around the entire mantel and wall.

Floor-to-ceiling windows made up the entire north wall of the room, making the forest feel a part of the room itself.

I walked closer to the glass. The image of Selkie crumpled on the floor with blood oozing from her neck burned in my mind, along with the memory of the blood I'd found on the office floor this morning.

Did the same person who attacked my mom attack Selkie? What if what happened to Selkie also happened to my mom?

My whole body clenched.

I have to find her.

I looked up at the sky and sent out a silent prayer. *Please let my mom be okay. Please keep her safe.*

"Everly."

Startled, I turned toward the voice.

"I apologize, my dear. I didn't mean to frighten you," said Felix.

A ray of sunlight streaked through the windows, lighting up his regal features. Bright blue eyes met mine, and I knew I was looking into eyes that had seen many years and maybe many centuries. If he was human, I would guess his age to be around sixty, but I knew he wasn't human. Humans didn't radiate the energy he emitted. He had a handsome and stoic face, his long, straight nose lined by the faintest of age lines.

"There is no mistaking that face," he said. "You are the mirror image of our lovely Cacsha, and quite the powerful Empath as well. Welcome to my home. I am Felix." He placed one hand on his heart and one on his abdomen and lowered his head in a bow, sending silky waves of champagne hair cascading forward.

There was something very soothing about the way his words flowed off his tongue like poetry. I felt safe here in his presence.

"Thank you," I replied. "And what do you mean by Empath?"

His long and graceful arms motioned toward the windows and around the property. "You can feel the energy force around this place, correct? You know how I'm feeling at this moment, do you not?"

I nodded my agreement.

"You come from a powerful bloodline. Your dominant gift is that of an Empath, and I can tell you that you have many talents yet to be discovered."

He spoke as though he knew much about me; things I didn't know myself. It made me feel both vulnerable and oddly reassured.

But the only gifts I care about are the ones that will help me save my mom.

"You know my mom? Did Calista tell you she's missing?" The high pitch returned to my voice.

He watched me with a studying gaze. "I have known your mother her entire life. She means a great deal to me."

Felix spoke with sincerity, and his presence exuded a unique sense of stability and wisdom.

Something about him urged me to keep talking. "When I discovered her missing, I found blood where she'd last been, a lot of blood. It makes me sick to think that whatever happened to Selkie might have happened to my mom, or could still happen. Can you help me find her?"

"There's no need to ask for my help. I would give my life for your mother without hesitation."

How could I have never met this man before who holds my mother's life so dear?

A twinge hit my heart. *She has so many secrets.*

Felix continued studying me as though he were deciphering my thoughts.

"Will you take a walk with me, child?"

I paused. But he said *child* not in a demeaning way, to make me feel less than him, and so I followed him out onto the porch.

It was magnificent up here on the mountain. The air smelled of fresh pine, pure and intoxicating. A clearing of trees allowed for an amazing view of Mount St. Helens. The crisp white mountain appeared to float in the crimson sky from our viewpoint. The flat top of its peak, a constant reminder of the threat hidden beneath the soft white layers of delicate snow.

Felix stood at my side.

He inhaled and exhaled a long breath. "What happened to Selkie is a terrible offense among our kind and strictly forbidden. Our people discovered long ago that by drinking the blood of one another, they could absorb not just the powers of that unique soul but also knowledge. Blood exchange for the sake of absorbing another's unique life force is like underage drinking to young Earthlings: taboo and irresistible. Most who indulge in the forbidden ritual do so in small quantities, only to experience the rush of the energy transfer, and are careful not to injure the one they are drinking from by draining too much. We're also able to use the transfer of our blood, and thus our energy, to save another life, as you have just witnessed."

He glanced sideways in my direction. "However, the one who committed this atrocity on our dear Selkie intended to absorb everything, thereby ending her life. This leaves the question as to whether he was after her knowledge or power … Perhaps both."

"Do you think the same person who attacked Selkie took my mother?"

His eyes narrowed. "Yes, unfortunately, I believe it is the same individual who took your mother. I'm told Darion is on this planet. He would not be so if not ordered by Siobhan. From what I've learned about Darion, he is extremely loyal to Siobhan, which leads me to believe that she is most likely behind these recent attacks."

Unwanted images of Darion tearing into Selkie's flesh filled my mind. "Is this what people are like on our planet, vengeful and murderous?"

Felix took a moment, as if to contemplate his words. "Good and evil are present in all facets and forms of life, my young one. Our planet is no exception, but the actions of these few do not represent the whole. Aenoas-Vita is a place of magic and unmatched beauty, but where there is beauty and light, you will also find their polar opposites."

I groaned in frustration.

I don't care how much beauty and light there is on Aenoas-Vita. All I care about is that the polar opposite of those things has my mom, and I'm getting tired of waiting around.

"How can you help me find my mom?" I asked, staring at the faraway snow.

"I have already initiated a summons to our allies to pool together all our resources to see if we can find any clues about where Darion may have taken her."

I spun to face him. "What do you mean, initiated a summons?"

The corner of his mouth twitched as if amused by my naivete. "Through magical means, of course."

"Of course," I said, slightly exasperated.

I believed Felix was sincere, and I was grateful for his reassurance, but I felt powerless and had no idea how we would find and save my mom. Magic or no magic.

I walked to the other end of the porch, where the view was a thick sea of Douglas fir and pine trees. The thought of someone draining my mom of her blood or causing her pain in any way filled my entire body with a burning rage. I wanted to scream out at the trees and howl up to the sky and tear through the wind. I wanted to release everything I was feeling on those who had threatened and harmed my loved ones.

I'm going to find my mom, and when I do ... I'm going to kill Darion.

My hair lifted as the still air suddenly stirred restlessly, and a violent wind roared through the trees. I closed my eyes and reveled in the ferocity of it, in the way it rippled around my body. It felt as though the wind were responding to my despair with a call of its own.

Felix came up behind me and placed a comforting hand on my shoulder. "It has been a very long day for you. You need some rest," he suggested.

His words calmed my raging thoughts and, oddly, the wind with it.

He looked out at the forest with a thoughtful expression and then back at me. "It would be safer for you to stay here. I have extra rooms on the top floor. Let's get you situated, and then I must speak with Calista."

He was right. The exhaustion of the day was taking its toll, but if he and Calista were going to be making any plans that had to do with saving my mom, I would be a part of it.

I stood firmly in place and stared him in the eye. "If you two decide what to do next, don't exclude me," I asserted firmly. "I've had enough of secrets and lies."

Felix looked at me as though he were taking my measure.

I refused to back down.

Looking into his eyes was like looking into the mysterious depths of the ocean: beautiful and serene on the surface, with its deeper depths the keeper of many dark secrets.

He spoke cautiously, his words firm. "I give you my word, my dear, that I will include you in all matters of import and I will not lie to you. But right now, the best thing you can do to help is to get some rest." He paused and arched his eyebrows. "I expect to begin your training first thing tomorrow morning, and trust me when I say you will need all of your strength."

Felix turned and walked back toward the front door of the cabin.

"What exactly do you mean by training, anyway?" I followed him. "Time is of the essence, and I don't plan to waste mine learning new magic tricks."

He stopped and turned back to face me, not a hint of impatience in his composure. "I understand your frustration, Everly, but you will help your mother by learning to master your gifts. Darion alone is powerful, but if others have traveled here with him, we must all be at our full strength if we stand a chance of rescuing Cacsha. Darion is keeping your mother alive, for now. He must be biding his time for a reason. And we will use that time to our advantage."

I flinched at his words and the thought that Darion was playing some devious game with my mom's life. And for what reason? Because Siobhan felt scorned.

Is he such a monster that he would take lives to satisfy the sick request of a betrayed woman?

I tried to push away the fear of what could happen to my mom and to remain strong for her sake, but it was too late. Fear had already etched itself into my very core.

Felix seemed to sense my warring thoughts. "I apologize for my bluntness. I don't get off the mountain much."

I swiped away the angry tear that I'd been trying to hold back. "Please don't apologize. Thank you for your honesty, Felix. Even if it's hard to hear, it's refreshing."

"Of course, my dear."

His expression softened. "Most of us have one dominant power accompanied by companionable gifts. Your dominant gift is that of an Empath. Mine is that of a Healer. Because I'm a Healer, I'm able to sense when certain forces are out of balance."

He squeezed my arm. "You are having difficulties with maintaining control over your ability, am I right?"

I hesitated to admit my weakness, but then nodded.

Felix showed no signs of judgment, only compassion. "Tomorrow, we will test your physical and mental strengths. Your magic has lain dormant for too long, and I believe this to be the reason for your current predicament. Our total sum of gifts works together in tandem, but you have never fully tapped into yours, and it's time we change that. Will you agree to at least begin your training in the morning?"

Felix was being honest with me, and for that I owed him

trust. But more than that, I believed him when he said he will give his life for my mother's, and for that I would try things his way. *For the time being*.

"I agree," I said.

With that, he turned and led the way back into the cabin.

CHAPTER 7

*T*he room Felix offered me was compact but comfortable. A futon that folded out to a twin-sized mattress decorated one wall. It was smaller than I was used to, but the cushion that doubled as the mattress felt thick and firm, with just the right amount of softness. Using the set of sheets Felix had left in the room, I finished turning the futon into a bed and went to use the bathroom in the hall to wash my face and brush my teeth with the spare tooth-brush Felix provided.

Wearing just my T-shirt, I sat on the edge of the futon, wondering how I could sleep while my mother was in danger and being held against her will.

I sighed, squeezing the pillow I held in my lap.

Felix is right. I'm going to need my strength. Maybe once I learn to use my companionable gifts, they'll be useful in helping me locate Darion and find where he's keeping her.

I tossed the pillow back onto the mattress, resolved to at least try to get some rest, but I just lay restless, staring at the ceiling and feeling completely useless. The windows were bare of coverings, just like every other window I'd seen so far. I supposed with no neighbors and a protective force field, Felix didn't have to worry about prying eyes.

Night shadows danced on the other side of the glass as the windows rattled in their frames in response to the whistling windstorm. I ignored the dark, twisting shapes that tried to play tricks on my mind and instead focused on the whispering sound of the wind. As time passed, my eyelids grew heavy with the feeling of night sand, and eventually, the pull of exhaustion lulled me into the world of dreams.

A voice echoed deep in my subconscious. It called out to me, drawing me back to the surface of consciousness. The sound of my mom's voice echoed in my ears, filled with a desperate plea for help. My eyes flew open, and I sprang upright. My mind still buzzed with sleep, and my heart hammered in my chest as I tried to orient myself, searching the dark room for a presence.

I held my breath and listened intently for the sound of her voice again, but all I could hear was the pounding of my heart beating with adrenaline.

Was I just dreaming?

Rushing out of bed, I yanked my pants on. I tried peering through the bedroom window, but it was too dark to see anything but my own reflection in the glass.

Hurrying down the dark hall, I searched the cabin. At first, all was silent, but then I heard her again, louder this time.

"Everly—help me—he's killing me."

Darion! Is he here with her?

I stumbled forward, both thankful to hear her voice and terrified that Darion was hurting her.

"Felix! Calista!" I shouted their names as I ran down the dark staircase, my hand skimming the top of the banister to keep from tumbling down.

The cabin was pitch-black, and I couldn't see a thing. I called out to her. "Mom—I'm coming. Where are you?"

"Help me. Everly—please."

Her voice came from the other side of the front door.

My throat seized as I pulled open the heavy wooden door and ran barefoot outside. I scanned the surrounding porch. No one was there. I hurried down the porch steps into the open wooded area. Heavy wind on my back propelled me forward.

"Mom!" I called out into the darkness.

The wind shifted, and my hair blew across my face, cutting into my eyes and making it impossible to see anything. I gathered it away from my eyes and mouth, and held it back while I called out again.

"Mom—please tell me where you are."

I turned, frantically searching for any sign of her, but without any kind of light, it was too dark to see anything except the shadows of trees thrashing in the wind. Their leaves hissed warnings.

An owl hooted from somewhere atop a tree, and then someone had me by the hair. My head was violently jerked backwards. Cold steel eyes stared down. I spun and twisted out of my captor's grasp, falling backward onto the hard ground.

Pain shot up my back. I expected him to be on me the instant I fell, but as I scrambled back to my feet, no one else was there.

"Everly?" Calista said questioningly as she came down the porch steps with Felix by her side.

Felix held his hands up with a bluish-white light swimming around them, lighting the area in front of them as they made their way toward me.

"What on earth are you doing out here?"

"I …" I was about to tell them I'd heard my mom's voice

calling to me and that someone had attacked me from behind just moments ago, but the worried looks on their faces halted me. I glanced around. My mom obviously wasn't out here, nor was any assailant.

What the hell is happening to me? First, I can't control my power, and now I'm hearing voices and seeing things that aren't there.

"I'm sorry I woke the both of you. I must have been sleep-walking." I rubbed the back of my scalp.

But why does my hair feel like someone just ripped out a chunk?

Felix quietly surveyed the area.

"Come on, sweetie." Calista wrapped her arm around my back. "You must be freezing."

∼

Still exhausted from lack of sleep, but relieved that it was finally daylight, I pulled the sweat-dampened blanket away from my sticky skin. I hadn't slept well after Calista brought me back up to my room last night. Cold silver eyes haunted every corner of my room and my mind, and I awoke with a start several times throughout the night to my hands fending off an invisible attacker.

What had happened last night?

I was sure I had heard my mom's voice and felt the pain when someone ripped my head back. I applied pressure to the painful muscle in my neck.

Could I have been in some weird sleepwalk dream the entire time?

I'd sleepwalked a few times over the years, but this time had felt different: *I felt awake. Nothing about last night felt like a dream.*

A nauseating feeling washed over me as rancid acid bubbled within my stomach.

Am I losing a grip on reality? No! Stop it right now, Everly, or Darion has won already.

I inhaled a shaky breath and pushed away the negative thoughts that threatened to swallow me whole. Scooting to the edge of the bed, I rubbed my face and massaged my temples. *I have to stay strong.*

A chill spread across my chest from my cold-sweat-soaked shirt. I stretched it away from my skin, wishing for a change of clean clothes. A thump on the other side of the door drew my attention. I opened the bedroom door and peeked out. A suitcase and duffel bag sat on the floor outside my room. The hall was empty. I unfolded a note propped atop the suitcase: *I thought you might like some of your things, C.*

I couldn't help but smile as I grabbed the bags and carried them inside. I placed them on the futon mattress and opened the suitcase first.

"Ahh … Calista, you wonderful woman."

She had filled the suitcase with as many of my clothes as she could fit, as well as some of my toiletries and other items. I grabbed a clean pair of stretchy skinny jeans, underwear, and a cotton T-shirt and went to take a shower.

The aroma of fresh-brewed coffee filled the cabin, and my olfactory senses led me to the kitchen, where I was met with a pair of mysterious blue-green eyes. My stomach immediately twisted with knots.

Arden returned my gaze with a grin.

"Good morning, Everly," he greeted me warmly as he moved away from the counter he was leaning on and handed me a steaming cup of coffee that looked to have the perfect amount of cream. *Hmm … just the way I like it.*

"I thought you might need this," he offered with a

knowing smile. "Calista said you prefer coconut milk. I hope I didn't add too much."

"Um. It's perfect, thanks," I uttered in my unusual tongue-tied state that he seemed to bring out in me.

"Hey, sweetheart," Calista greeted me from behind. "I see you got the gift this handsome devil brought for you."

"And what would that be?" I asked.

"You're wearing it," she replied casually with a wink.

My cheeks burned at the thought of Arden going through my personal things.

"I thought you brought the suitcase?" I asked her.

"I asked Arden to bring your things. I hope that's okay."

I definitely wasn't happy about it, but there was nothing I could do about it now, so I shrugged it off and changed the subject.

"So, what's the plan?" I asked while taking a sip from my mug and sneaking in a quick glance at Arden, who stood quietly observing our conversation. The dark gray shirt he wore set off the blue in his eyes.

"Felix left this morning to meet with some contacts," Calista said.

I pulled my gaze away from Arden to look at her. She'd left her hair down today, and long, wild curls flowed past her shoulders.

"Selkie's still too weak to be left alone," she added. "I'll look after her while you begin your training with Arden immediately."

I coughed as I choked down a swallow of coffee.

"You okay, honey?" Calista asked.

"Yeah. I just swallowed wrong." I waved off her concern. "But I was kind of under the impression that Felix would train me." I glanced at Arden. "No offense."

"None taken," Arden replied without a hint of emotion. His long body leaned against the counter. His posture was casual, but there was a hint of something guarded in the way his intense eyes continued to watch me.

I shifted nervously.

He was probably sizing me up to determine if I was a worthy trainee.

Was that why he was at the café, studying me so closely?

I'd thought his guarded looks were for another reason. The room suddenly became too warm and too small, and my skin flushed with heat.

Calista quirked her eyebrow.

"I'll leave you two alone," Arden said.

As he walked past me, the air filled with cedar and sandalwood.

I held my tongue until I thought he was out of earshot. "Who is he? And why is he training me instead of Felix?"

Calista reached for the large glass French press and filled her coffee mug. She omitted any cream but added a dash of honey instead to her black coffee as usual.

"Sweetie," she said, turning back to face me, "I know Arden is a stranger to you, but he was a close and trusted friend of Creagan's, and he came to Earth at your father's request before his death. He can teach you to connect with your innate magic and to develop your abilities to their fullest potential."

I remembered how my energy had felt drawn to him at the café. "Is he some kind of magic trainer or something on your planet?"

Calista grinned mischievously. "You could say that's one of his responsibilities." She took a deep drink of her coffee. "Creagan wanted Arden to be your trainer, and he's here to honor that wish and to help us, and we need all the help we can get. Your father trusted him completely."

I stared at the dried garlic stalks tied in knots around a thick cord of string that hung along two large kitchen windows. Each window took up half of two separate walls, joining in one corner. Like the rest of the house, the windows were bare, and morning fog floated by in thick, smoky patches.

The warmth of Calista's body pressed nearer as she slid closer.

"It's so strange," I said, "to hear someone refer to my father after all of these years of thinking of him as a faceless donor instead of a real person."

"I know this is hard for you, Ev, and I'm sorry that we kept the truth from you. I know it's asking a lot, but please trust that we made the choice in your best interest."

Looking at Calista made me miss my mom all the more. The two women had always been as close as sisters and alike in so many ways. I just couldn't believe this was all really happening, that someone had actually taken my mom—someone from another planet, the same other planet that we supposedly came from.

Calista must have sensed my thoughts, because she said, "We will find your mom and bring her home."

Even though she spoke with conviction, her words did little to lift my spirits.

"I need some air," I said, and started to walk away.

"Everly," Calista called after me, and I turned to look back at her.

She tried to smile reassuringly, but the unspoken worries in her eyes gave away the emotions she kept guarded from me. "I'm here if you need to talk."

"I know," was all I said, and I hurried out to the front porch.

I stood on the porch and breathed in the brisk morning air. My exposed skin immediately prickled from the sting of the cold, and my damp hair chilled the back of my neck. I could've gone back inside to grab a sweater, but I preferred the numbness of the bitter chill. It helped dull the building fear beginning to dominate my emotions. I sat down on the wooden porch steps and tugged my phone out of my pocket. The screen lit up with unread text notifications.

Molly: *Are you okay?*

Ty: *Has the sheriff found anything?*

Jasper: *Where r u?*

Jasper: *Call me! I'm worried about you!*

I listened to the voice mail Jasper had left:

"I heard about your mom. I'm so sorry, Ev. I'll do everything I can to help. I tried to find you at your place and the café. Calista's not home either. Are you with her? Where are you? Please call me and tell me where you are, so I can come to you. I'm here for you, Ev. Call me, please."

My stomach twisted with an ache. So much had happened yesterday that I hadn't thought to call Jasper. He must have been freaking out. I didn't feel like I could handle talking about everything right now, so I sent him a quick reply.

I'm okay, I promise.

I'm sorry I haven't called.

I'm with Calista and her friend. We are going to find my mom.

I will call u soon to explain everything.

I stared at my phone screen, not sure what to do next. I opened up my camera and clicked on the last photo I'd taken of my mom. It had been one of those rare moments when she'd faced the camera, and she was smiling ear to ear and had a sprig of lavender tucked in her hair.

How am I supposed to help you?

If only we could get help from the police.

But what can the police do against inhuman beings with magical powers? For all I know, some of them can shoot lasers from their eyes.

I released a long breath. *Where are you?*

The porch creaked from behind me. I *felt* Arden's energy as he approached my side. He sent out warm vibrations. He wanted me to trust him. *But trust will need to be earned.*

"May I join you?" he asked.

I responded by scooting over to make more room on the step.

The air filled with the scent of cedar as he sat down beside me on the steps.

He was quiet at first as he stared ahead into the mass of trees. "I'm sorry about your father," he spoke softly. "Creagan wasn't only my friend, but also a mentor. He meant a great deal to me."

"Thank you." I peeked over at him. The sun was breaking through the morning clouds, and his honey-gold hair sparkled in a stream of sunlight.

"I didn't really know Creagan. I only just found out two days ago that he was my father. These last couple of days"—I picked at a cracked piece of wood on the step—"have been filled with some overwhelming and disturbing revelations. I'm sorry you lost someone you cared for. It must be difficult for you."

Arden stared at me in silence. His intense gaze sent a shiver tingling down my spine.

Then he said, almost under his breath, "You're not at all what I expected."

A pang hit my chest. After years of blocking out what others felt, it was perplexing to me that I should care so much about what this stranger thought.

"How do you mean?" I asked, hoping he didn't notice the disappointment in my voice.

"Well, with you having grown up on this planet, I guess I expected you to be more like most humans: less intuitive and more selfish. Humans are a destructive, greedy, and less evolved race of beings." He said the last part with obvious distaste in his tone.

A wave of heat rushed through me, but this time it wasn't from attraction but anger. I had grown up believing I was human; my friends were human, and his arrogant assumptions insulted me. My left brow poised in an arch, as it often did when I was about to go on defense.

"Ha! Considering the things I've recently learned about 'our kind,' I would have to conclude that *we* are not so immune to selfish tendencies ourselves."

His eyes widened slightly at my reproach. "Touché," he said, looking at me with a puzzled expression and hands held up in defense. "I apologize if I offended you. It wasn't my intention."

My eyebrow dropped, and I huffed out a breath. "It's okay, but I think we all fall prey to selfish tendencies at times," I added less aggressively while glancing down at my cell phone cradled in my hands.

"Do you feel like talking about it?" he asked, nodding toward my phone. A short lock of honeyed hair fell over his forehead with the movement.

I wasn't about to share with him specifics, so I went with an abbreviated version. "Well, my relationship with my best friend has recently become … more complicated. And then there's the part about finding out I'm from another planet. I don't want to keep secrets from him. I know first-hand how it feels to be lied to, and I don't want to do that to him, but I also don't want to drag him into a dangerous situation."

"That's understandable," Arden agreed, waiting for me to continue.

Arden listened as though he truly cared about what I said. Except for his arrogant behavior towards humans, he had a laid-back demeanor, and interacting with him felt comfortable. It reminded me of how I used to feel with Jasper before things changed between us.

"Jasper knows that I'm different, and he'd probably think it's cool that I'm from another planet, but it would be selfish of me to tell him when knowing the truth could put his life in danger. And—" I stopped, feeling like I'd already talked too much. Arden was here to train me, not listen to my personal issues.

"What is it?" he asked. His curious expression appeared genuine, urging me to continue.

"It's just … I can't stop thinking about the night before someone took my mom, or maybe someone took her in the night. I don't know. We had an argument that night at the café. She shared with me about Creagan and our origins, and I felt hurt and angry, so I ran out and left her alone."

I buried my face in my hands, and my hair fell forward, creating a thick ebony veil. "If only I had stayed with her instead of abandoning her, I would have been there to prevent Darion from taking her. Oh, my God!" My head shot out of my hands. I remembered something from that night.

"What's wrong?" Arden's entire demeanor became alert as he surveyed the surrounding area. He looked back at me, concern etched in his brow.

"After our argument, I drove off. I was too upset to drive, so I stopped in the middle of the street for a moment, and when I looked in my rear-view mirror, someone was standing behind my car, but when I looked back over my shoulder, through the back window, they'd disappeared. I thought I'd just imagined it, but now I'm not so sure. What if it was him lurking around? He saw me leave and knew my mom was alone and vulnerable. It's my fault."

It's all my fault. If I hadn't stormed out … If I'd just stayed and given her a chance to explain, then Darion wouldn't have …

A sharp pain stabbed through my heart. I wanted to crush

something, anything. *I want to crush Darion into a thousand pieces, and when I find him, that's exactly what I'm going to do.*

Arden smoothed my hair back. "You can't blame yourself, Everly. There's no way you could have known what would happen, and had you stayed, Darion may have captured you both."

I turned my head so that his hand fell away. I didn't want to be comforted. "At least if he'd taken us both, I'd be with her right now, protecting her."

"Hey," he said, lifting my chin so that our eyes met. "You should know that your mother is a strong woman; she'll be able to hold her own until we find her," he said with certainty.

He placed his large hand over my own, and an immediate rush of warmth spread through me. A connection buzzed between us, its meaning unknown, but I'd felt it the first time we met, when he came to the café.

Does he feel it too?

The look in his eyes said yes, but he firmly guarded his emotions from me now.

The sound of his smooth voice brought me out of my thoughts. "I have a few things to take care of before we start your training." He lifted his hand from mine, and the lingering warmth from our skin contact blew away with the morning breeze.

Arden got up and disappeared back inside the cabin while I sat staring at my phone, feeling indecisive. Making up my mind, I tapped Jasper's name and held the phone to my ear.

I heard his voice after the third ring. "Evy, thank God. I went to the café and saw the police tape everywhere. What the hell happened, and where are you?"

Guilt stabbed at my insides. "I'm so sorry that I haven't called. Some things have happened that we need to talk about, but I can't talk about it over the phone."

"Where are you?" he demanded. "I'll come meet you right now."

"Jasper—please calm down. I know you're worried. I'm safe, but my mom has gone missing. She was at the café alone. There was blood on the office floor and she had vanished, although her car was still in the front. I can't tell you more than that right now, but I'm with people who can help. I'll tell you everything soon—I promise. It's best if you stay away from a potentially dangerous situation."

"What dangerous situation? And I don't care how dangerous it is. I can protect you. There are things I need to tell you, too. Please—just tell me where you are."

I closed my eyes, torn with indecision. "Listen, I have to go. I'll call you back as soon as I can, okay?"

I hung up before Jasper could convince me to tell him where I was. He had always been relentless and would be even more so now that he was worried about me. Since we were kids, he'd always taken it upon himself to be my protector, regardless of my objections that I could take care of myself.

CHAPTER 8

*A*rden designated a clearing behind Felix's cabin as our training space. The ground was mostly solid dirt covered in sprinkles of pine needles. Small patches of wild grass sprouted up here and there throughout the area. Felix had a large picnic table near a fire pit dug out in the ground, which had thick rock inlays, and he had layered the ground around the picnic area with gravel. A soft clucking issued from a chicken coop that stood next to a double horse stall and shed at the far side of the cabin.

I stood facing Arden for our first training session at the edge of the clearing. "This is pointless. Nothing feels any different. How is this supposed to help me?" I fidgeted with irritation.

He watched me from several feet away with an amused expression. "You're not focusing. Just be still, and focus on what you feel at this moment. Pay attention to the slightest difference."

I twisted my hair over one shoulder. "What I feel is antsy and awkward, which is making it impossible to focus," I said, rubbing my sweaty palms on the fronts of my thighs.

"Okay," he said, walking closer, so we stood face-to-face. He placed a finger on each of my temples. "Now take a deep breath and as you release it, imagine the tension melting away from your muscles."

"Really?" I said sarcastically.

"Just try it," he insisted.

Our faces were mere inches apart. The color of green moss circled his black pupils and streaked through the dominant cerulean blue of his irises.

I closed my eyes because I found it impossible to concentrate with him in my line of sight. The way he stood: tall and so sure of himself, his perfectly toned biceps pressing against the short dark gray sleeves of his shirt.

The temperature had warmed since earlier this morning, and I was thankful for the still-lingering warmth of a fading summer. *Okay—that's it! I'm closing my eyes now!*

With my eyes closed, I focused on the feeling of Arden's fingers pressing against my temples. The surface of his skin had a roughness to it that made me curious about his daily habits. A tingling sensation spread throughout my body. The sensation was pleasant. It made me feel elated and content. It was like being bathed in sunlight. The feeling ended abruptly, and I opened my eyes.

"What was that?" I asked.

"That was me penetrating your sensorium and altering your emotions," he explained. "The purpose of this exercise will be for you to learn to *feel* when I am attempting to do this and to repel my attempt."

"Felix told me that Empaths can manipulate the emotions of others. Are you an Empath too?" I asked with a renewed feeling of embarrassment as I realized he must have sensed my reactions toward him, which explained the way he'd been watching me at the café with that amused expression.

How humiliating! I'd have to keep my feelings more closely guarded around him.

"It's one of my gifts, but not my dominant. Our abilities develop differently in each of us. Our companionable gifts greatly influence this, as well as the amount of effort we dedicate to mastering our power. No one, Empath, is exactly the same, and I should warn you that Darion has absorbed some power as an Empath as well. It's not one of his natural gifts, so your ability will be stronger than his once you learn how to control it properly, but Darion has many other abilities as well—many that he has taken from others, and he will use them against you. He'll try to weaken you by inflicting as much pain as possible."

I rubbed my neck as I remembered the silver eyes of my invisible attacker. "You mean he intends to take my power and kill me?" I threw my hands up. "Why is he doing this to us? We don't even know him."

Arden's features hardened. "Darion does many vile things, either out of his own demented desires or at the wish of Siobhan. He is her loyal subject and does everything she commands of him. I won't let him hurt you—I give you my word."

His eyes held mine with intensity. I couldn't bring myself to look away. The blue of his eyes evaporated into a blaze of emerald. I wondered if the intense pull between us had anything to do with our shared gift. My body moved of its own accord, closing the minuscule space between us.

"Ahem." Arden cleared his throat and took a quick step back, breaking our trance. The blue returned to his eyes. "Let's get back to training." He turned and walked back to the other side of the meadow.

A sting of disappointment stabbed me as he moved away.

It took several attempts before I could build up any sort of resistance to the tingling sensations of Arden entering my sensorium. Each time I felt the familiar buzz of his energy, I locked on it and imagined it to be a tangible element moving in my body. I pictured it melting and disintegrating into nothing, and the tingling stopped each time.

"Good," Arden said. "Let's try moving on to something more difficult."

I nodded and waited until the familiar sensation returned as Arden began peeling away the layers of my emotional barrier, but when I locked on it, it was different this time, stronger. I could not resist the power it had over me, and my entire body felt like it was burning from the inside. The pain brought me to my knees. My muscles yearned to give in and crumble to the ground, but I resisted, recognizing that Arden was pushing my limits.

I fought the urge to give up, and I forced myself back to standing. It was like fighting against an invisible weight holding me down, and it took every ounce of strength I had. Closing my eyes, I concentrated on the pain, transforming it into a potent force of anger. I mentally gripped the emotion and refused to let it slip away from me. I imagined it gathering together into a pulsing ball of energy, and then I released it, projecting the blast toward Arden, repelling him from my mind. The pain vanished, and an unseen force thrust Arden backwards. His body hit a large tree directly behind him, and he slid down to the ground and slumped motionless with his head hanging forward.

"Arden!" I cried out as I ran to him. "Oh, crap. Are you okay?"

His body lightly shook, and as I got closer, I realized he was laughing. Infuriated by his audacity, I ignored his annoyingly sexy laugh as all concern flew by the trees.

"What the hell!" I fumed. "I was worried I'd injured or maybe killed you, and here you are, laughing at me like I'm a joke." I turned to leave him chuckling on his ass, but he reached out and grabbed my hand before I could get away.

"Everly—please, stay. I'm sorry I offended you … again. It seems that I have a talent for doing that. I don't think you're a joke. Your strength surprised me for one so young and untrained. You learn quickly. I want to show you something." He tapped the ground, indicating the spot directly in front of him. "Please, take a seat here—facing me."

I became less annoyed with his apology, and his request sparked my curiosity, so I complied. We sat cross-legged on the ground, facing each other. Arden scooted closer so that our knees touched and lifted his hands up to his chest with his palms facing me.

"Join your palms to mine," he instructed.

I placed my palms flat with his. His rough skin contrasted with the smoothness of my own, and my hands looked tiny compared to his large ones. There was an intimacy in touching hands with another person in this manner, and my cheeks flushed. Suddenly I remembered Arden had the ability of an Empath and could *feel* what I was feeling. I remembered the look he'd given me at the café when I'd had the sense that he'd known how I was feeling toward him, and my cheeks burned even hotter knowing I'd been right. *Ugh … I should have listened to my intuition the first time I saw him.*

Lost in my thoughts, his voice jolted me back to reality. "Look into my eyes and don't be afraid."

His eyes shimmered, and I instinctively started to pull my hands away, but he cautioned, "Maintain eye contact or we'll lose the connection. Touching enhances our ability to project a feeling or an experience."

A slight dizziness overcame me, and warmth swept over my body. This time, the warm feeling was euphoric, and I had the sensation that I was leaving my body and floating through space. Flashes of shooting beams of light and swirling colors emerged in the darkness. A pulsing energy moved through me that was stronger than anything I'd ever felt. The energy beckoned, urging me closer. Layers of space and then sky peeled back to reveal a scene of magnificent colors. An intoxicating scent of flowers filled my senses that made me think of stargazer lilies mingled with star jasmine. Suddenly I could see the flower. It was the largest flower I'd ever seen, and it was beaming with energy. Glowing hues of crimson, white, and violet surrounded it. The image was reminiscent of a colossal dahlia, its vibrant yellow center pulsating with energy. It was the most beautiful flower I'd ever seen, but not the first time I'd seen it. It was the same flower from my mother's paintings.

I longed to reach out and feel the flower's petals, but my hands remained firmly fixed, reminding me that this was an unreal scene. The vision faded as I felt myself being drawn away, returning to my body. My consciousness woke as if from a dream. The green and brown shades of the forest took the place of the swirling colors of space. The dizziness subsided as my body grounded in place, and everything around me came back into focus.

My hands stayed tightly clasped with Arden's, our fingers intertwined. A glow emitted from within our skin, similar to the glow I'd seen when Felix had healed Selkie. Arden appeared to still be recovering from whatever had just happened. His skin glistened with sweat, and he looked slightly out of sorts. For the first time since I'd met him, his guard was completely down. An electric energy flowed between us, stronger than it had before. When he looked at me, I felt everything he felt: attraction, desire, confusion, guilt, and sadness. A tear slid down my cheek, and I realized our clasped hands were acting like jumper cables, and my body was siphoning his emotions. The glowing light spread up my forearms, and Arden quickly separated his hands from mine, breaking the connection. I was afraid I was going to be sick as my stomach tightened with nausea. I leaned forward and placed my hands flat on the ground. The earth's coolness seeped into my body, providing relief from the nausea, while the emotions I had absorbed from Arden gradually receded, making me feel better.

"Everly! Are you okay?" Arden leaned over me. "Your gift is much stronger than I realized. I only meant to show you something beautiful from our planet. I never meant for you to suffer in any way."

"I'm okay," I said, trying to keep my voice from giving away how shaken up I really was. "This experience has made me realize just how much I still need to learn about my magic. If I'm going to protect myself against Darion, I need to learn everything about being an Empath."

"And you will," Arden said as he lifted himself off the ground and stood. "Can you stand?" he asked, offering his hand.

I wasn't sure my mental guard was sturdy enough to block out his emotions if we touched again so soon, so I pretended to dust debris off my pants as I stood on my own. Changing the subject, I asked, "What were those images I saw?"

His expression turned thoughtful. He nodded toward a path leading into the forest. "Walk with me."

I walked quietly to Arden's side, waiting for him to explain.

"What you saw was one of my memories of Aenoas-Vita. There are many beautiful wonders on our home planet, but one of the most beautiful places is the Ever Gardens. The flower you saw from my memory is called the ever flower."

I stopped in my tracks.

"I've seen the flower before in my mother's paintings. At least one is always present in her work. She told me once that it was a very special flower from her dreams. Now I know it's a memory of her home that she's carried with her."

Arden watched me with a contemplative look.

"It's more than that," he said. "Creagan once told me you were named after the ever flower. He hoped that someday the two of you would walk through the Ever Gardens together, and I know that he would have wanted you to see your namesake for yourself, even if only in representation."

"My father talked about me with you?" It felt strange to think Arden knew things about me I didn't even know.

"Creagan trusted me. He knew I would guard his secrets as if they were my own." A hint of sadness darkened Arden's expression, and he glanced away.

"Did he say why he and my mother named me after the ever flower?"

"He did not, but Creagan spent much time walking the sacred gardens. You see, the flowers of the Ever Gardens are unique—they will never fade or die as long as they remain planted in their sacred soil. It's a crime to pick a flower from the Ever Garden. Some say the flowers hold the essence of our people who have passed to the next life. If you touch the flower, it may share a memory of the past with you."

My eyes widened at the thought of a flower holding such power.

"That's incredible. It sounds like a magical place." I bent down to pick up a twig so Arden wouldn't see me wiping the tears from my eyes. "I never knew my name came from anywhere special, but how were you able to share one of your memories with me?"

The scent of pine deepened the farther we walked.

"The ability to share memories is one of my gifts. I can show you another sometime if you'd like, perhaps of your father?"

I sucked in an excited breath, and thought hopefully

about getting the chance to see my father again, if only in memory. "Yes. I would like that."

Questions whirled in my head, and it was hard to pick out one from the other. There was so much to do, but so much to know at the same time. "Why did our skin glow when we touched hands? I saw the same thing happen when Felix healed Selkie."

Arden gazed out at the forest. "Our magic recognizes when it's joined with another of its own kind. When this happens, our energies bond together, and I guess you could say that they feed off one another, igniting a spark. The magic that fills us comes from our planet. In a way, we are all connected through our shared link with Aenoas-Vita. Perhaps, Aenoas-Vita has gifted us with the ability to sustain life as a defense mechanism to protect its offspring. Take these trees, for instance," he said, extending his arm out in an arch. "They all appear independent of one another, but underneath this ground"—Arden bent down and smoothed his hand atop the dirt—"their roots connect, and they share and transfer their resources through their root systems for survival."

He stood back up. "I think you could use a break. I can sense that your energy has weakened."

I shook my head. "No. I want to keep going. My mom needs me. I can do this for her."

"I have no doubt that you can do anything you put your mind to," Arden said, his voice filled with conviction. "But you're just learning to use your magic in this new way, and we don't yet know your limits."

I took a step toward him. "Then let's find out."

His eyelids lowered slightly, and the corners of his lips turned up in a sly grin.

"What?" I asked.

"You remind me of your father. Creagan had a bit of a stubborn streak."

I put my hand on my hip for dramatic show. "Oh, so I'm stubborn?"

"A bit," he said, and laughed at my display. The sound sent a shiver down my spine, and once again my body reacted without my consent. I fought back the urge to move closer to him.

His eyes glazed over as if he, too, were suddenly struggling to subdue an impulse. He looked away and continued walking forward, and the moment was gone. "Come on. Let's get some lunch, and then we'll continue your training."

Just before we reached the cabin steps, Arden grabbed my hand and stopped me.

"Everly, wait."

When I turned to face him, the vulnerability I sensed surprised me, and I had the feeling it surprised him, too.

He answered my unspoken question. "When our energies were linked, you experienced some of my emotions and they caused you pain. I want you to know that I'm sorry for that. Creagan was a dear friend and an important man. I feel the loss of him greatly, but I never meant for you to endure that feeling."

I remembered the intensity of his emotions and the deep sense of guilt he suffered. I was on the verge of questioning him about his guilt, but I held back, worried that the inquiry would be too personal.

"There's nothing to apologize for. I only wish I had had the chance to know him as well as you."

I turned and walked away a few steps, and he followed behind. The light danced over the cabin windows, but I couldn't see anyone inside.

"When I think of all the years he and I have passed in greeting, I can't help but think that if I'd just paid closer attention, or if I'd understood how to use my abilities better, maybe I could've figured it out on my own and things would be different now."

"Hey." Arden reached for my shoulder.

I stopped and turned back to face him.

He moved closer, looking down at me. "I understand why you feel that way, but don't torture yourself with maybes and should haves, Everly. Regret and guilt will only weaken you, and you are not weak. You're brave and strong."

A deep sigh escaped from me. "I'm not feeling brave or strong right now. I have absolutely no clue what I'm doing. All I know is I have to do whatever it takes to save my mother." I made to move past him toward the cabin, but Arden stepped sideways to block my path and reached for my hand. I looked up at him questioningly.

"You're not alone in this."

I stared down at the ground. "I know," I whispered.

"Hey, look at me."

I lifted my gaze to his.

"Your mother is alive, and we will bring her home. And you're learning to use your magic—magic that will strengthen you. You're doing exactly what both of your parents would want you to do, and what Creagan asked me to help you do."

"I'm glad you're here," I admitted sheepishly, and swallowed the lump in my throat.

"Me too," he whispered as our bodies instinctively moved closer and his thumb circled the inside of my palm. His head tilted down slightly toward mine, and the same lock of golden hair from earlier fell over his cheekbone.

Our bodies pressed lightly together. The air stirred around us, as everything but the two of us spun out of existence. Arden awakened something deep within me, and I could feel our energies syncing with an invisible thread. He ran his free hand up my back and continued trailing his fingertips up the back of my neck, caressing the skin just beneath my hairline. Goose bumps spread across my body. My head slowly tilted to the side while my mouth lifted toward his, and his down toward mine.

"Hey, you two," Calista called from the top of the porch.

The world snapped back into place, and I took a quick awkward step back and glanced up at Arden. He was still looking at me with a hunger in his eyes that sent shivers from my head down to my toes. Neither of us had noticed Calista come out of the cabin.

"Hey, Calista. We … um … were just taking a break from training."

"I can see that." She shot Arden a look filled with warning. "I made veggie sandwiches. I thought you two might be hungry. They're in here on the table, if you want 'em," she said with one final glare in Arden's direction, and then turned and walked back inside the cabin.

～

The veggie sandwiches hit the spot. Calista always made them just the way I liked, with cashew cream cheese, broccoli sprouts, black olives, and thin-sliced cucumbers to add a light crunch. I quickly polished off my second sandwich as I hurried to catch up with Arden.

"How are your fighting skills?" Arden asked as we walked through the meadow to continue my training.

"Um … if you mean punching and kicking fighting skills, then I can hold my own," I declared proudly. "I've been studying martial arts with Jasper since we were kids. He insisted I take classes with him, and I quickly fell in love with the study." My gut sank. Thinking of Jasper made me realize how much I missed him and wished he was here. I quickly steeled myself. *No*. The less he knew, the safer he'd be.

Arden didn't look impressed with my declaration of skill. "That knowledge will be a good base level for your training."

"Base level?" I responded with a sharp edge to my voice. "I'm a fifth-degree black belt in Jiu-Jitsu."

Arden lifted a brow. "Impressive. For human technique. But human fighting skills do not compare to the fighting skills of a Vitarian."

I glowered at him and blew out an exasperated breath. His continued smug demeanor toward humans irked me.

"Looking for a fight, are we?"

Startled, I jumped at the unexpected presence. We both turned toward the direction of the voice. A woman appeared in the clearing.

My body moved on instinct, positioning itself into a fighting stance. I looked her up and down.

It wasn't her impressive height or threatening posture that I found intimidating. It was the dangerously sharp sword casually dangling from her hand, and the battle-ax tucked neatly in her belt. Her leather uniform molded to her body, accentuating every curve and taut muscle. This woman appeared to be a true warrior from another time and place. She reminded me of a character straight out of the old *Xena: Warrior Princess* reruns I'd seen. Instinctively, I tuned into her vibrations, and she was oozing confidence and superiority.

As if sensing my appraisal, she looked at me dismissively. "Aren't you sweet?" she said. She turned her sharp glare to Arden, her green eyes raking him up and down. "Not too smart being out here unarmed with so many enemies lurking about."

"You would know." Arden positioned himself in front of me, but I maneuvered to his side. I would not let him take this bitch on alone.

The woman grinned at Arden as she twirled her sword and then sheathed it in one quick maneuver.

"Show-off," Arden accused as he casually walked toward her.

"I learned from the best." The woman's aggressive demeanor completely vanished as she moved to meet Arden.

Arden smiled and closed the remaining distance between them in two quick strides. "Rheya, it's good to see you. I've missed you."

"And I you, my liege." She inclined her head with a slight bow.

"My liege"? What's going on here, and who is this strange woman?

The two clasped arms in some kind of salute and then embraced.

A sharp pain twisted in my chest.

No. I'm not jealous. I have no reason to be jealous. Arden is just my trainer and nothing more.

I stood watching the new dynamics with some confusion and suddenly felt like an awkward third wheel. I didn't enjoy seeing Arden in this woman's arms. It was clear that not only were the two familiar with one another, but they shared a friendship.

"Where are Malakai and Rhal? I expected them to arrive with you."

"We had some trouble with the queen's guard on our way to the portal. Malakai and Rhal came through right behind me. They should arrive any minute. Come, I'll take you to the portal." She turned to leave without giving a second thought to my presence.

"Rheya."

"Yes, my liege." She turned back with a taunting smirk.

"That's enough with the formalities. I'd like to introduce you to Everly, Creagan's daughter."

As all eyes turned towards me, I shifted awkwardly, determined to maintain a strong facade. I lifted my shoulders back and shook off the chill of Rheya's cold appraisal. I met her icy-green stare with equal authority and reached out my hand in an attempt at a friendly greeting. "It's nice to meet you, Rheya."

She sneered at my gesture and looked at my outreached hand as though I were offering her a disease.

Her eyes softened for an instant. "I'm sorry for your loss," she said with sincerity. "Creagan was an exceptional leader, and his passing will leave a void that many will feel." Without another word, she turned and headed back into the woods from where she'd come.

Arden scowled after her and then turned back toward me. "I'm sorry about that. Rheya's not much of a people person."

"Well, she certainly doesn't like me. Who is she, and why was she calling you 'my liege'? What aren't you telling me?"

"I'll explain later. As for Rheya, she's a trusted friend and a skilled warrior. And here at my request. It may not seem like it now, but you'll be glad to have her fighting at your side."

Arden deliberately evaded the second part of my question, and before I could press him further, he fled to catch up with Rheya.

She moved stealthily through the woods without a glance back at us. The sun waned as the day settled into dusk, and the forest came alive with the chirping of hidden frogs and crickets. A peaceful rhythm of nature. I glimpsed two squirrels chasing each other up a tree, probably in search of their next meal. We passed a family of deer, who quickly trotted off deeper into the trees at the sound of our approach. Being used to living in a heavily wooded area and spending much of my free time hiking the local terrain, the meandering trek through the woods did not bother me. It felt like a familiar blanket of safety.

Rheya slowed her pace when we came to a running stream. We followed it to a rock cave, nearly blocked from view by a massive tree trunk. A small waterfall cascaded over the entrance, making it difficult to make out the actual size of the cavern.

"This is the place," Rheya said, facing the cave. "They should be arriving."

The three of us stood staring at the waterfall. The rushing water lulled me into a thoughtful trance. Water gurgled and sprayed as it bounced off moss-covered rocks. Suddenly, the waterfall bubbled out and separated into the air. The inside of the cave slowly became visible. It was much larger than I expected. Two men dressed in battle armor and hooded cloaks walked out of the dark depths of the cavern and leaped over the stream to meet us.

Arden and Rheya clasped arms with the two men as they greeted them. The two new arrivals simultaneously turned their attention to me. Unexpectedly, each dropped to a knee and put their fist to their hearts. "My lady," they both said in unison.

Worried that this was a customary greeting, I didn't want to insult either of them by not following suit, so I mimicked their motions and knelt on one knee with fist to heart and said, "Hello."

Rheya barked out a laugh. I looked up and caught Arden giving her a dark scowl. Her green eyes continued to watch me with mock amusement.

I quickly stood up, feeling like an idiot. My cheeks burned, and I was sure they were as red as the huckleberries on the nearby bush. I took a deep breath to calm the ball of irritation mounting in the pit of my stomach. There was no point in getting upset. Individuals who repeatedly used sarcasm and mocked people did so out of habit to mask deeper-rooted issues. I flashed Rheya a knowing look, and she glanced away.

As beautiful as she is, she lacks an inner confidence. I couldn't help but wonder what she kept buried below the surface of her alluring beauty.

I redirected my attention to the two men, who were straightening their posture.

"Everly," Arden said. "This is Malakai and Rhal."

Without thinking, my hand shot out in front of me. "It's nice to meet you," I said, looking up at the towering form of Rhal.

He wrapped his two giant hands warmly over mine and bowed his bald head. His midnight skin shone under the sunlight. He lifted his form and studied my face. "There's no mistaking the daughter of Creagan. It is my great honor to meet you, Everly. You have my deepest condolences. We all loved Creagan."

My muscles relaxed slightly. "Thank you for your kind words, Rhal."

He nodded and stepped aside.

Malakai stepped forward. He had an unusual aura. Multiple threads of vibrations came off him that differed from any other person I'd felt. Some of his vibrations didn't seem directly linked to his own emotions. They felt raw and primal, and bounced off him from multiple directions while channeling through him. There was something wild in his characteristics, and I was immediately curious to learn more about him. He reached out his golden-brown hand and took my hand in his.

"It is my pleasure to meet you, Everly." His silky ink-black hair cascaded over his shoulders as he bowed his head to kiss the top of my hand.

I smiled in response. "It's nice to meet you as well, Malakai."

He beamed a smile of his own, and the appearance of his eyes startled me. Like his unique vibrations, these, too, had unusual qualities. His pupils continuously expanded and contracted. Their shape shifted from oval to round, and his irises changed colors with each transition, reminding me of the eyes of cats and snakes.

How unusual.

"We must close the portal," Rheya interrupted. She stood in front of the cave and chanted some words in the same language I'd heard both Felix and Calista use. *The Vitarian language.*

The waterfall returned to its natural appearance and flowed as if nothing out of the ordinary had just taken place.

~

*I*t was full dusk by the time the five of us returned to the cabin. Felix was back from wherever he'd gone, and he and Calista were setting the dining table with enough food to feed half a nation. Something told me they expected our visitors.

"Friends, welcome," Felix greeted our guests with outstretched arms. "It's good to see so many familiar faces."

"Felix," I interrupted. "Did you find out any information about where Darion is keeping my mom?"

Felix turned in my direction, and his eyebrows lowered. "I'm sorry, my dear," he said in a weary voice. "There's been no sign of Darion, and the magic guarding their location is impenetrable."

Damn it.

My chest tightened as the hope I'd clung to in Felix's

absence shattered. I gripped the back of a dining chair and took a few deep breaths to push away the urge to lash out and swipe all the colorful steaming dishes of food onto the floor.

"Darion has a warlock with him. One of Siobhan's," Rheya announced.

Felix nodded at her pronouncement. "Yes, I surmised as much." He looked back at me, his eyes warm. "Do not lose hope, my dear. I met with an old friend who has supplied me with a spell that might help your mother. The spell will not tell us her location, but it offers us a way to provide Cacsha with aid for now, though it's a difficult and complicated spell." Felix glanced at Calista, and her eyes tightened with concern.

"I don't care how hard it is," I said. "I want to do it."

Felix put a hand on my shoulder. "I knew that would be your answer. The spell is old and requires a blood sacrifice."

"A blood spell," Calista gasped. "Felix!" she said, louder this time. "It's too dangerous."

"What's the big deal?" Rheya scoffed. "Just pluck one of those chickens from the coop we passed and make the sacrifice." She walked over to the table of food and popped a grape in her mouth.

"These spells wouldn't be so well guarded if it were that easy," Felix remarked, looking at her.

He reached into his pocket and pulled out a small vial of syrupy red liquid. "You see, in order for the spell to work, you must have the blood of a warlock." He held the vial out for all to see. "And warlocks aren't usually so generous with their blood." He turned his gaze on me. "And the blood sacrifice must be a blood relation of the one you seek to make your offering to."

"No!" Calista stepped in front of me. "I won't allow this. This is dark magic, Felix. I won't let Everly put her life in jeopardy. Cacsha would not agree with this."

I moved out of Calista's shadow.

"I'm sorry, Calista, but this is my choice, and if it means helping my mom, I'll make any sacrifice necessary. And besides, it's just a little blood."

Calista closed her eyes and shook her head.

"You don't understand, Everly. If it were just a little blood, I would not be so against this, but the blood sacrifice requires a great deal more." She shot Felix a glare.

"But the vial of warlock blood is so small," I pointed at the glass vial Felix held. "How much of my blood will it take?"

"All of it," Arden said, his voice cold and emotionless. "And this spell is out of the question."

"What!" I fumed. "This is my choice, and none of you can tell me otherwise."

I looked around the room, eyeing each of them and daring them to challenge me. To my surprise, I found Rheya watching me with a huge smile on her face, as if my response pleased her.

Arden, on the other hand, was bristling. "Creagan put me in charge of your safety, and if I allow you to do this, I fail him, and that won't happen again." His posture stiffened as he stared me down with blazing green eyes.

"I'm sorry, Arden, but if I have to trade my life for my mom's, then that's what I'll do. You promised to help me, so please … help me do this."

His eyes narrowed, and I could see the struggle raging behind them.

"She's right," Rhal said, stepping forward and placing his hand on Arden's shoulder. "This should be her choice."

"Thank you," I said to Rhal, who bowed his head in response.

The room went silent as I stood, meeting Arden's hard glare. The soft crackling of firewood coming from the living room grew louder with each passing second. Smoke lingered in the back of my throat.

"Everly's life will not be in jeopardy." Felix spoke with authority. "My warlock friend provided me with a loophole to the spell, and it will require the assistance of all of you." He gave everyone a pointed look.

"And what type of assistance would that be?" Rheya said with a note of hostility.

"Everly is an Empath. She can siphon the energy of others. We will each take part in the ritual, allowing her to siphon from us as she sacrifices her blood. The warlock has written me two spells to cast together and provided enough of his blood for both. The intertwining spells will allow Everly to transfer her energy to Cacsha through the blood sacrifice while at the same time siphoning both blood and energy from all of us."

"Will this work?" Calista asked, her voice hesitant.

"I believe it will, or I wouldn't have offered the spell as an option. But there are no guarantees." Felix slipped the warlock blood back into his pocket. "Do you all agree to take part?"

Calista looked at me with indecision.

"Please," I whispered.

She nodded her assent.

Rhal and Malakai both stepped forward in agreement.

I looked to Arden, who still warred with his emotions. I pleaded with him silently to accept my choice. He held my gaze and stepped forward, nodding.

Rheya stood back, watching the scene with an unamused expression.

"It will take all of us," Felix said to her.

She glanced at Arden and stepped forward without a word.

Felix clapped his hands together. "It's settled. We'll all

need our strength. We will eat and then prepare for the spell." He sat down at the table and began filling his plate.

Our three visitors wasted no time in following suit and digging right in. Unable to muster an appetite, I picked at a rosemary roll until most of it was broken up into pieces on my plate.

"Now, friends," Felix said in a serious tone. "Please, tell us how things fare on Aenoas-Vita? I've not seen my home in quite some time."

Rheya turned to Arden. He inclined his head. "There is much unrest back home," she said as she added another heaped scoop of saffron rice to her plate and topped it with a spoonful of curry. "The people have noticed Creagan's prolonged absence and are becoming suspicious of the queen. And there are rumors." Rheya paused, glancing in my direction.

"Continue," urged Felix.

"There are rumors that the king secretly married another before he wed the queen and that the queen's claim to the throne is not legitimate."

Felix waited patiently as Rheya chewed and swallowed a mouthful of curry and rice, and washed it down with a long drink from her glass of red wine. She leaned back, swirling the crimson liquid inside her glass. "The queen has become enraged and more dangerous than ever. We've not been able to locate her whereabouts, and we have an informant who confirms that she has or will travel to Earth."

Felix refilled Calista's wine and then his own. "That confirms what I've learned as well." His brow furrowed. "I fear that if Siobhan is not already on this planet, then it's only a matter of time before she arrives, and that means our plight is worse than we originally thought."

The mood in the room became grim as everyone at the table sat in quiet contemplation. The fire spat and crackled.

"You speak as if Siobhan and the queen are the same person?" I asked, breaking the eerie silence.

"They are one and the same, my dear," Felix answered.

"But if Siobhan is the queen of Aenoas-Vita, then ... that would make Creagan ... the king?"

"That's right, Princess," Rheya said sarcastically.

"Rheya," Arden growled.

I ignored Rheya's snarky comment as I threaded together bits and pieces from my memory about my mom telling me of the powerful enemy she'd made on her planet. And now I knew the enemy was her queen.

I remembered Rhal and Malakai's greeting when we'd first met, and Rheya's mocking laughter when I had responded in kind. My eyes slid to meet Rheya's. The knowing grin melted from her face, leaving behind not empathy or compassion, but some deeper understanding of my pain. She tore her gaze from mine and turned to hide what her expression gave away.

I stood from my chair, clutching the end of the table. All eyes except Rheya's were on me. "I don't understand. If there are rumors of Creagan being married prior to his union with Siobhan, then the rumors could only be about my mom. And if he and my mom were already secretly married, then why would Siobhan's threats have mattered, and why would he have still gone through with his arranged marriage to Siobhan?" Pain pulsed in my temples.

Calista rose from her seat and came to stand beside me. "Only your mother can answer that question. I had no knowledge of a marriage between her and Creagan, if this rumor is even true, but if it is, Siobhan is even more of a threat. She desires nothing more than her throne and will stop at nothing to eradicate anything that threatens her rule. It makes sense now why she would travel here. This is about more than revenge to her."

I walked away through the kitchen and looked out at the serene lavender sky. Its calmness was the polar opposite of the turmoil boiling in my mind. "Even if it is true," I said, watching a hawk swoop down from the sky and land on a treetop, "my mother doesn't want Siobhan's throne. Can't we just reason with her?"

"It won't matter," Calista said, her voice strained. "On our planet, only one marriage is permissible. If the council rules that Creagan and Cacsha's union happened before his with Siobhan, and they validate it, then they will remove Siobhan and crown your mother as queen, or her next of kin." Calista's lips turned down at the corners. "Siobhan will want to remove all chances of either scenario happening."

Malakai scooted his chair forward. The flame of the candle centerpiece highlighted the sharp angles of his high cheekbones. "Siobhan has powerful allies in the council, but the people have become vocal about their unhappiness with her." He rested both hands on the table. "In Creagan's absence, she has proved to be a wicked ruler. When the people learn of their king's death, they will look for any reason to strip Siobhan of her status."

I walked back toward the table and looked down at them all. A coldness gripped my heart. "So that's why she's sent Darion after us after all these years—to remove all evidence of the threat to her throne? She must have had Creagan murdered or committed the deed herself, and now she plans to do the same to my mother and me."

My answer came not in words but in the truth *vibrating* from those sitting around the table. Even though they didn't say as much, they all felt sorry for me, and that meant they thought Siobhan would win. What little food I'd eaten curdled, and my belly swelled with rage. A red haze blurred my vision. Suddenly, a warm hand rested on top of mine, and calming waves of emotion passed through me.

"Everly," Arden said in a gentle voice. "You must control your emotions. You're using your power without intending to."

"What are you talking about?" I snapped my eyes open and drew in a breath. Four pairs of eyes stared back at me with seething rage. Arden and Felix seemed to be the only ones unaffected. As Arden used his own power to calm me, the boiling rage I felt dulled into a permanent ache in the pit of my stomach. The faces around the table relaxed as everyone regained control of their own emotions.

"Wow!" Malakai exclaimed. "That was intense. I've never been around an Empath with that much ability before."

"I'm sorry," I said to everyone. "I didn't mean to affect you all like that." Exhaustion laced my voice. The day's activities and this new knowledge were taking their toll.

Calista looked at me with loving eyes. "It's all right, honey. You're still learning to use your gift in this manner. In time, you'll be able to control it."

The table rattled as Rheya's hand came down hard against the wood. "No. It's not all right," she said, scowling at Arden's hand on mine. "She can't even control her own power, and you"—she pointed at Felix—"want us to risk our own lives doing some spell that she'll most likely fail at."

"Rheya! That's enough." Arden marched toward Rheya, who stood and met him fury with fury.

"I'm sorry, Commander, but I don't share the same faith in her as you do." She stormed out the front door, slamming it behind her.

Arden sighed. "I have to go after her."

I nodded. "Of course. It's okay. Go."

My attention shifted to Rhal and Malakai. "I'm so sorry about what I did to you both. I hope I haven't made you hate me as much as Rheya does."

"All is forgiven," Rhal said. "And Rheya doesn't hate you;

she's just protective of the commander. They've been looking out for each other for many years, with her as his second-in-command. She sees he cares about you, and to her, that's a weakness."

"That's ridiculous." I clenched my jaw as I considered his words.

Rheya thinks I'm a threat to Arden.

"Rheya's a complicated woman," Malakai said as he and Rhal both stood and stretched their legs while Felix and Calista cleared the table. "But don't worry. She'll come around, eventually. The commander will calm her down."

"What exactly is Arden, the commander of?"

Malakai's eyes widened, as if surprised by my lack of knowledge. "Arden is the liege commander of the king's army."

"Oh," I muttered. I remembered how Calista had grinned mischievously when I'd asked her if Arden was a magic trainer, and she'd said that was "one of his responsibilities."

I'm being trained by the king's army commander. He must think I'm a joke next to a warrior like Rheya.

～

*A*t nightfall, we all met in the clearing outside the cabin for the ritual. A full moon shone brightly over the eight torches Felix and Rhal arranged into the large shape of an octagon. Felix had explained that the energy of the full moon would aid our spell as he placed seven large milky-white stones in a wide circle within the octagon. I recognized the stones from the box Calista had grabbed when we left her house.

"Each of us will be linked to a healing stone and to each other," Felix informed us. "Everly, you will take your place in the center of the stones. For the entire duration of the spell, our lives will be connected to yours. I've mixed the warlock blood into a potion, and we all must drink until it's depleted." Felix passed around the bowl.

I pushed away my disgust at drinking blood. If it meant saving my mom, I'd drink gallons of it. We each took turns until we drained the bowl dry.

Felix unsheathed a jeweled blade from his side and walked around the circle. He stopped at each person and pierced their palms as he recited words from the warlock's spell.

When he completed the task, he joined me in the center of the circle. "Are you ready, my dear?"

I met his bright blue stare and turned my wrists up in response. He had already explained the process—that I would offer my blood to the spell, and in doing so, my energy would be linked with my mom's, strengthening her. Felix was confident this would work, and I trusted him, though a shudder still ran through me.

"Do it," I commanded.

He sliced open his own palms first and then drew the blade down the length of each of my forearms, ending at my wrists. I ignored the searing pain that burned down my arms as the blade cut through my skin. I lifted my arms up toward the sky as Felix continued his chant and took his place in the circle.

I expected my blood to stream down my arms, but instead, it trickled out into the air, as did the blood of the others. As my body siphoned their blood, my own vanished into the darkness in thicker and thicker pools. A glowing light traveled through my skin, mingling with my blood. My strength gradually diminished as I lost more and more light. As my legs trembled, numb and weak, I collapsed to the ground, feeling my consciousness slipping away. It was in that very instant that I became aware of my mom's essence and felt an undeniable connection between us. She called out to me, her voice an echo in my mind. "Everly."

Mom ...

I heard Calista yell to Felix, her words gliding on the wind. "Felix! Stop the spell. It's too much."

"It's nearly complete." He continued chanting. And then all went quiet.

When my eyes opened, Felix was wrapping my arms in bandages. His brows knitted tightly with concern as he studied my face.

"Did it work?" I asked. My words came out dry and hoarse.

"We completed the spell, so I can only assume it did. How are you feeling?"

"Like I got hit by a truck." I tried sitting up, but the room swam around in circles.

Felix put his hand behind my head and guided it back down. "You lost quite a bit of blood. You need to rest."

"I felt my mom's presence during the spell, Felix. It was her. I know it. And ... I think she sensed me, too. I'm sure I heard her call out to me."

"In that case," he said, "we can be sure the spell worked as intended, and your mother is going to be quite furious with us when we rescue her. But at least she'll be stronger for the time being."

"Yeah." I smiled up at the three Felix heads circling above me, and then all went dark again.

∿

I twisted, trying to find a comfortable position, but the surface below me was nothing but solid bumps, and then my body was floating through the air.

"Everly. Wake up." The voice was so close its warm breath brushed my cheeks.

My eyes flew open as I realized I was being carried.

"You're okay. I've got you."

My entire body shivered uncontrollably. I clung tightly to Arden as he moved up the porch steps into the cabin. Confusion shook me as I tried to piece together what had happened and why Arden was carrying me to my room.

He set me gently on my bed. "You're freezing," he said as he wrapped me tightly in my blanket. "What were you doing outside in the middle of the night?"

"I don't know," I muttered through chattering teeth, and I pulled the blanket even tighter. "The last thing I remember was waking up to Felix wrapping my wrists, and then I passed back out. I must have been sleepwalking again."

Arden's brow furrowed in a worried arch. "Do you often sleepwalk?"

"Occasionally, when I was younger, but it hadn't happened for years, until recently. Ever since my mom's been missing, I've been having these strange dreams that I hear her voice calling out to me from the woods. I follow the sound, but when I get there, no one's there. Except ..." I hesitated, worried he might think I was crazy. "Except the first time it happened."

"May I?" Arden indicated the spot next to me.

I scooted over to make room.

"Tell me about the first time it happened."

"Well ... I could have sworn someone grabbed me from behind, but after I twisted from their grasp and fell on the ground, no one was there, but my head ached the next day from where he'd grabbed my hair."

Arden's expression became guarded. "How do you know it was a he?"

Because I'd never forget those chilling silver eyes.

"When my head was pulled back, I glimpsed Darion before I broke free and fell. But then he was gone and Felix and Calista were rushing out of the cabin."

I stared across the room at my reflection in the mirror hanging on the wall and flinched at the sight of me. My skin had an almost blue tint, and my cheeks appeared sunken in.

Arden nudged closer. "You just need some rest. You had a tough night. I'll talk to Felix in the morning about mixing you a tonic to help ward off the dreams."

I had the feeling Arden was holding something back, but my thoughts were too groggy to push him further. "What were you doing outside this time of night?" I asked through a deep yawn.

"I haven't slept well since I've been on Earth. I was tired of turning restlessly, so I went out for some fresh air. When I got outside, I saw you lying on the ground near the tree line."

My body shivered, not only from the chill but from the thought of what might have happened had Arden not found me when he did. "Thank you. And not just for finding and bringing me back in, but for what you all did tonight to help me and my mom. I'm sorry that I put you all in a dangerous situation, but I'm grateful for what each of you did. We helped her. I felt my energy go into her during the spell."

"That's good." His mouth turned up in a tired smile. "You're still shivering," he said, and stood from the bed. "Lie down. I'm going to get you another blanket."

~

J awoke with a pounding headache and in desperate need of a strong cup of coffee. Sunlight streamed in through the uncovered windows, and I lifted my arms to block the stinging light from my eyes. Stiffness pulled at my muscles, and I ached as I moved my arms. The bandages reminded me I had finally done something to help my mom. We still didn't know where Darion had her, but the spell had worked last night. There had been a moment when I felt my energy connect with hers, and for now, that small success drove me forward. She was stronger now, but for how long, I didn't know. I only hoped it was long enough.

Soft sounds of sleep coming from the floor below my bed startled me out of my thoughts. I rolled over to the edge and peered down to see Arden's long form slumbering below me. Everything from the night before came rushing back, along with the memory of Arden carrying me to my room.

He must have sensed my motion, because he roused and slowly rolled over, propping himself up on an elbow.

"Hey, you. How are you feeling?" he asked through a long yawn.

I smiled at the sight of his tousled hair as I pushed myself up to a sitting position. "My muscles are pretty sore, and my head feels like someone clocked me with a baseball bat, and I'd kill for a cup of coffee right now." I began massaging my temples.

Arden stood from his bedroll on the floor, still fully dressed in the clothes he'd worn last night. The mattress sank as he positioned himself beside me.

Even with pulsing temples and aching muscles, my body responded to the nearness of his.

"Hold out your arm," he instructed.

I lifted my eyebrows in question.

"I'm going to massage the stiffness from your muscles," he replied to my questioning look. "You're going to need full mobility for your training today."

That made sense. I felt safe with Arden, but I couldn't help feeling nervous at the thought of him touching me in such an intimate way. Not because I didn't want him to, but because I did.

He took hold of my hand and began softly massaging my fingers and then circling the inside of my palms, hitting all of my pressure points. He slowly moved up my arm, carefully avoiding my bandages, and a warm, tingling sensation heated my skin.

A sparkling glow spread across the area he massaged. He was using one of his gifts to remove the ache from my locked-up muscles. He performed the same procedure on my other arm, and the tension completely melted away.

"Turn your back toward me," he said.

I held down the long T-shirt I'd slept in as I carefully twisted around.

Arden's strong hands moved along my spine and shoulders. He lifted my long hair and carefully laid it over one shoulder, then began massaging my neck and head and finally my temples. My headache faded, and my body shivered at his touch. His warm breath lingered on the back of my neck. I scooted back and pressed my back against his chest. My heart pounded as I felt his lips tenderly kiss the back of my neck and move up along my neckline to my earlobe. I wanted to feel his lips on mine. I turned so our bodies faced each other. Green that burned with the fire of passion had vanquished the blue in his eyes. I peeled his shirt off and moved my hands along his hard muscles. His hands glided into my hair, spilling black locks over both of my shoulders. My heart skipped a beat as his head slowly inched down toward mine. Our lips were nearly touching when a loud thump on my door broke the spell.

"Hey, Princess," Rheya shouted. "It's time to start your training. Be down in ten."

Rheya's interruption killed the moment. "Bossy much, isn't she," I said, more as a statement than a question.

"With Rheya, you get what you see. She's a soldier through and through, and she's the best at what she does."

Ouch.

Arden's quick defense of her stung my pride. She was obviously important to him. The mood in the room had quickly changed from hot and steamy to cool and awkward, and I suddenly felt self-conscious about being in bed in just my T-shirt. I pulled the blanket back over me while Arden put his shirt on and stood fully clothed.

"I better get down there before they all get suspicious of our whereabouts," he said, and closed the door behind him.

I threw my blanket back off, resolved not to let Arden's quick change in demeanor affect me. I reminded myself that I didn't really know him that well, and it was for the best that we had been interrupted before anything further could happen. But I couldn't deny the pang of disappointment that lingered.

After a quick shower, I dressed in flexible clothing and made my way to the kitchen, where the air was infused with the uplifting aromas of rosemary, ginger, basil, and fresh coffee. I filled a large mug to the brim with coffee and skipped my normal addition of coconut milk. I took a long pull of the straight-up black brew. It went down bitter at first but had a nutty finish. It surprised me that I actually kind of enjoyed it without the added cream. Calista pushed a full plate of scrambled eggs filled with veggies and herbs in front of me.

"The others are already out front," she said.

I nodded my thanks as I took large bites in between deep gulps of coffee, my energy building with each. I finished my plate within minutes and started working on my second mug of coffee.

"I'm glad to see you've gotten your appetite back," Calista said with a smile. "And your wounds have healed."

I turned my arms over. "Yeah. Thanks to whatever Felix did before wrapping them, the cuts were completely sealed when I removed the bandages. It's like nothing ever happened."

Calista's smile faded and her expression became serious. "Well, something did happen, and I need you to promise me you won't do anything that reckless again. Your mother would never have forgiven me had something happened to you."

"I'm fine." I sighed. "Everything worked out. We're all okay." I walked to the sink and washed my plate and fork.

"I read your mom's lifeline this morning, and she's stronger than she's been in days. At least the spell worked," she said, her expression still somber.

I glanced out of the kitchen window and saw the others outside. "If you know the spell worked, why are you still so upset?"

Calista leaned against the counter opposite me and ran her hand through her mass of chestnut curls. "You could have died last night. Your mom is counting on me to protect you. She'll know it was your energy linked to her through the spell, and she's going to be worried beyond measure about your safety. She won't know that we had the secondary spell to protect you. All she'll know is that you performed an extremely dangerous blood spell."

For the first time in my entire life, I saw dark circles forming under Calista's eyes, and it made me realize I wasn't the only one suffering. "I'm sorry." I wrapped my arms around her. "I'm sorry I put you through that. When we get my mom back, I'll explain everything, and she'll understand that I gave her no choice."

"She's going to be furious with you too, you know," she said, kissing my forehead.

"Oh, yes. I'm expecting as much." I gave her a reassuring smile.

"I better go take Selkie her breakfast. She's getting feistier by the day and nearly back to her old self."

My smile widened with genuine happiness and then faded in an instant. "Promise me you won't tell her about the blood spell. She's just getting her strength back, and I don't want to worry her."

Calista paused in thought. "Only until she's fully recovered, and then I'll let you be the one to tell her. Deal?"

"Deal." I gave Calista another hug and then headed outside to join the group.

The ringing of clashing swords echoed over the field. Rheya and Rhal battled like two gladiators in a tournament of life and death. With each step, their movements exuded a sense of vitality and vigor. Sparks flew as steel met steel with each powerful thrust.

Watching them made me reconsider my judgment of Arden's opinion of human fighting skills. I quickly began to have doubts about my ability against either of these two.

Malakai stood off to the side, studying the battle with intense concentration. I walked to stand beside him. "They're incredible," I said. Rheya was an amazing sight. Her long, bright red braid sparkled with golden streaks as it whipped through the air, acting as a weapon in its own right. The thick braid whipped Rhal across the back of the head as she maneuvered around him. Her lengthy, toned body moved with a grace and agility that should have been impossible to achieve by moving at her speed, but she made it look effortless. Regardless of our prior interactions, her skill and technique as a fighter were admirable.

Poor Rhal doesn't stand a chance.

Malakai's voice brought me out of my reverie. "Rhal's been trying to beat Rheya in a sword fight for decades, but she wins every time."

Just at that moment, Rheya swept her long leg out and

knocked Rhal off his feet. "You're sluggish," she taunted, and reached out an arm to lift him off the ground.

"Argh …" Rhal moaned as he sat upright. "The air on this planet sits heavy in my lungs," he groaned while rubbing his chest with one hand, and the spot on his head where Rheya's braid had assaulted him with the other.

"Yes, I feel it too, brother. It's the pollutants. We're not used to them." The two walked arm in arm, carrying on in a friendly manner as if they hadn't just been ferociously fighting one another.

Rheya spotted me standing watch next to Malakai. "What about you, *Princess*? Shall we see what you're made of?" she asked in a mocking tone.

My defiant sapphire eyes met her daring emerald ones. "Listen, Xena, I'd appreciate it if you'd stop calling me that. I'm not a princess, nor have I ever wanted to be one. My name is Everly. Got it?"

"Okay … Everly," she said in a more serious tone. "But what is this Xena you call me?"

"Just a TV character you sort of reminded me of when I first saw you."

"TV character?" she asked with an arch of her eyebrow.

"You know, from a television show."

"Ahh … yes, the television. We don't have television on Aenoas-Vita—it weakens the mind." Rheya glanced at Malakai like she thought I was dense.

I couldn't help but roll my eyes. I was tiring of this Vitarian superiority mindset.

"Now," Rheya said, changing the subject. "Let's see what kind of endurance you have." She walked over to the nearby picnic table, where they had spread out a variety of swords, staffs, and knives. She collected a pair of wooden staffs, both as long as a sword and with the same handle diameter, and offered me one. "We'll start with these."

The weight of the staff was light, but the wood itself felt durable. It was the color of white oak and covered in beautiful carvings from top to bottom. "What are these carvings?"

"They're Vitarian runes," Malakai answered. "This one here"—he pointed—"means 'life and magic.' And this one," he said, pointing at another, "means 'strength and honor.'"

"They're exquisite." I turned the staff around, examining the many symbols covering the entire length and circumference of the wood.

"Yes, they are," he agreed, gesturing for the staff. He held it respectfully. "Crafted from the ancient wood of an ever tree, the staffs possess a unique quality. They embody the magic of our home. These runes contain powerful spells that awaken one's inner warrior. If one's strength is weak, the magic of the staff will not work for them." He passed the staff back to me.

I gripped it, running one hand over the smooth carvings. An energy vibrated within, as if the staff had suddenly come to life. It reached out to me, and I felt my energy respond and connect with that of the staff. A glow ignited from within my arms. I swallowed. "What's happening?"

Malakai gestured toward the staff. "It's the magic of Aenoas-Vita. It senses you are Vitarian and is connecting with your inner magic and testing your strength. Do you feel it awakening something within you? If a human were to hold one of these, nothing would happen. The magic of Aenoas-Vita only flows through a child of its womb."

"Enough with the history lesson," Rheya interrupted. "It's time we begin."

Arden met us in the clearing. He took the staff Rheya held and stood beside me. The scowl she gave him let him know his action did not please her.

"You place one hand here like this"—he demonstrated by placing one hand about a quarter of the way up the staff—

"and the other here, just below the higher one. Let all mental and emotional guards down, and allow the magic of the staff to bind with your own. Ancient Vitarian warriors spelled these runes with powerful magic. The staffs tested the abilities of the one wielding them and ruled out those unworthy of guarding the royal families. If the magic of the staff deems you a worthy warrior, its magic will bind with yours, and it will awaken the warrior within and yield to your command."

He moved to stand directly in front of me. "Are you ready?"

I nodded, and he motioned to Rheya and handed her back the staff. She moved in front of me with the look of a panther ready to pounce.

I held the staff as instructed. I wasn't entirely sure exactly how I was supposed to invoke the staff's power, but I didn't have time to contemplate before I felt an overwhelming amount of energy vibrating from within the wood. My entire body buzzed as the staff's magic pulsed through my body. It moved through me as if it were seeking my very soul. A ghostlike voice whispered my name. No one else seemed to notice. The voice was inside my head, waking something dormant inside me.

Rheya did not hold back. She came at me with full force. Her speed was incredible. She was even quicker now than when I saw her battling with Rhal. She sprang, striking me with her staff and pivoting away before I could attempt any counter attack of my own. With every step, my arms burned and my legs grew heavier, yet she continued on, undeterred. She was faster than me, but I had to strike back if I ever stood a chance of earning her respect.

The others watched us with rapt attention as Rheya stalked toward me with a hungry glint in her eye. I gripped my staff and swung at her, only to miss and nearly topple over. Beads of sweat trickled down my shirt, and my ponytail annoyingly clung to the back of my sticky neck. I knew I couldn't continue holding her off for long, so I backed up, putting as much distance between us as I could, while I planned my next move.

Arden made to come between us, but I halted him with a gesture of my arm. If I was going to stand a chance of beating a Vitarian, I needed to learn to fight like a Vitarian. Frustration and sheer will pushed me forward. I knew what I had to do. I had to use my ability, as she obviously used some gift of speed and strength.

I stayed back while she continued pacing around me, showing no signs of getting tired. Just like in my training with Arden, I focused on forging energy together. I released my mental barrier and allowed the surrounding energy to flow through me, absorbing and merging it into a single pulsating entity.

Excitement filled me as the energy easily responded to my will. It's getting easier each time I do it.

The energy was hot and burned to be released, but I held it inside me, waiting for the right moment to discharge my invisible weapon.

"Is that all you have, Xena?" I taunted Rheya.

Her eyes flared, and she stormed toward me, just as I wanted.

I smiled as I raced to meet her, bringing my staff down toward her own. When we made contact, I released the pulsing mass, and the shocking force threw her backward.

She recovered quicker than I'd expected.

"Nice," she said before moving in for another attack of her own, but she was slower than before. Her speed now matched my own. The force of the energy blast must have taken a toll on her.

I met her blow for blow. The surrounding trees became a blur as we continued in our dance for control. Just as I thought I might gain the upper hand, Rheya performed a move that defied human capabilities. Her body left the ground as she leaped into the air toward me. Her staff smashed into mine, bringing me crashing to my knees.

"Argh …" I cried out as pain radiated from my arms and down through my kneecaps as they banged on the ground.

"LEAVE HER ALONE!" A voice roared from nearby. In the next instant, Jasper was standing in front of me. Rheya was in the grip of rage as she spun and swung toward Jasper with a deadly force.

"NO!" I wailed.

The staff slammed down with a force that could crush a skull, but instead of making contact with Jasper, it struck an invisible barrier, which forcefully propelled Rheya backward through the air, causing her body to collide with one of the surrounding oaks. Because of my ability, I could see the vibrations coming from the energy that Jasper was releasing. It was incredible. He stood with his palms facing out, and a heavy current of energy poured from them, encasing us in some kind of live shield. I'd never seen anything like it. In an instant, a crushing realization hit me: Jasper had been lying to me, too.

Losing all drive to fight anymore, I dropped my staff to the ground. In a flash, Rheya picked herself up and retrieved my fallen staff, then tossed it to Jasper, who caught it midair.

"So, the princess has a personal Shield, and judging by the look on her face, one she didn't know about."

I watched in disbelief as Jasper's skin lit up with the magic of the staff, confirming what I already knew to be true, that he was Vitarian. Rheya was in full warrior mode as she began her attack. Jasper met each of Rheya's strikes with graceful precision. In all our years of practicing martial arts together, I'd never seen him move the way he moved now. The two battled on with equal strength.

"Enough!" commanded Arden.

Rheya and Jasper both halted.

Jasper returned the staff to the table, where I'd moved to sit. He turned to me. "Ev, I ... I'm so sorry. I wanted to tell you the truth, but I was sworn by an oath to my king."

"You mean ... my father." The words seared the tip of my tongue.

I shook my head. This couldn't possibly be happening. Jasper, of all people. The only true friend I'd ever had. Anger replaced the shock I felt. I grasped onto it to quell the heartbreak that threatened to cripple me. "How could you keep this from me, Jasper? You're supposed to be my best friend and the person I trust with all of my secrets, and you've been lying to me like everyone else for our entire friendship."

He reached out to take my hand. Pain shrouded my vision. I struggled to take a breath and leaned forward to put my head between my knees. Jasper crouched down beside me and placed his forehead against mine. The heartache came crashing all at once. My own intertwined with Jasper's, and the combination of emotions crushed my heart.

Jasper lifted his head. The pain in his expression mirrored my own. My ability had gotten stronger, and I realized that, without intending to, I'd been projecting my own emotions into him while siphoning his. Tears slid from his golden eyes and trailed down his cheeks. I understood the agony he felt from betraying me, and he understood mine. He hated himself for lying to me, but he'd still done it. I pulled away, but he tightened his hold on my hand.

"Please give me a chance to explain," he pleaded.

I yanked my hand free of his. I didn't want to feel his guilt or understand his sorrow. His betrayal was unforgivable. I got up and ran to the cabin, ignoring Jasper's plea to stay. I burst through the cabin door. Calista and Felix both jumped up from their seats, startled at the sound of the door banging off the wall. "Everly, honey. What's wrong? What's happened?" Calista glanced behind me, as if expecting a threat to be close behind.

"Did you know about Jasper?" I asked. "Did you know he's like the rest of you?" I demanded.

The guilty look in her eyes said she did. "Everly, please calm down. Let us explain."

I didn't want an explanation. I didn't want to hear anymore of their lies. On a nearby stand, I spotted Calista's keys and quickly snatched them up. I ran to her car, started the engine, and peeled away. The tires screeched as I hit the brakes hard to make the sharp corner I'd come to too quickly. I released a breath as I cleared the tight turn and pressed on the gas. I sped down the bumpy road, twisting and turning at each bend, and sped up as the sound of a motorcycle behind alerted me to Jasper following. He quickly closed the distance between us, so I slammed on the gas pedal, gaining speed. The car jostled and bounced over potholes and large rocks in the dirt road. Mustangs were not designed for off-roading. Calista would not be happy if I marred her baby, but I wasn't happy with being constantly lied to.

I caught sight of a massive shadow out of the corner of my eye. At first, I thought Jasper was moving alongside me, but I was struck with surprise when the shadow leaped from the tree line. I slammed on the brakes; the tires skidded, kicking up rocks and dirt as the Mustang slid to a stop. My heart pounded as I waited for the dust to clear to see if what I thought I'd seen was what I'd actually seen. As the dust settled, an enormous shape emerged. It paced just inches in front of the vehicle. My eyes widened in disbelief when I could finally see what had leaped from the trees and was now blocking my path to freedom. The mountain lion's roar filled my ears. I sat stunned and staring at the ferocious beast. The animal made eye contact with me and opened its jaw wide as it released another terrifying roar.

"Holy crap!" I shouted.

The news had been reporting more and more sightings of mountain lions recently, because of urban development and lack of wild food sources, but this was the first time I'd ever seen one this close. It was even more intimidating than I could've imagined. I leaned closer to the windshield to get a better look at it. It stared straight back at me.

What's it doing, and why is it looking at me like it recognizes me?

The crunching of feet on gravel reminded me that Jasper had stopped right behind and was now walking to the driver's door of the Mustang.

"Jasper, no. Get back on your bike," I yelled out of the cracked window, afraid he hadn't noticed the beast pacing in front of us. It roared at his approach.

"Malakai," Jasper yelled at the aggravated lion. "That's enough." The beast quieted as it continued to pace.

I rolled down the driver-side window. "What do you mean, Malakai?" I asked, pointing at the uneasy animal that watched us with careful eyes.

Jasper shot a glance at the lion. "Malakai's inhabiting the mountain lion. He's taken over its consciousness. It's his dominant gift. He can inhabit the mind of any animal and control its actions." He walked over and rubbed the lion's head, which it didn't seem to appreciate. "Malakai can hear through the animal's ears and see through its eyes. He can hear and see us now, and he intends to block your path until you turn around and come back with me. It's not safe for you to be alone, with our enemies searching for you."

I got out of the car and looked at the lion in disbelief. Just when I thought I was getting used to my strange new reality, some new discovery bewildered me. I walked carefully toward the lion. It sat and allowed me to approach, something it wouldn't have done in its natural state. As I got closer to it, I recognized the vibrations it was sending off. They weren't the typical vibrations of an animal; they were the same ones I'd sensed from Malakai. As crazy as it sounded, Jasper was right: Malakai was inhabiting this animal.

Being this close to such a creature in nature was a rare opportunity. Its wild eyes studied me as I reached out a shaky hand and stroked its coarse golden fur. It shifted uneasily. I pulled my hand back and gave it space. I wasn't confident about how much control Malakai maintained over the lion's actions, and didn't want to risk it attacking.

"Okay." I turned and walked past Jasper without stopping. "I'll follow you back."

Turning the Mustang around was a bit of a challenge. The mountain lion followed along the tree line as we made our way back up the road toward the cabin until it eventually disappeared into the forest.

Jasper stood waiting for me as I parked the Mustang. A part of me wanted to turn back around and floor it off this mountain, but I'd agreed to come back, so I turned off the ignition, and pushed open the door.

"Will you walk with me?" Jasper reached out his hand as I lifted myself out of the driver's seat. I ignored his gesture and brushed past him.

After walking a few feet, I turned back to face him. "Why didn't you tell me? It was one thing finding out that my mom and all the others were keeping secrets from me, but you? How could you pretend to be my best friend these years while secretly knowing the answers to all of my deepest questions, questions I shared with you?" I choked the last word out and fought back burning tears as I struggled to breathe.

I clenched my hands into fists to quell the flood of rumbling emotions. "These last few days, not telling you what's been going on has torn me up. I've wanted nothing more than to tell you everything, and the only thing that's held me back was my worry for your safety. I didn't want to drag you into a dangerous situation. And it's been eating me up, keeping these things from you, and it's only been a few days. You've been lying to me for years. I don't know how we can come back from that." I turned my back on him and stared into the thick trees. Their long branches lifted and twisted in the air, as if acknowledging the truth of my words.

Jasper moved close behind me. His warm energy vibrated all around him. The sorrow, guilt, and shame emanating from his aura was too much. I brought up my guard, but once again, it refused to respond.

Why does this keep happening? I squeezed my eyes shut, hoping to block everything out.

Jasper gently placed his hand on my shoulder and moved in front of me.

"Open your eyes, Ev."

I shook my head.

"Please—look at me."

My eyelids snapped open, and when I looked into the eyes of my best friend, who I'd counted on for so many years, the tears I'd been forcing back burst free.

Jasper swiped them away with his thumbs and bowed his head against mine. "I've wanted to tell you so many times. Every time we've been together lately, I've tried to tell you, but I always lose my nerve. I was afraid that if you knew I'd kept this secret, you'd hate me, and I'd lose you. You mean everything to me. Please forgive me, Evy. What can I do? Tell me, and I'll do it."

I inhaled a deep breath and stepped back from him. "I

want to know everything. How old are you? Were you born on Earth like me? What do you know about my parents?"

"Okay," he said, and nodded toward the cabin porch steps. "I'll tell you everything I know. No more secrets."

We sat next to each other on the steps, and I waited for him to speak.

He fiddled with his hands. "I'm nineteen," he finally said. "The same age as you. My mother was pregnant with me at the same time yours was with you. I was born on Aenoas-Vita, not Earth. My father was in the royal guard, but our parents were also friends before your mom traveled to Earth."

His long back leaned forward, and he propped his elbows on his knees.

"Why did your parents bring you here?" I asked.

He ran a hand through his dark waves as he sat back up. "You were exhibiting your abilities as an Empath and began isolating yourself from the human children. Since you weren't raised honing your gifts, it took you some time to learn how to block out the overwhelming emotions of others. I'd begun developing my skills as a Shield early and had already begun my training for the royal guard when the king confided in my father about your struggles. My parents wanted to help, so they agreed to bring me to Earth as your Shield and companion."

"So," I interrupted, "our friendship has been nothing more than your duty?" I wasn't angry anymore. My heart ached as though someone had just ripped into my chest and tore into it.

I started to get up from the steps, but Jasper snatched my hand and refused to release it. He stood, staring down at me. "Everly, please," he pleaded. "You know our friendship is more than that. Yes, it was my duty that brought me here to this planet to protect you, but our bond is real. It has always been real, from the first moment I walked into the classroom and saw you hunched over your desk. You were in so much pain trying to block out everyone's emotions. I instantly wanted to protect you, to shield you from everything that caused you pain. Then you looked up and smiled at me. I knew right then that I'd do anything for you. And every moment we've shared since, every secret, laugh, disagreement, every feeling I have for you, has been genuine friendship and has had nothing to do with duty. I love you, Everly, and I think you know that love goes deeper than just friendship."

The stairs swayed. It was too much. I'd known Jasper's feelings for me had grown beyond friendship, and I'd known he would express them eventually, but now that I knew he'd hidden so much more from me, I couldn't even think about addressing those feelings.

"Jasper, I—"

"It's okay." He pulled me into his arms. "You don't have to say anything. I know you've known how I feel, but I wanted you to hear the words from me. I'm not asking for anything except your forgiveness. Please forgive me."

I allowed myself to relax into the familiar, safe feeling of being with Jasper. He tightened his hold, and for just a moment, I imagined everything was back to normal, but I knew things would never be *normal* again.

I turned my head so that one cheek rested against his chest, and his heartbeat quickened at my movement. "I know you had your obligations, but you didn't just betray me. You betrayed our friendship. My heart is breaking, Jasp, and I'm angry. I'm so angry with everyone for not believing that I could handle the truth. Look where these lies have gotten us. My father is dead, and some psychotic queen and her lackey have taken my mom. I don't want to lose you too."

I itched my nose on his shirt and breathed in the familiar

scent of cypress. "The thought of losing our friendship feels like a piece of me being ripped out, but I don't know how to forgive you right now."

He tucked his head onto my shoulder while holding me tighter than he ever had. "I understand. I know I messed up. All I ask is that you give me a chance to earn your forgiveness." He lifted his head from my shoulder. "Will you come someplace with me?"

I leaned back, glancing up at him with surprise. "What? Where?"

"A place where you can blow off some steam. Someplace I've wanted to take you to for a long time."

"But I thought I wasn't supposed to leave."

"You're not, not alone, anyway. I'm your Shield, remember? It's my job to protect you."

The look on his face said he was loving having this new reason to be overprotective. "And now that I finally know that you're *my* Shield, you're going to take full advantage of using it against me, I'm sure." I nudged him on the shoulder.

"You know I will. Now come on." He tugged me toward his motorcycle.

"Should we tell anyone we're going?" I asked, nodding toward the cabin.

"No, they'll most likely have a problem with it. Let's just go before anyone notices us out here. Do you trust me?" He climbed onto his bike and kicked up the kickstand, then handed me a helmet.

Did I still trust him? My body answered for me as I snapped on the helmet and instinctively climbed onto the back of Jasper's bike like I'd done so many times over the years. I wrapped my arms tightly around his waist before he sped away from the cabin.

CHAPTER 9

*W*e reached the bottom of the mountain and popped out on a back road, where we made our way down to Highway 30 and headed toward the Columbia River. The sun was setting, and Mount St. Helens illuminated the rosy sky with its snow-white reflection. I clung tightly to Jasper as he leaned the motorcycle near the ground and turned us off the highway. Our bodies jostled up and down as we crossed over train tracks and emerged onto an unmarked road that ran side by side with the river. Sparkling hues of yellow and gold bounced off the murky water under the setting sun.

As we continued west, the tree line steadily thickened until the river was no longer visible from the road. Jasper slowed and turned down an unmaintained drive marked with a No Trespassing sign. We slowly drove along the tree-lined, bumpy road until we arrived at a wide grass field that contained an enormous two-story house shaped like a boxy warehouse. Both the top and bottom levels had wooden decks that wrapped around the entire building. To prevent anyone from peering in, they had tinted all the windows.

Several vehicles parked throughout the field, and a loud, thumping bass boomed from within the building.

My neck felt the instant relief of weight being lifted as I pulled the heavy helmet from atop my head. I surveyed the area. A thick mass of trees surrounded the clearing, guarding the building, so it wasn't visible from the main road up above. "What is this place?" It didn't look like much from the outside.

"Come on, I'll show you." Jasper hauled me toward the building.

We came to a door with another No Trespassing sign. "Are you sure we should be here?" I whispered, trying to resist, but Jasper confidently pushed the door open as if he belonged there and pulled me in with him.

Once inside, the decor was a full 360 compared to the outside. The small foyer we stood in held a Victorian mahogany desk and plush red velvet chairs. A pair of red Converse flexed up and down atop the desk. The man wearing the shoes was sitting with his feet kicked up and a hardback book in his hands. How he could read with the loud music pumping throughout the building was beyond me. My chest was literally vibrating with each beat of the bass.

"Jasper!" Book Guy stood and came around the desk. "Long time no see, my friend." The two gave each other a quick hug and pat on the back. He stood about a head shorter than Jasper. His attire was full-on nerd–tech–geek with a flair of retro: black-collared dress shirt with a deep red necktie, black-rimmed square retro glasses, black skinny jeans, and red Converse shoes to tie it all together. He turned to me. "And who is this lovely creature with you tonight?"

"Neil, this is Everly. Ev, this is Neil. He owns the place."

"Nice to meet you, Neil," I shouted over the music coming from an unseen room.

"The pleasure is all mine." His voice echoed in my head, but his lips didn't actually move.

My eyes grew wide. *What the hell? Did he just speak to me telepathically?*

Neil must have noticed the confused look on my face, because his mouth spread in a wide, friendly smile, and he winked at me.

"You two kids have fun now," he said aloud this time. "There's a great band on tonight."

Neil said something to Jasper in another language. I recognized it as the Vitarian language I'd heard the others use. Jasper responded in kind. Hearing him speak in Vitarian was like ripping a scab off a wound. My stomach twisted at the reminder of his secrets.

I pushed away the anger. When I'd gotten on the back of Jasper's bike, it had been a choice, a choice to forgive. Forgiveness was the only way for us to move forward. I took a deep breath. The knots in my stomach eased as I watched Jasper smiling at something Neil had just said to him and remembered all the times we'd laughed together like that.

Jasper saw me watching him. I couldn't help but return his smile. It had always been infectious.

"Ready?" he asked, putting his arm around my waist and leading me toward the red velvet curtains separating the foyer from another room.

"Neil's Vitarian?" I asked as he parted the curtains.

"Yes. This club has a ... restricted membership policy."

I paused before we went through the curtains. "When you introduced us, and he spoke to me, I heard his words in my mind, but his mouth never moved. Is he a telepath?"

"Ahh ... I'm so used to Neil speaking that way that I don't even notice the difference anymore. He's sort of like a telepath, only he can't read minds. His abilities are limited to projecting thoughts and sounds."

"Wow! That's incredible."

Jasper laughed. "Yeah, it's a pretty cool ability. Now come on. Let's go have some fun."

It was good to hear Jasper's laugh. It reminded me of happier, carefree times.

We pulled aside the velvet curtains and entered an enormous room filled with people dancing and congregating all around.

My breath caught, and my heart skipped nervously. "Are all of these people Vitarian?"

Jasper nodded.

I looked around the room in amazement.

So many. There are so many here.

I scanned the room for familiar faces, wondering if some of them were regulars at the café or people I had gone to school with. I noticed a couple of faces that seemed familiar, people I'd seen buying herbs from my mom, but other than that, I didn't recognize anyone.

"Do all of them live in town?"

Jasper shook his head. "No. Most come from out of town to be around their own kind, and some of them come to the club by portal. Aenoas-Vita doesn't really have clubs, so once the word spread about Neil's place, it's basically been a Vitarian magnet."

"Oh." It felt strange encountering so many individuals from Aenoas-Vita. Some people blended into the crowd wearing ordinary street clothes, while others stood out in their unique and extravagant outfits. A few were dressed in similar uniforms as Rhal, Rheya, and Malakai when they'd arrived from the portal. I assumed those were the ones who got here by portal.

I began to realize the special aura that Vitarians emitted. Their energy differed slightly from humans'—stronger. It contained a spark that human energy didn't have. The room hummed with the vibrations of so many gifted individuals, with so much *magic*.

A live band filled the stage at the other end of the room. The instruments pumped out exotic beats matched with sensual vocals. I couldn't understand the lyrics, since the vocalist was singing in Vitarian, but my body resonated with the rhythm of the music. Staircases on either side of the stage led up to a second floor that was occupied by more dancers and socialites.

Jasper led us toward a bar lining an entire wall of the bottom floor. The top piece of the bar sat atop one long glass fish tank that spanned the entire width of the bar. All kinds of exotic, glowing fish and coral filled it. The bartender lifted a section of the bar and tossed in a scoop of food, causing the sea life to swarm toward their sinking meal.

The bartender nodded at us and asked something in Vitarian. Jasper responded, and the bartender turned and poured two shots of a glowing lavender-colored liquid, then handed them to us. A fog-like vapor floated above the drink. I wasn't sure this was something that was meant to be ingested.

"What is this stuff, and aren't they going to card us and find out we're not twenty-one?"

"Vitarians don't live by the same laws as humans. And this isn't exactly alcohol. It's a potion made from the pressed oil of an ever flower harvested on Aenoas-Vita. Neil has a contact who smuggles him the flowers. The effects are similar to alcohol because it lessens your inhibitions, but much more intense. Try it."

Jasper lifted his shot glass out, and we clinked glasses and downed our shots.

"I don't feel anything." I set my empty glass down on the bar.

Jasper grinned. "It might be a magic potion, but it still

takes a couple of minutes to kick in." He added his glass next to mine and nodded to the bartender to refill them.

"Cheers," we said in unison, and drained the second shot.

The flavor was sweet and flowery. It made me think of lavender and chamomile with a hint of orange peel.

"How often do you come here?" I asked over the music.

"Occasionally. I've wanted to bring you here for so long."

Jasper stepped in front of me. "Come dance with me."

"Oh …" I was feeling slightly light-headed, and the multi-colored and decorative glass-blown lights hanging from the walls and ceiling left streaking impressions in the air as I looked around.

Jasper took hold of my hand, and I followed him out onto the dance floor. He wrapped an arm around my waist and pulled me in close. I roped both of my arms around his neck, and our bodies moved in sync as we swayed to the beats. The music lulled me into a calm trance, and all the other bodies that swayed on the dance floor faded into the background.

With the potion-induced sense of freedom, my mental guard dissolved like ice under a warm sun. Everything but this moment felt surreal and far away. As the energy in the room surged, I allowed it to pass through me, embracing its force. Each sense felt heightened, making every sight, sound, smell, and touch more vivid.

Jasper was definitely feeling the effects of the potion, too. The world melted away, and all that remained was the pure bliss of the moment. In response to his desire, my body moved instinctively, as I ran my fingers up his neck, feeling the soft strands of his hair intertwine with my fingertips. He looked down at me questioningly, and when I smiled, he ran his hands through my hair, lifting it up and letting the black waves fall free. There was no space between us: no anger, no betrayal, nothing but this moment, this moment of pure, intoxicating freedom.

His hands traced a path from my hips up my back, sending shivers down my spine. I had a flash of the night we'd almost given in to our passion—the same passion ignited between us now. I couldn't tear my gaze away from Jasper's piercing golden-amber eyes. As his mouth moved closer to mine, I could feel the heat emanating from his body. Tension charged the air as I braced myself for his kiss, fully aware that I desired it just as much as he did. Just as his lips grazed mine, someone suddenly yanked him back away from me.

"What the hell do you think you're doing, bringing her out in the open like this, boy?" Arden growled at Jasper.

I glanced around in a daze to see Arden, Rheya, Rhal, Malakai, and Calista all circled around the two of us. My cheeks burned with embarrassment, knowing they must have witnessed how Jasper and I were dancing. Arden threw an angry glance in my direction before returning to berate Jasper.

"I'm her Shield!" Jasper defended himself. "She's safe with me."

"You are an ignorant child. You have spent your short years on this planet and do not know the dangers of our kind. Your actions could have put both of your lives in danger."

Suddenly my skin felt too hot and tingled all over with biting pin-pricks; everything faded out in a dizzying rush. My knees hit the cold concrete floor, and I caught myself with my hands before falling forward.

Calista was down on the floor in an instant, helping me back up. "What did you give her?" she snapped.

My vision clouded over, and my ears buzzed. I worried I was going to pass out, but suddenly my head cleared and my senses sharpened, though the sights and sounds around me seemed incomprehensible. I saw myself from a distance, on the floor, hunched over my knees, with Calista bending over me and Arden holding Jasper by the shirt collar. Looking down from above, my eyes burned with an intense hatred as I took in the scene. As the dizziness passed, I came to the startling realization that I was no longer seeing things from my own point of view, but from the vantage point of someone watching from high above. *The balcony.* Instantly I recognized his unique vibrations, and I knew whose eyes I was looking through.

"He's here," I muttered as I pulled myself unsteadily to my feet. It was disconcerting, trying to stand while seeing myself from someone else's perspective.

Arden and Jasper were arguing like two schoolboys, so I stumbled toward them with Calista supporting me by the arm. "HE'S HERE!" I said, louder this time, finally getting their attention. "He's watching us from the balcony."

We were drawing attention from the bystanders, and the music had quieted down. Arden and Jasper both went utterly silent as someone started clapping from above.

"Well, well, well ... this is a pleasant surprise. How considerate of all of you to save me the trouble of hunting you down."

"Darion," Arden hissed.

Another wave of dizziness came on, and my vision returned to normal. I turned to see Darion looking down at us. We were the only seven people still standing. Everyone around us had bent down on one knee with their fists held to their hearts. It was the same bow Rhal and Malakai had performed when we first met.

"I must admit, Arden"—Darion's voice echoed off the walls—"I expected more stealth from the king's army commander. Instead, you have delivered the prey directly to me. For that, I may make your execution swift."

Several guards dressed as gladiators appeared from every corner of the room. Each held a sword ready for battle.

"Capture them," Darion commanded.

The guards closed in around us.

"Get Everly out of here." Arden shoved me into Jasper's arms.

Before Jasper realized my intention, I broke free of his grasp and ran for the staircase leading up to where Darion stood. A guard moved to grab me, but I kicked him in the groin and leaped up the stairs two at a time. When I reached the top, I stood face-to-face with the man who had taken my mother.

This time, he didn't guard his emotions from me. He wanted me to know how much he detested me. "So, we finally meet again. Are you so eager to be my captive?"

"Where's my mother, you bastard?"

Darion's menacing gaze raked me up and down. "Come with me, and I'll take you to her." He reached his hand out in invitation.

"You admit that you have her?"

"Oh, yes, I've kept her alive for you." He made a motion of flicking lint off his sleeve and added, "Barely."

"Why are you doing this? Why did you take her?"

"Your mother has earned her punishment for her betrayal of her queen."

"If you've hurt her, I'll kill you."

His brow twitched. "Hmm … it's a little late on the first part, but as for the latter, you can try."

I lunged at him, but a vision of my mom chained to a wall assaulted my mind. She lay lifeless on a stone floor.

Darion took advantage of my stunned state and grabbed me by my hair and throat. He yanked my head back as he squeezed the air from my lungs. My only thought was that I could not fail my mom.

"Does this seem familiar?" he whispered smugly in my ear.

My returning nightmare flashed before my eyes. It wasn't my memory creating the images, though. Darion was sending me visions through some ability of his. I forced the images from my mind and focused furiously on gathering as much energy into me as I could.

"I'll admit," he continued, pulling my hair harder, "your mother's strength has impressed me. She's put up quite the fight, but I don't think she'll last much longer." His hot breath skimmed my cheek.

Everything about him repulsed me. I struggled in his grasp. My heart pounded against my chest as I felt my consciousness slipping away. I refused to let Darion win. The battle below raged. Steel clashing against steel. I opened myself up to receive the current of energy being expelled by the warriors below: rage, fear, lust, valor. It now all flowed through me, fueling my strength. I forged the energy together, infusing it with every ounce of pain I'd felt over the last several days, and projected all of it into Darion. He staggered backward as I twisted out of his grasp. I threw my hands out in front of me, and they emanated an electrical current. Sparks of electricity surged up and down my arms. *This is a new development.*

Darion recovered and regained his posture, but he still seemed off-balance. "Your power is unlike any I've encountered before. I'm going to enjoy draining it from you."

I ignored his threat. "Where's my mom, you sick creep?"

"Everly," a voice called out from behind me. I turned just briefly to see Jasper running up the stairs. When I looked back, Darion had just leaped over the balcony. I looked over to see him land on his feet and disappear into a mass of guards.

"No!" I squeezed the balcony railing, scanning the bodies below for any sign of him, but he'd escaped.

"Ev," Jasper said, staring at the bolts of light flashing up and down my arms.

"Let's go," Rheya yelled from below.

Jasper looked up from my arms. "We need to leave … now!" he said with renewed urgency, and pulled me down the steps. His shirt had a tear, and a long bleeding cut crossed his chest.

"You're hurt," I said.

"It's fine. Felix will heal me when we get back. We need to leave now before more guards show up."

"I have to find Darion!" I tried to yank free.

"This isn't the time," Arden said as he flanked my other side. Rheya and Malakai joined, taking the lead as we made our way out of the club. My stomach churned as we stepped over bodies. Something tight gripped my ankle, causing me to fall forward. My hands slid through a sticky red puddle on the floor. I gagged as I breathed in the sharp, metallic scent of blood. I heard a thump behind me as the fallen guard cried out, and Rheya pried my ankle free.

"Take my hand." Arden's shadow hovered above me.

Shaking my head, I took shallow breaths to avoid the nauseating smell and picked myself up from the floor. I rushed behind the bar and turned on the small sink the bartender used for washing his hands and bar utensils. I scratched the blood from my hands and arms until my skin burned raw under the scalding water. Even though no blood remained visible on my skin, the smell stained the inside of my nose. Guilt plagued me as I stepped out from the bar and looked around. Wreckage covered the inside of the club, and it was all my fault.

Arden waited for me to follow him. We found a tied-up and blindfolded Neil in the field. Calista undid his bindings.

"Those bastards grabbed me unawares. And the damn blindfold was spelled, so I couldn't project any warnings." Neil flicked the blindfold to the ground with indignation.

"I'm sorry about the club, Neil," Jasper said to his friend.

"Hey, man. Don't worry about it. It's nothing a couple of favors owed can't take care of. You guys get out of here and leave the rest to me."

We hurried to Jasper's motorcycle. I was about to climb onto the back when Arden stepped in front of the bike. "Everly will ride back with us."

"I brought her here and I'll take her back," Jasper shot back. His aura still surged with the heat of the battle.

Not in the mood for another of their testosterone-fueled arguments, I stepped in. "It's fine, Jasp. I'll see you back at the cabin." I glanced at his cut. "Besides, you're injured, and it'll be easier for you not to have the extra weight to balance."

I placed my hand flat on his chest, avoiding his wound, and released a calming energy. The anger immediately faded from him. I was really getting the hang of this energy projection.

"I'm sorry I put you in danger," Jasper said, undoing the strap on his helmet.

"It wasn't your fault. Neither of us could've known that Darion would show up here. And if it's anyone's fault, it's mine." My chest tightened when I thought of the damage caused just by my being here.

Jasper shook his head, and a dark-cocoa wave fell over his forehead. "I hate to admit it, but Arden is right. I should have been more cautious. My actions were reckless and selfish. As your Shield, it's my duty to keep you safe."

Out of habit, I reached up and combed his fallen hair back with my hand. "Stop beating yourself up. I wanted to come with you. Now get back to the cabin so Felix can heal that nasty cut."

Jasper kick-started his bike and strapped on his helmet. He squeezed my hand and sped away. I watched him go until his bike faded into the shadowy night. When I turned around, I saw Arden had been silently watching our interaction. The only feature giving away any hint of emotion was the color of his eyes: they had lost all shades of blue and practically glowed green.

We all piled into Calista's Mustang. Rhal, being the tallest in the group, rode shotgun, while the rest of us squeezed into the back seat. It was a tight fit. Rheya offered to sit on Arden's lap to make more room. She looked to be enjoying herself immensely and winked at me when she caught me scowling at her.

An awkward silence filled the car, and the musty scent of sweat didn't help. The energy was still high from the events at the club, and by the way Arden avoided eye contact with me, I was sure he'd seen Jasper and me together on the dance floor. My skin flushed with heat as I thought about how we must have looked. Rheya watched me mischievously as she smoothed Arden's hair. He didn't reject her fondling, and she smiled when she saw the fire in my eyes. I swallowed the urge to poke her eyes out and avoided her watchful glare.

Jasper's motorcycle was already parked outside the cabin when we arrived. I breathed a sigh of relief that he was nowhere in sight and most likely in the process of being healed by Felix. The thought of another confrontation between him and Arden made me cringe.

"Finally." Rheya flung the car door open before the wheels had even come to a full stop.

"Hey," Calista shouted from the front. "If you scratch my baby, there'll be—"

Before Calista finished her sentence, Rheya had already hopped off Arden's lap through the open door, landing in the grass with a graceful thump on both feet. Once the car was parked, the others quickly followed suit, eager to leave behind the uncomfortable atmosphere inside the Mustang.

I glanced at Arden, who hung back while everyone disappeared inside the cabin. Without saying a word, he slid out of the car and headed for the forest. Unsure what to do, I followed him as he slipped off into the trees.

When I caught up to him, he was casually leaning against a tree trunk, his silhouette a shadow in the inky night. "Arden … I …" His lips were on mine before I could utter another word. The intensity of his kiss was like a spark that ignited a raging fire of desire and longing deep within me. As I responded to him with equal abandon, everything around us faded away. Energy surged between us. Every touch sent a jolt of electricity through our bodies, igniting a fierce desire that consumed us both. Arden pressed me against the tree, his body firmly against mine. His mouth explored my neck as his hands moved under my shirt.

When he bent down and kissed my abdomen, a soft moan escaped my lips. His tongue traced the sides of my waist, causing a shiver to ripple across my skin, before returning to claim my lips once more.

A sobering sense of guilt hit me when I remembered Jasper in the cabin. "Arden, we have to stop." I gently held him back.

"I know," he whispered, his warm breath brushing against my forehead as we stood there, our breaths intertwining and slowly syncing. "I shouldn't have kissed you like that. When I saw you in his arms the way you were, I didn't like the way it made me feel."

He lifted his head from mine. "He's in love with you. You're the same age and you have a history together. It would make sense for the two of you to be together. You also have feelings for him. I sensed them when you were with him."

I stepped away from him and drew in a deep breath of the

crisp air. "Yes," I admitted to both Arden, and finally, myself. "I have feelings for Jasper. He's my best friend. He's always been there for me, and I love him for that, and I think there is something more between us or could be if I …" A cool breeze hit my cheek. "The truth is. I feel a strong connection to you, Arden. I felt it the first time I saw you. And it's different from how I feel about Jasper. Being with you. It's like … I'm finally awake."

Frustration gnawed at me. I kicked at a mound of fallen leaves, sending them fluttering up into the light breeze. I surprised myself with how forthcoming I was being about my feelings for the two of them. Perhaps I was still feeling the effects of the ever flower.

Arden watched patiently as he moved toward me. He gently ran his hand up the side of my face. "I think maybe you owe it to yourself and him to find out what those feelings mean." He placed a soft kiss on my forehead and walked away.

I stayed behind for a moment. I needed to make a choice. After being in Arden's arms tonight, I knew without a doubt what I had to do. But it wouldn't be easy. By the time I got back to the cabin, my head was pounding and my stomach felt like it'd been turned upside down. As soon as I walked in, the scent of herbs and something else made my stomach turn even more.

"Ugh … what are you two brewing up in there?" I called out to Calista and Felix, who were working side by side in the kitchen, mixing some concoction. "It smells awful." I plopped down on the old sofa, sending up a plume of dust, and slid down so that my head rested on the back cushion. I rubbed my stomach, hoping that the motion would help ease the nausea, but it only made it worse.

"You'll thank us after you've drunk this." Calista handed me a teacup sized beverage. "The distilled ever flower you two drank can leave you with quite a nasty hangover when you're not used to its effects. This rejuvenation tea will detoxify your body, and you'll recover quicker."

"I don't know." I wrinkled my nose at it. "It doesn't smell very rejuvenating."

"Don't worry, my dear." Felix chuckled. "It doesn't taste nearly as bad as it smells."

Just as I looked down into the green, bubbling liquid, a popping bubble released a disgustingly foul smell. I shoved the mug back into Calista's hands and dashed out of the cabin. I barely made it down the porch steps before the contents of my stomach spilled from my mouth.

Calista held out the mug to me as I dragged myself back inside the cabin. "Drink up," she encouraged.

I held my breath and downed the tea. The flavor wasn't bad after all. I tipped my head back to make sure I drained all the liquid. "Hmm … you're right. It didn't taste as bad as I thought it would." I handed Calista back the empty mug.

"You'll feel better soon. Here." Calista handed me a second mug. "Take this one to your partner in crime." She nodded toward the back room, where we'd taken Selkie the day we arrived.

I found Jasper lying down on the twin-sized bed. His shirt was off, and the wound was completely sealed and covered in a thick salve. One of his arms lay across his eyes. He sat up when he saw me.

"Rejuvenation tea, courtesy of Calista and Felix." I handed him the mug, taking a seat next to him on the mattress. "It looks and smells something awful, but the taste isn't bad, and it really helps. I felt like death until just a minute ago, but I'm starting to feel hu— I mean, normal again."

"You were going to say 'human'?"

"Yeah." I looked down at my shaky hands. "I guess I'll always think of myself as human in a way. Finding out that

I'm from another planet has been like losing my identity. I don't even know what to call myself. I'm not human, but I don't think of myself as Vitarian either."

"I'm sorry, Ev." Jasper put his hand on my knee.

He didn't waste any time analyzing the contents of the cup like I had, and just downed the liquid in an instant.

"Ahh," he said, letting his head fall back down onto the pillow. "I suppose we should go out and face the music," he moaned from under his arm.

I followed Jasper out of the room. Rheya stood gawking at his chest as he pulled his shirt over his head. She brushed past me. "I see why you're attracted to him," she whispered, loud enough for Arden to hear, who stood nearby.

I shot her a look, but she only smirked and kept moving to the other side of the room to stand next to Arden, who showed no reaction to Rheya's taunt. But his eyes followed my movements as I sat down next to Jasper on the sofa.

"How are you feeling?" I asked Jasper.

"Could've been worse. How about you? Are you okay?"

"I'm fine, but I need to ask you something, and I need you to be honest with me."

He winced at my words. "I told you, I will never keep any secrets from you again. What do you need to know?"

"Back at the club, when Darion appeared on the balcony, everyone in the club bowed to him. Who is he?" I feared I already knew the answer to my question, but I needed to hear someone else confirm it.

Jasper stared directly at Arden, who was quietly watching us. "None of you have told her?"

"It was for her own protection," Arden defended the group.

"Told me what?" I asked them both, though I already knew.

Jasper looked me straight in the eyes. "Darion is Siobhan's son."

"And Creagan was his father?" I whispered as my gut twisted.

Jasper nodded, confirming my suspicion.

I understood now why I'd thought there was something familiar about Darion's eyes when I'd first seen him at Creagan's funeral. He had *our* father's eyes.

"My half brother wants to kill me …" The heavy words were unbelievably true. I'd often fantasized about what it would've been like to have a brother or sister when I was young, but I had never imagined it would be like this. I remembered the picture of the little boy with the silver eyes that I'd found hidden in my mom's room. She must have known about Darion. *But why does she keep a picture of him?* And there had been a lock of hair with the picture that could only belong to him. *Why does she have those things?*

"Do you think Darion knows Creagan was also your father?" Jasper wondered aloud.

"He knows," I said with absolute certainty, understanding now the strange comments he had made to me at the cemetery.

"We're very sorry we didn't tell you before," Calista said as she and Felix entered the room together, both carrying steaming mugs. "We didn't want to add to your pain."

I tried to stifle the fury raging inside me. "It's okay. I understand. Of course, you wouldn't want to tell me that my long-lost psychopath half brother from another planet, who is also the son of the man that I just found out is my dead father, kidnapped my mother and wants to kill us all for some sick and twisted reason."

Calista's face fell, and she looked away to hide the tears welling in her eyes.

I hated hurting her, but there had been too many secrets and lies.

Jasper wrapped his arm around my back and pulled me closer to his side. The motion didn't go unnoticed by Arden.

"Calista, I—"

"No." She stopped me before I could continue. "Don't apologize. You have every right to be upset. We should have told you everything." She took a seat in the armchair across from the sofa Jasper and I occupied.

"No more secrets, okay? All of you." I looked around the room. "If you want me to trust you, then you have to trust that I can handle the truth."

"No more," Calista agreed.

"Do you think Darion killed Creagan?" I asked her.

She held her mug in both hands and blew over the top of its contents. "In all honesty, we really don't know how Creagan died, but from what I know of Darion, he's as dangerous as his mother. But that doesn't mean he's capable of taking the life of his own father."

Another question popped into my mind. "How old is Darion? He appears to be the same age as me."

Calista paused and set down her mug. "Everly ... Siobhan carried Darion at the same time that your mother carried you. You were born on the same day on two separate planets."

I leaned forward, feeling nauseous all over again. "I don't understand. If Creagan loved my mother so much, how could he have also conceived a child with Siobhan at the same time?"

Calista shook her head. "Honey, I wish I had all the answers, but I don't know."

"My dear," said Felix, moving to stand near Calista, "none of us can claim to know or understand all the decisions others make, but we know that Creagan and Cacsha had their reasons for what they did. What's important now is not what happened in the past, but focusing on the present. We must continue your training, and we need to trust that you both—" he paused and gave both Jasper and me a serious glare, "will take more caution with your safety in the future."

The front door blew open before I could answer, and Malakai entered the room, followed by Rhal.

"We've reinforced the wards. No spell will detect our presence here," Rhal assured everyone.

At least there was that.

CHAPTER 10

*I*n the morning, I got up early, intending to find Felix. I'd noticed he'd been an early riser since our arrival here. It was still early dawn, and I had at least another hour before the sun cracked through the dark purple sky and everyone else started rising.

The memory of my experience at the club consumed my mind. I couldn't shake the surreal connection I had with Darion, where I saw the world through his eyes and felt his emotions as if they were my own. I needed to know if what happened was some new facet of being an Empath or a side effect of drinking the ever flower. I hoped for the latter. As fascinating as some might find it to see the world from someone else's perspective, I'd experienced enough of others' emotions to last me a lifetime.

I pulled aside the sheet I'd tacked up over the window and peeked outside. *Good.*

I tiptoed down the hall and quietly made my way to the first floor. The living room and kitchen were both dark and silent. A half-empty French press sat on the kitchen counter.

I pressed my hand to the side of the glass. The coffee inside was still warm.

The sound of creaking wood alerted me to someone moving along the porch outside. When I opened the door, I saw the silhouette of Felix slipping into the forest. His name was on the tip of my tongue when I stopped myself before calling out to him, worried that the noise would wake the others.

Pulling the door closed behind me, I hurried to follow him into the woods. He moved quicker than I expected, and I couldn't tell which direction he'd gone in once he'd entered the dark canopy of trees. I stopped moving and listened intently until I heard a soft crunching of leaves, and followed the sound. Felix continued to move deeper into the forest.

Where is he going?

When I caught up to him, I recognized the cave entrance. Just as I was about to make my presence known, Felix began chanting the same incantation that Rheya had the day Malakai and Rhal had come through the portal. I stepped back into the shadow of the trees as the water separated.

A figure stepped out of the cave. He spoke in Vitarian, and a swirl of glowing light floated at the top of a tall staff he carried. The light cast a soft glow that illuminated his long silver dreadlocks.

"Torin," Felix greeted him. "Thank you for answering my call."

The stranger walked with his tall staff, though his strong, fluid movements indicated no need for support. "Your message said you have knowledge of Oria's chosen heir," Torin replied.

Felix nodded. "I do."

"How do I know you speak the truth?" There was no hostility in Torin's words, just an air of authority.

Felix pulled something from his pocket, causing a drastic

shift in Torin's expression. "The royal ring. Where did you get that? It was thought to have disappeared along with Oria."

I moved slightly closer while keeping in the shadows.

Torin waved his staff in the air, causing the swirling light to move closer to them. He stared down into Felix's open palm with a look of astonishment before Felix snapped his palm closed. Torin's eyes followed Felix's hand as he tucked the ring back inside his pocket.

"Oria herself entrusted the ring to my family, along with her only child. My family promised to keep a safe watch over both, hiding them in secret, until the day came for her blood-line to reclaim the throne."

Torin listened intently while Felix spoke.

"Before Oria left both her ring and child with my family, she shared with them a premonition of the one who would reunite her people. Her premonition has finally come to fruition. And here's proof." Felix pulled a small vial of blood from his other pocket.

What the hell! Who is he talking about, and whose blood is that?

I ached to move closer, but the sun was highlighting the sky, and I didn't want to give myself away.

Torin reached for the vial, only to be halted by Felix. "I must have your word as the high councilman that you will protect her identity until Siobhan is properly removed from her rule."

Torin's face contorted. "You dare to question my loyalty? You forget who you speak to, Healer."

Felix stood his ground. "I forget nothing. But you cannot deny that some in the council have sided with Siobhan."

Torin's features smoothed. "I give you my word that as high councilman, I will protect both your secret and Oria's heir with my own life."

Felix seemed to trust Torin's promise, because he held out the vial of blood and released it to him.

I cringed as Torin popped the top off the small glass tube and drank the blood. His entire body went rigid as he appeared to go into some kind of trance. Curiosity got the better of me, and I crawled on the ground nearer them and tucked myself into a bush to hear them better. Minutes passed before Torin regained his normal posture.

"She's here on Earth. She was born here?" Torin asked with a hint of distaste.

I froze in place. *Born here? Are they talking about me?*

Felix nodded. "And she has no knowledge of her lineage and is only just learning the true depth of her powers. But I've sensed great strength in her. She was born to rule. She's the descendant of Oria's vision."

Torin's expression was somber, his mouth turned down in a frown. "How can you be sure?"

Felix paused in consideration, as if he were having an inner debate with himself before answering. "She exhibits the gifts of Oria. When Oria came to my family and told them of her vision, she instructed that the ring only be given to the descendant who inherits her very own gifts."

My elbows shook, and my arms burned from holding my crouched position for so long, but it was too bright now to move without giving myself away.

"And one more thing," Felix added. "Siobhan is here and has taken her mother. We've not been able to locate her whereabouts."

My mom. Oh my God. Now I know they're talking about me. Who is Oria, and what am I the heir of?

Torin looked up at Felix. "Her mother is of the Ever bloodline." The concern in his voice was in complete contrast to the angry scowl marring his features. "I must return home and speak with our allies. It's time we put an end to Siobhan's control over the council. You have my word that I'll do everything in my power to help save the girl's mother and return Oria's heirs to their rightful place."

The two men bowed their heads to each other before Torin stepped back into the cave and disappeared. Once again, the waterfall flowed down over the cave, hiding it from existence.

"You can come out from behind the bush now, Everly," Felix called out.

I stood up, and Felix answered my question before I asked. "I saw you scurrying over toward that bush. Thankfully, you escaped Torin's view, or he may have insisted on bringing you back to Aenoas-Vita with him."

I marched over to face Felix, unapologetic for eavesdropping. "Who was that man, Felix, and who is Oria?" My arms and legs trembled with anxious energy.

As if lost in thought, Felix's eyes glazed over. He took a step away and bent to pick up a walnut shell. He smoothed his fingers over the nubby shell as he answered. "Oria was the last ruler of the Ever bloodline. The Evers were the original royal family and ruled over Aenoas-Vita for centuries before Oria's twin brother, Orien, went mad with jealousy after their mother, named Oria queen. He wasn't happy with the position Oria gave him in the council. Consumed by dark magic, he killed his entire family to seize the throne. His own power never satisfied him. He took the lives of countless Vitarians, stealing their powers for himself."

I bit my tongue, eager to ask questions but not wanting to interrupt.

"Oria was beside herself with grief for what Orien had done to their family and their people," he continued. "When he came for her, she was prepared. She stripped Orien of his powers and had him locked away. He died shortly after. Losing the will to rule, Oria hid her daughter with my family, along with her royal ring, and disappeared into the Ever Forest. Some say she relinquished her soul to the trees, feeding them all the power she'd taken from Orien, as well as her own. But no one really knows. My family has watched over Oria's descendants, keeping their identities secret, ever since."

He stopped rubbing the shell and looked up at me. "You and your mother are the last of the Ever bloodline."

"This is crazy." I walked over to the nearby stream and picked up a handful of rocks. With a swift motion, I hurled a rock into the stream, watching as it glided effortlessly over the shimmering water before disappearing into its depths. I peered over the edge into the water. The reflection staring back at me was of a girl I no longer knew. The life I'd shaped for myself was only a facade now. I threw the rest of the rocks into the water, causing a splash of droplets to ricochet back in my direction. I reached up and used my shirt-sleeve to wipe the drops of water from my forehead and cheek. Felix came and stood beside me; his reflection rippled into mine.

My stomach twisted with knots. "First, I find out I'm from another planet. Then I discover who my father is, and that someone has murdered him. My mother has been abducted, and to my astonishment, the person responsible for it is my half brother, who is determined to ruin my life, and now you're telling me I'm descended from an ancient bloodline and that my ancestor murdered his entire family." I barked out a hysterical laugh. "These things aren't supposed to happen in real-life. This sort of crap is meant for movies and TV shows."

Felix glanced sideways at me, and a wrinkle of concern formed across his brow. He exhaled a long breath, then turned and nodded toward a spot with rocks large enough to sit on. His reflection stretched across the water as he made his way over and took a seat. I noticed he left the rock with the smoother surface vacant for me. Rays of sunshine cut through the trees, and Felix shifted his body directly into the warm light. His long champagne hair glowed under the sun, and I noticed faint silver highlights that were normally invisible.

Clearing his throat, Felix continued speaking. "You're right, my dear. No one should suffer so. But life often presents challenges we're unprepared for. It's up to us how we respond to those challenges."

I huffed and kicked at a mound of dirt. Felix was right, but that didn't help untangle the knots in my stomach.

"There is something that's been nagging at me," Felix said. "It's a conundrum, really."

"What is it?" I asked as I sat across from him.

Felix crossed his legs and sat quietly for a moment. I knew by the faraway look in his eyes that his mind was adrift with memories.

"Well," he finally answered. "After the atrocities Orien had committed, Oria had a new law enacted and bound with a spell. It was a law, made permanent by magic, that allowed each Vitarian to conceive only one child. Only a descendant of the Ever bloodline has the power to create such a spell or vanquish it. How Creagan conceived two children is a question that has haunted me. It should not have been possible."

My head spun with Felix's revelation. I knew so little about where I came from. If Oria could take away an entire planet's ability to conceive more than one child, she must have had unimaginable power. "How did she have the ability to cast such a spell, and how could she have done that to her people?" I shook my head. "Her brother was crazy, so she punished all of her people by taking away their freedom to conceive. I'm glad I won't ever meet Oria. She sounds as ruthless as her brother."

Felix winced at my words. "Oria was queen, and she made a hard choice that she thought best for her people. The origin of the Ever bloodline magic remains a mystery, but only individuals born of it had that kind of magic."

I smoothed my hand over the grainy surface of the rock and picked at some moss. "Maybe the spell just weakened over time," I offered.

"I've considered that possibility. But you see, Oria was a master spell crafter. Some of her spells remain locked in the royal library, and there are rumors of many more hidden in other locations for safekeeping. It should not be possible for anyone outside of the Ever bloodline to break the spell. I fear there is something that I'm missing."

I caught my hair in the wind and twisted it into a bun. "You told Torin of a premonition Oria had. What did that mean?"

"Yes. Oria had the gift of premonition," he answered while removing his beige linen tunic and folding it next to him on the rock. "She was confident that her line would one day rule Aenoas-Vita again. You are the first of her descendants to be born with Oria's gifts. I believe you are the one she saw."

My fingers clenched. Felix had to be wrong about me. "Just because I have some of Oria's gifts doesn't mean I'm the one from her premonition. I don't have the gift of premonition, and I can't even manage my life right now, and the last thing I ever plan to do is rule a planet of people." My palms burned, and I relaxed my fingers and rubbed at the indents where my nails had cut into my skin.

Felix glanced at my hands and continued, undeterred. "Don't be so hard on yourself. Knowledge and skill come with time and practice, and the gift of premonition may yet come," he insisted, lifting his face into the sun and closing his eyes.

"No," I said flatly. "It doesn't matter to me how many of Oria's gifts I receive. I'm never going to be the ruler she foresaw." I was ready to change the subject. "If Oria and Orien were twins, how did Oria come to rule and not Orien?" I asked.

Felix's hand slipped into his pocket, the same pocket I'd seen him tuck Oria's ring into. "Their mother was an Ever queen. She made the choice of who would take her place as ruler. But she had guidance," he said, and added nothing more.

I wondered at the ring in his pocket, and why Torin had responded so strongly to it. I moved off my rock and bent down over the stream, and slowly dipped my fingers into the cold water near a tiny flock of fish. The cool temperature calmed the burn from the tiny cuts in my palms. "How can you be sure you can trust Torin?" I asked. "What if he gives Siobhan our location?" The tiny fish pecked at the tips of my fingers, hoping to find food. Their slippery skin brushed against my hand as they glided onward. I stood up and wiped my wet hands on my pants, and took a seat next to Felix on the rock.

"Torin is my great uncle," Felix revealed, still reveling in the sunshine. "And he despises Siobhan. Since he's taken his place as high councilman, he's worked with your father to filter out the corrupt council members. He will help us. That I'm sure of."

Since Felix knew Torin better than I did, I'd just have to take his word for it.

"Did my mom know about her lineage? Do the others know about me?"

Felix shifted his face out of the sun. "The others know nothing of your relation to Oria. When I learned of your mother's exile to Earth, I told her of her birthright, hoping that she would claim her rightful place and remain on

Aenoas-Vita. But she disregarded my disclosure. She was adamant in her decision that my news was too late and no longer made a difference. She refused to tell me more and made me promise to never speak of it again. And until this day, I've kept my word."

"It doesn't make sense. If my mom had knowledge that she's Oria's heir and the rightful queen, then why didn't she fight Siobhan to stay on her planet and stay with the love of her life? She could have ruled with Creagan, and we could have been a family."

Felix looked over sympathetically. "As much as your mother's choice confused me, a part of me knew before I told her that she would not accept it. Your mother isn't an Empath, and Oria was clear that the next Ever to rule would be an Empath, as she was."

A light crunching noise caught my attention. Two chipmunks chased each other across the trail and scurried up a large oak tree, disappearing into its branches. I turned my attention back to Felix.

"There has to be more to it, and I need to find out what." I stood from the rock and paced through the fallen leaves on the ground.

Felix moved toward me. "I understand your frustration, but your mother's decision was well-intentioned. She knew how evil Siobhan was and is still, and she also knew that Siobhan would not give up her rule without a fight. Siobhan's family had been coveting the crown for many generations. When it passed to Creagan's line, Siobhan's family wasted no time in arranging a marriage between the two newborns. Cacsha knew that challenging the line of succession would put your life in danger, and made the choice she thought best."

"I know … She's sacrificed so much for me, but I still think there's more to it than that. My mom's a fighter, and I don't think she would've given up so easily. It's not like her."

Felix reached for my shoulder. "Is that how you see it? You think your mother gave up? Leaving her home to protect her child took great strength and courage. Cacsha made a brave and selfless choice."

Felix is right, but I know in my gut there's something missing that we don't know, some piece of the puzzle that will explain why my mom let Siobhan win when she could have used her birthright to crush her.

Instead of arguing the point further, I just nodded, and we turned back onto the trail. As we neared the cabin, I remembered why I'd followed Felix. I was just about to bring it up when the sight of someone sitting on the porch steps filled me with joy.

"Selkie!" She sat wrapped in a cardigan. Her skin had shed the sickly gray it'd taken on and recovered its former glow. "You look so refreshed." I sat down next to her and wrapped my arms around her. "It's such a relief to know you're going to be okay. I was so scared." I breathed in her hair, and it smelled sweet, like cherry almond. The fragrance reminded me of twirling my fingers in Selkie's hair when I was a child.

"It's good to see you too, sweetie." Her eyes watered. "I'm so sorry about your mother. I can't believe any of this is happening." She took a deep breath and wiped at her eyes. "I'm sorry. I don't mean to make it worse. Cacsha's strong. I know she'll survive this."

A familiar scent rose from Selkie's tea mug. She couldn't resist a smile at my scrunched expression. "Calista's famous rejuvenation tea. It smells like crap—don't tell her I said that—but it does the trick." She took another drink from her cup.

"Yeah." I stared at the bubbly green liquid. "I've had my own encounter with that brew recently." I wrinkled my nose.

"Ahh … I heard about your little escapade to Neil's

place," Selkie said, her tone feigning disapproval, but I could tell by her sly grin that she wasn't really upset with me.

"It's okay," she said. "I get why you and Jasper went, but you need to use more caution." She tipped her mug to her lips, draining its contents.

Watching Selkie finish her rejuvenation tea, I couldn't help but feel guilty over what Darion had done to her. I knew it was irrational to blame myself, but knowing he and I shared blood and why he was here somehow made me feel responsible for his actions.

"Selkie. I'm sorry about what Darion did to you. It never would have happened if he wasn't after me and my mom."

She knitted her brow and shook her head, causing her strawberry hair to bounce in its loose bun. "None of this is your fault, or Cacsha's. Neither of you is to blame for the actions of others. I'm just glad that you're safe." She smiled, and the warmth of her words shone in her hazel eyes. "Do you hear me?"

I lifted my head up and nodded, then my stomach released an agitated growl.

"The others are finishing up with breakfast. Why don't you hurry in there before that feisty bunch eats all the sustenance?"

∾

*A*fter I'd scarfed down some breakfast, I followed the others outside and joined Malakai at the picnic table. Arden and Rhal walked the perimeter of the cabin while Rheya taunted Jasper into a fight. Malakai's attention seemed far away when his head slowly turned toward me.

"Holy crap." I jumped up from the bench. His sockets were all marbled yellow eyes with tiny oval black slits.

Malakai's eyes, resembling those of a snake, watched my every move.

Then he blinked, and his eyes returned to their normal, unusual form. "*Crotalus viridis*—western rattlesnake," he said. "Their bite is extremely venomous to humans. Not so much to our kind, but it still packs a nasty punch if a bite injects enough venom. The wards around the mountain are strong, and I found no other Vitarian lurking about," he said with a tone of disappointment.

"I'm sorry about my reaction." I rejoined Malakai on the bench.

His lip quirked. "It's quite all right. Not something you're used to seeing every day."

"Definitely not," I said, embarrassed by the shakiness of my voice.

Malakai smiled and leaned back against the picnic table, stretching out his long form. His golden-brown skin glowed in the sunlight, and sparks of light twinkled off the silver beads woven into the twists of shining black hair tied behind his head.

"What you can do is incredible. I can't imagine what it must feel like to occupy the bodies of different animals." A thought occurred to me. "Malakai—are you able to occupy the minds of people as well?"

He sat upright, crossing one leg over the other. "The gift of sight, as well as all others, can differ depending on the Vitarian. My particular ability only extends to animals. I've not come across another Vitarian with the gift of sight who could occupy the mind of another Vitarian. I believe that ability faded with the original royal family of Aenoas-Vita."

Crap. Maybe my experience had nothing to do with the ever flower drink after all and more to do with my blood.

"Would you like to experience it for yourself?" he asked.

"Huh? What do you mean?" I folded my leg up onto the bench.

"Would you like to join me?" He nodded up at the sky as a bald eagle glided over the treetops.

The thought of being able to take over the mind and body of an animal both terrified and excited me. "Is that possible?"

"Through touch, we can share the experience of our gifts. Take my hand."

I hesitated only for a moment before I slipped my hand into his. My stomach contracted as I suddenly felt like I was soaring off the ground. My eyes opened, and I looked out over a dense mass of treetops. The eyes I peered through could see farther into the distance than I'd ever known was possible. It was like seeing through binoculars. A long, dark yellow beak protruded from my face, and I let out a loud squawk. Enormous black-and-brown-feathered wings spread out on either side of me and beat into the wind. The ground was thousands of feet below, and the wings flapped of their own accord. Malakai had to be controlling the gigantic bird we occupied.

Its body twisted in the sky, and I was suddenly diving toward the ground. The bird's feathers rippled as it propelled itself through a thick, dewy cloud. Another squawk screeched from its beak as I flew down toward the river. Giant claws reached down and snatched a trout swimming near the surface of the water. The reflection of a magnificent bald eagle skimmed the water. The bird's responses were all instinct as it dropped the flopping fish on the ground and drove its beak through the slippery silver skin and pulled loose a hunk of flesh. Once the bird's belly was full, we flew once more over the forest. The bird descended onto a branch and wrapped its claws around the rough surface, easily maintaining its balance.

My vision blurred as my consciousness slipped out of the

bird and traveled back into my body, which was still sitting on the picnic bench next to Malakai. It took a moment to feel grounded back in my own skin. I could almost still taste the fresh, salty flavor of the trout on my tongue.

"Wow! That was absolutely amazing. Every movement felt like pure instinct, as if they were my own. My skin is still buzzing from the rush." I looked up at the sky and couldn't believe I'd just been soaring that high through the puffy white clouds. The eagle leaped from the tree and continued its journey as if nothing out of the ordinary had taken place.

I ran my hand through my hair, expecting to feel frizzy bits standing up all over the place from spiraling through the wind, but my hair remained neatly brushed in its snug pony-tail. Only our consciousnesses had left the ground, while our bodies had remained. My arms shook with goose bumps. The thought of my body sitting idly, empty of thought and vulnerable to the world, gave me the creeps. "What happens to the animal's consciousness when you're occupying its mind?" I asked.

Malakai hadn't lost a bit of his casual composure as his eyes shifted back from the beady eyes of an eagle. "The animal's consciousness is essentially asleep when I move into their mind. When I leave, they resume as if I were never there. I'm happy to share the experience with you again whenever you like."

I smiled at the possibilities. "I think I'll be taking you up on that offer soon."

"And what offer would that be?" Jasper asked, walking toward us and seeming slightly out of breath.

"Malakai shared the most amazing experience with me. What happened to you? You look like you just wrestled a bear." His wavy hair stood in a wild mess, and his shirt appeared rumpled and torn.

"I warmed Lover Boy up for you," Rheya said, coming up

behind Jasper. He scowled at her, but she just winked at him and said, "Not bad, Shield, but there's room for improvement." She turned and walked off to join Arden and Rhal.

"You should consider that a compliment, coming from Rheya," Malakai offered. "She's Arden's second-in-command and nearly an undefeated warrior, bested only by the commander himself, and she doesn't give compliments lightly."

I found it amusing that Jasper's cheeks brightened at Malakai's declaration. Rheya's voice boomed from across the field, and I looked over to see her laughing with Arden and Rhal. They interacted so naturally, as if they'd been friends for decades. I couldn't help the pang of jealousy that twisted in my chest as Arden continued to laugh whole-heartedly at whatever story Rheya was telling.

I turned to find Jasper watching me with an odd expression and instantly felt guilty over my jealousy of Rheya with Arden. Jasper and I needed to have *the talk*, but now wasn't the right time. "What do you say to showing me some of those moves that Rheya found so impressive, huh?" I playfully punched Jasper's shoulder.

∾

"*Y*ou're going to need these." Jasper tossed me two ever staffs.

"Cocky much, aren't you? Where's your weapon?"

He held up his hands and wiggled his fingers. "All the weapons I'll need." He smiled his wicked, flirtatious smile, that usually had girls falling all over themselves to get his attention.

"Okay, but no holding back on me anymore."

"I won't if you won't," he agreed.

We circled each other in the field. I noticed that Rheya, Arden, and Rhal joined Malakai to watch us.

With one staff in each hand, I felt the surge of power as it intertwined with mine. I assumed a Qwan Ki Do stance, with one arm held high over my head and the other held near my bent knee.

Jasper stood sideways in an Aikikai Aikido stance, with his back knee slightly bent and both hands held up near his face. He bounced lightly toward me.

I swung my extended leg forward and leaped and spun in the air, bringing down my arm behind me in attack. When I collided with his invisible shield, it felt like hitting a solid wall, causing me to stumble backwards and nearly lose my footing.

I tried to focus on Jasper's counter-attack, but his body blurred out of view, and everything around me suddenly went dark. I stumbled sideways until my hand skimmed the rough bark of a tree, and I let my body sag against it for support. A cutting pain shot through my head like something had sliced into my brain. I slid down the nubby tree to the ground and buried my head in my hands.

"Everly!" Jasper crouched over me. "What's going on? Did I hurt you? Where are you hurt?" His hands searched my body for an invisible injury.

"It wasn't you," I whispered through the earsplitting pain.

I tried prying my eyes open, but when I did, the dizziness only got worse, because what I saw wasn't what I knew I should see. My body was in one place, but my mind was in another.

What's happening to me? And then I knew. I remembered this feeling from the club.

Worried voices circled me, but they were nothing more than the fading sounds of a faraway place—someplace near my body. My consciousness existed elsewhere. *But where?*

The dizziness subsided, and I recognized his vibrations. He looked down at a piece of paper. His hands were shaking. His mind was a coiled mess of emotions, but what stood out most was an aching sense of loneliness and loss. I focused on what he was looking at, and artfully written letters formed before my eyes.

I'm sorry I was not the father you deserved. I know you feel I failed you. And you're right. I failed you. I should have protected you from her. There was a time in the beginning I thought you might actually change her. She doted on you as a child, but then she distanced herself from you, and the resentment returned. I hope a day will come when you'll understand the choices your mother and I made to protect you. And when you do truly understand, take care of them both, and protect them the way I never could. I've always loved you, son.

He crumpled the letter in his palm. When he looked up, he spun his body around so quickly the surrounding scenery blurred by. I glimpsed an old brick building, but I couldn't make out any recognizable details. As Darion's fist slammed into the heaped mountain of rotting pallets, the vibrations reverberated through the air, snapping me back into my own consciousness.

The clamor of voices persisted around me.

I slowly rose from my crouched position. "I'm fine …" I was about to tell them what had happened when I remembered what Malakai had said, that the only other Vitarians with the gift of sight who could connect to the minds of people were from the Ever bloodline. Felix hadn't told them about my lineage, and I wasn't ready for them to know.

I pushed away Jasper's worried hands. "I'm okay. It's just a migraine. It came on suddenly is all, but it's subsided a bit now."

Arden stepped forward. His sudden nearness caused my

heart to skip a beat. My skin tingled with a warm flush, causing a light sheen of sweat to form on my forehead.

"Perhaps you should rest awhile," he suggested.

What I really craved wasn't rest, but rather a peaceful moment alone, to delve into Darion's thoughts intentionally. *If I can see what he sees, then I can find my mom.*

I lay in my room for over an hour, trying to force my mind into Darion's, to no avail. The first time it happened, the ever flower potion lowered my inhibitions, and the second time, Jasper's energy force stunned me when I hit his shield. Maybe it only worked when there was a shock to my body. Or maybe it had something to do with Darion himself. He'd obviously been reading a letter written to him by Creagan. I didn't know who Creagan thought he should have protected Darion from, but I had a feeling he referred to me and my mom in the last part of the letter, though I couldn't imagine why he'd asked Darion to protect us. I'd connected with Darion's emotions. He hated us and would sooner see us dead than protect us. But if Creagan had been referring to us, then maybe Darion had been thinking about me before I entered his consciousness. And he'd also been watching us at the club before it happened the first time.

Frustrated with the ifs, hows, and whys, I tossed my pillow across the room. I finally had a power that could actually be of some use, and I had no idea how to use it.

I lifted myself off the bed with renewed intention. Felix had spoken of working with my ability to detect auras. Is there a link between my gift of sight and channeling into auras? If I could master that ability, maybe I could figure out how to get into Darion's head.

I need to keep training. It's the only way I'm going to learn to control my powers.

∿

J tracked down Felix for our lesson and followed him through the woods until we arrived near a narrow creek. "This is the place," he declared. "My favorite spot on the mountain to come for meditation."

Although I was antsy to get started, the gentle rush and quiet trickle of water bouncing off the moss-covered rocks elicited a mindful peacefulness. "It's lovely," I agreed. "The air smells so pure up here." I breathed in a long, cleansing breath filled with the scents of pine needle and oak. The area was thick with trees, but I spotted a plush-looking patch of grass where I tossed my jacket. My feet crunched over fallen leaves as I walked toward the creek.

"When in nature," Felix said, standing beside me, "regardless of planet, our innate magic flows more freely and unhindered from the chaos of the outside world."

We took a seat in the soft patch of green grass, and over the next couple of hours, Felix had me sitting and standing in multiple positions to learn to control my energy flow and to direct it in a series of pathways throughout my meridians. I understood now why he thought this exercise was helpful. By the end of our session, I could channel my energy with purpose along my meridians and better project it at will. The meridian exercise was a warm-up for what Felix called "aura detection."

We spent the next several hours developing my ability to see past the outer biofield surrounding one's aura. In the past, I'd always found the swirling colors to be dizzying, but now that I knew how to channel the energy emitted by the biofield properly, I could mentally peel the layers back and see into the multiple layers of ever-changing colors without being overwhelmed by them. I practiced my new skill on Felix. Each aura was unique and embodied the personality traits, and in our case, Felix had informed me, the magical traits of its owner.

A warm and welcoming glow surrounded the surface of Felix's aura, its outer shades of gray representing knowledge, wisdom, and deep intellect. I moved past the outer biofield and into the next layers, and my body immediately filled with the sensation of well-being. It was no surprise that his inner aura was a whirlpool of green shades, the color of healing. In the center beamed a harmonious white light. The light drew me into its warmth. The desire to be inside it grew stronger the closer I got, and my body floated weightlessly into its depths.

"Everly, dear." Felix's voice broke my trance. He stood over me with light emanating from his hands, and he was moving them around my sitting form in a circular motion. "You must remember to remain present when reading the aura of another. If you go too deep, you may find it difficult to make your way back out." He held his hands steady on either side of my head. The warm energy he released worked to ground me back into my body. "The aura is a projection of the inner spirit of the one it belongs to. If you lose your connection with your own when you transcend into another, theirs may envelop you completely."

"I'll be more careful the next time," I replied, rubbing my eyes. With a slight pinch on my cheeks, I delighted in the invigorating tingle and the reassuring presence of my own body. "I hadn't realized how far I'd gone until you brought me back. The further I ventured, the more I felt myself being lured into a different plane of existence, making it nearly impossible to break free." I rubbed my arms, still trying to feel attached to my own skin.

"You were in the midst of astral projection; your spirit was separating from its physical form. Before now, you've only sensed the aura on the surface level. This was my purpose with the meridian exercise: to teach you to channel your own energy and to be aware of your connection with it when using your gifts. Losing yourself in the dark energy of an evil soul or getting lost in the astral realms is something you wouldn't want. Without proper practice, you may not find your way back to your body on your own."

"Oh—" The thought of being lost in a spirit world outside my body sent a sudden chill through me. I snatched my jacket from the ground and slid my arms into its sleeves, reveling in its snug warmth.

~

*F*amished by the time we got back to the cabin, I dug into the trays of food Calista was setting out on the picnic table when we arrived.

"Hey, honey. You look like you could use a pick-me-up. I just brought out a thermos of fresh coffee." Calista nodded toward the thermos.

"Caffeine sounds amazing. Mental training is more exhausting than the physical." I quickly chowed down on two of the veggie sandwiches and a plate of grapes, followed by lots of coffee.

"Better?" Felix asked with a grin as he finished his own plate of food.

"Much," I answered, leaning my back against the picnic table as my belly swelled with gluten and coffee.

"Rheya," Felix called out to her.

She stood in front of the nearby fire pit, watching her plate disintegrate into ash. She looked up with dancing flames reflected in her sharp green eyes.

"Will you allow Everly to read your aura?"

Oh. I wasn't entirely sure I wanted anything to do with Rheya's aura.

In three quick strides, Rheya hovered in front of me. By her expression, I could tell she didn't want me having anything to do with her aura, either. "What's the point in all these mental exercises? She should learn to use her physical strengths and weapons."

"The point is," Felix answered in a disappointed tone, "when we are out of sync with one of our gifts, the others do not function at their fullest capacity. Mastery of our sub gifts makes our dominant gift all the stronger." Felix narrowed his eyes, and I felt both a pang of pity for Rheya and glad not to be the recipient of Felix's displeasure.

He swirled his coffee inside his cup and continued in a stern tone. "You know this, Rheya, from your own years of training. Everly has only just begun and has barely scratched the surface of testing her abilities. It's our duty to guide her the best we can."

Rheya's cheeks brightened, and she looked at the ground, kicking at some leaves. "Of course, I will help in any way I can."

"Good. I'll leave you two to it, then." Felix stood from the picnic bench we sat on. "Remember to stay present." He patted my shoulder as he walked away.

Rheya took Felix's place on the bench beside me. "Healers are always such know-it-alls."

"He's just trying to help, Rheya."

"Yeah, yeah, I know. Let's get this over with." She scowled.

I lifted one leg over the bench so I could turn my whole body to fully face Rheya. Her scowl transformed into a look of intrigue, and even though she probably wouldn't admit it, I sensed an excited curiosity coming from her.

"What are you smiling at?" Rheya asked.

"Nothing at all. Now let me focus." I cleared my mind and tuned into Rheya's energy field. It took a moment to move past the protective wall she'd built around herself. She kept her emotions guarded, and not in the way the others did when they were near me. This was something different, something Rheya did to protect herself. It made me curious about her past and what made her so defensive of herself. As I moved into her aura, I passed through layers of ice-blue and then searing crimson, and my body temperature changed from shivering to feverish. I'd assumed Rheya's gifts were all related to her physical strengths, but now I realized I didn't really know much about her magical abilities. Just as I was delving into her deeper layers, I sensed Arden and Jasper draw closer to us. Rheya's colors burst into shades of red, blue, and orange. Her loyalty and protectiveness emanated from her, practically radiating towards Arden. However, the orange shades hinted at a sexual attraction, leaving me uncertain if these feelings were for Arden or Jasper. Knowing now how guarded Rheya was of her feelings, an awkwardness settled over me, and my subconscious whispered that I was trespassing. I quickly pulled out of her aura, moving backward through the layers of fire and ice.

"Well?" Rheya asked in her usual sarcastic tone. "Did you learn anything useful?"

I had, but I'd keep those thoughts to myself. Instead, I said, "Your aura is unusual. I assumed your magic was all about your strength and speed, but you have other powers. What are they?"

Rheya quirked her head sideways and smirked. "You'll just have to wait and see." She resumed her tough-girl act. "I need a walk." She got up and headed toward the trees.

"Rheya," Arden called after her, "would you like company?"

"No, Commander. I want to be alone."

I could tell Rheya felt violated, even though she was too stubborn to talk about her feelings. Having been so connected to her emotions while in her aura, I had gained an understanding of her complexity. She had emotional pain that she kept hidden, maybe even from herself. As much as Rheya irked me, my heart went out to her. I wouldn't tell her that—she'd hate every word.

By the end of the day, exhaustion overwhelmed me and I practically fell into the bed that Felix had designated as mine. When I awoke in the night to the sound of my mother's voice, I realized I had gone to bed still fully dressed in the clothing I'd worn during training. Even my ponytail was still pulled tight against the back of my head. The voice called out to me as usual. This time I knew it was Darion inside my head, playing his game, but I followed my mother's call outside.

Darion walked out of the woods and met me in front of the cabin.

"How are you here?" I asked. "How did you get past the wards?"

"I'm not here in the physical sense. I'm an image in your mind."

I swung out to punch him, but my fist went right through his egotistical face as I lurched forward.

"I'm just an apparition. You can't touch me."

"What do you want, Darion?"

"To give you what you want, sister."

"Don't call me that! And what are you talking about?"

"You want your mother back? I'm here to offer a trade. Meet me at the abandoned paper mill, and trade yourself for your mother. If you come to me alone and willingly become my prisoner, I will set your mother free. You have my word."

His apparition faded.

"And what's your word worth?"

"I guess you'll just have to come and find out. If you don't, then you'll never know if you could have saved your precious mother."

He vanished, and I stood alone outside the cabin. The chilly midnight air would have been biting to the flesh, but instead, it fueled my adrenaline. I ran into the cabin and quietly retrieved the things I would need, including the ever staffs and Jasper's motorcycle keys. A sense of skepticism washed over me as I questioned Darion's honesty. His promise of releasing my mom felt like a ploy, a sinister trap waiting to be sprung. To outsmart him, I hastily scribbled a note to Jasper and set the alarm on my phone, timing it to go off in thirty minutes. This way, I could stay one step ahead and protect myself from any potential dangers. I taped the note to my phone, turned the volume to the max, and carefully slipped both into Jasper's room. Thirty minutes should give me enough time to get to the mill and confront Darion. If he was telling the truth, I'd trade myself for my mom, but if he was lying, I'd have backup on the way. I crept back outside and rolled the bike down the road and away from the cabin before starting the engine.

CHAPTER 11

*T*he night was dark and the sky was bright with constellations: Hercules, the hero, held his club high in the sky in pursuit of Hydra, the sea serpent. As I pursued my own malicious serpent, I hoped my story would end as successful as Hercules.

The roads were empty and ironically peaceful. I revved the motorcycle engine and sped toward the old paper mill.

Have they been this close all along?

Slowing my pace, I reached a small park behind the abandoned mill and carefully concealed Jasper's bike amidst some tall bushes. Keeping close to the trees, my eyes darted around the park, searching for any sign of movement in the stillness. Surprisingly, there were no guards patrolling the area as I made my way closer to the west end of the park, even though it was located just behind the mill's parking lot. I'd expected Darion to be more cunning in his strategy. Either he didn't find me to be a threat, or he was too cocky to consider the option. Either way, worked for my benefit. When I came to the end of the park where it met with the mill's parking lot, I found the mill's buildings blocked by heaped-up pallets of old milled paper stacked in rotting piles. These must have been the pallets I'd seen through Darion's eyes when he was reading Creagan's letter.

I moved out of the trees and wove through the pallets. Not wanting to fall into a trap, I erred on the side of caution and carefully assessed the strength of one pallet. Satisfied with its stability, I slowly climbed up, pulling myself all the way to the top of the stack. I crouched on all fours and surveyed the area. A flickering light in one of the building windows caught my attention, as well as the shadow of a body standing guard below the stacked pallets I crouched atop.

After its closure, the mill had been abandoned, so I was confident that the figure below was either Darion or one of his guards, most likely the latter. Darion didn't strike me as one to give himself away so easily. I quietly repositioned myself onto my feet and leaped down onto the shoulders of the figure below, knocking him to the ground. I grabbed him by the sides of the head and smashed his forehead against the concrete, knocking him out before he could make a sound.

I sprinted across the parking lot, the sound of my footsteps echoing in my ears, and pressed myself up against the closest building. Concealed in darkness, I observed for any signs of activity before silently maneuvering around the building's corner. There, I noticed two additional guards engaged in a heated discussion. I inched closer to catch their conversation.

"That spoiled prince has us on this rotting-pile-of-shit planet waiting for his bastard sister," one guard said to the other.

"Would you keep your thoughts to yourself? You're going to get us beheaded with that treasonous talk," said the other guard, who looked around nervously to make sure no one had heard them.

"You sniveling little coward." The pissed-off guard grabbed the other by the front of his uniform. "I'll—"

"Hey, boys." I stepped out from the side of the building.

The guard holding the other by the front stared at me with a look of shock and complete idiocy.

"It's me, the bastard sister. But if we're talking semantics here, rumor has it that Creagan was technically married to my mother first, which makes your spoiled prince the bastard." I smirked at the two, who separated themselves and stalked toward me.

I backed up, leading them into the shadows where I'd come from.

"You little bitch. I'm going to do the prince a favor and take care of you myself," said the guard with the big mouth.

The cowardly one looked over at his counterpart. "The prince said to bring her to him alive."

"Once I take care of her," Big Mouth growled, "I'm going to twist your whiny head off your neck."

The coward's eyes went wide, not with fear, but with rage. He stopped and drew his sword, and before Big Mouth could utter another word, he slashed open his throat. Big Mouth fell to his knees and gripped at his dripping neck. His eyes rolled up. He opened his mouth, and all that came out was a gurgle before he fell face-first onto the ground.

The remaining guard paid no further attention to his now-dead counterpart as he continued to stalk toward me in silence.

"I don't suppose you want to abandon your post and get lost?"

He answered my question by arching his sword in the air.

"I figured that was too much to ask," I said, and threw him a bolt of energy that sent his body flying backward. The clattering sound echoed in the night as his back slammed against a brick building, and his sword slipped from his fingers. I snatched the fallen sword off the ground and held the heavy steel pointed at his throat. "Last chance." I pressed the sharp tip into his skin, causing a drop of blood to spring forward. "Run or die."

It only took him a second to decide. "I'm tired of doing the dirty work for the dark queen and her son."

I backed up, and he took off running toward the park.

So much for loyalty.

I kept inching toward the building with the lit window. Only one guard guarded the entrance. I suspected Darion was making this too easy on purpose. He wanted me to get inside. He had probably stationed his worst guards out here intentionally. Now I knew what his word was worth. All I cared about was getting my mom back, and if that meant walking into his trap, then so be it.

The guard stood with his back facing toward me. I quietly sneaked up behind him, grabbed him by the arm, and twisted it into an arm bar, taking him down to the ground. His arm snapped and made a sick crunching sound. I moved my arm around his neck, cutting off his scream, and squeezed with all my strength until he lost consciousness.

The door to the entrance was on rusted hinges and squeaked as I pulled it open. I peeked to either side of the room and listened for movement before moving inside the dark space. The air was putrid and smelled of old, wet rust and decaying paper. Something scraped across the room. I pressed my body against a wall and waited. A group of rats scurried across the floor. I exhaled and pushed forward without hesitation. Light flickered at the other end of a dark hallway.

That has to be the light I saw from outside the building.

I stepped over a puddle of something I hoped was water, and walked face-first into a broken floorboard dangling from the ceiling. *Damn it!*

I cleared the cobwebs from my face, feeling their sticky threads against my skin, and brushed the dust from my eyes. Everything about this building made my skin crawl. When I got to the end of the hall, there was nowhere to go but straight into the shadowy room with the flickering light. It didn't surprise me to find guards lining the walls on either side. Balls of firelight floated above them in midair, casting the space in an eerie light. Darion stood at the other end of the room, holding my mother clutched in his hands.

"Mom!"

I reached behind my head and retrieved the staffs from their harness secured to my back and instantly felt their power link with my own. The guards stepped away from the walls with hands on their swords, waiting for their master's command.

"Let her go and take me. I'm here alone, just as I agreed. Now it's your turn to hold up your end."

Darion smirked at me. "Oh, I mean to release her, just not the way you thought. Take her." His tone carried the authority of someone accustomed to giving commands.

The room rang with the sound of steel being unsheathed. I backed up a step just as something hard and cold coiled around my neck. The staffs fell from my hands, and I gasped for air as the guards moved in quick succession to circle me. I looked once more at my mother hanging limp in Darion's arms. Her torn and ragged clothes hung loosely on her body, while dirt smudges marred her skin.

Whoever held the other end of the chain wrapped around my neck tugged me back hard. My throat burned from lack of air, and water leaked from my eyes. Two guards broke from the circle and stalked toward me. One fell to his knees, screaming, as I projected a hot, burning blast of energy into him. The other guard struck me across the cheek, and I stumbled backward. The guards laughed all around me, but I paid them no attention. *Let them think they have the upper hand.*

I used the moment to my advantage and twisted my body around while reaching for the slack in the chain. With all my strength, I pulled as forcefully as possible, causing the guard on the other end to stumble forward. I kicked her in the Adam's apple and quickly unraveled the chain from my neck. A hand snatched me by the back of my hair. Without hesitating, I slammed my head back into the guard who held me by my hair, knocking him backward. With the chain wrapped around my hand, I swung it like a lasso, hitting one attacker in the head and then wrapping it around the neck of another. I picked up the fallen staffs just in time to block the blow of a sword. I maneuvered around its bearer and snapped her arm from its socket. Her sword fell with a clatter, its noise blending with her blood-curdling scream.

Darion's voice cut through the ringing in my ears. "You impress me, sister. I didn't expect you to last this long."

I stepped over the heap of bodies and moved toward him. "Remove those chains from my mother, Darion. Now!"

"As you wish, sister." The chains fell from my mom's wrists, neck, and ankles. Darion released her, and she crumbled to the ground.

A lump cut down my throat as I looked from my mom's limp body to Darion's gloating face. "I'm going to beat the life from you," I growled.

"Bring it," Darion taunted.

His arrogant overconfidence incensed my hatred of him. I filled the room with a scream as I ran toward him. He flicked his hand and sent me flying backward in the air, causing me to crash against the wall. As Darion extended his arm, my body remained immobile while a fireball soared towards me. Rage filled me, and I tore my arm free of the wall and blocked the fireball with the staff. I fell to the ground and landed on my feet. Electricity flowed through my skin, coursing up and down both staffs as if they were a part of me. I realized I was siphoning power from the staffs.

More fireballs came at me, but I blocked them and sent them flying across the room. Darion whipped a sharp, long blade from his side and lunged at me. I pivoted and spun around to his other side while dodging unconscious bodies. My staffs met his blade, and we battled until my arms burned with exhaustion. Darion was unwavering and showed no signs of tiring.

"Everly," I heard my mother moan softly from the floor.

The sound of her voice fueled me with renewed energy. I pushed harder. I infused every hit with raw emotion, projecting it into Darion. He staggered, and I knocked the blade from his hand. I kicked him hard in his chest, and he fell to the floor. I spun to make the final blow, but just as my arms were swinging the staffs down toward his skull, my mother flung herself across Darion's body.

"NO!" she screamed. "Everly, no. Please stop. You can't kill Darion. You don't understand."

I halted. "Mom—move out of the way. I know he's Creagan's son, but he's a monster."

Her tired eyes pleaded with mine. "He's not just Creagan's son, Everly. He's my son too. Darion is your twin brother." Tears slid down her cheeks, leaving streaks from the dirt covering her face.

"What—?" I fell to my knees in front of her and Darion's slumped body. My arms, still surging with power, fell limp to my sides. "How can that be?"

"Cacsha!" Calista came running toward us, with the others following behind her, and they all swarmed around us.

Arden had his sword held at Darion's throat as Rhal

forced him onto his knees and bound his wrists behind his back.

Suddenly, a glowing whip wrapped around my mother's neck. Her sapphire eyes opened wide in surprise. Her fingertips shot out and grazed my temple, and in an instant, a flurry of images flooded my mind, before an abrupt force jerked her away from us.

"No!" I tried to reach for her, but crashed into an invisible barrier.

"Take that blade from my son's throat," demanded a cold, hard voice.

I looked up to find a woman standing in the open door-frame, behind where Darion had stood when I first entered the room. She held the other end of the whip that held my mother captive. Flaxen hair framed a cruel and beautiful face. Her dark eyes swept the room with a deadly glare and then settled on me. I could feel her hatred in my bones. She moved her gaze to Arden. "Whatever happens to my son, happens to your beloved Cacsha." And she vanished, along with my mother.

"Ahhh …" I slammed my fist into the floor. "I almost had her back." The defeat in my voice sickened me. I looked at Darion's pathetic face and didn't know what to feel. He watched me back with an odd expression. A strong desire to inflict pain upon him consumed me. I wanted him to feel the pain I felt, and I wanted to punish him for what he'd done to my mom and Selkie. As much as I wanted to, I couldn't hurt him. Not after seeing the look on my mom's face when she'd pleaded for his life.

Arms wrapped around me. "Come on, Ev. We need to get out of here." Jasper lifted me from the ground.

I sat on the porch steps, staring out at the forest. Nothing made sense anymore. I didn't know how life could ever go back to feeling normal, or at least what I thought was normal, again. The wood creaked from behind as Felix lowered himself onto the step beside me.

"How is it possible, Felix, that Darion is my twin brother and my mother's son?"

"I do not have the answer, my dear, but I sense dark magic at the root of this. This new knowledge helps me understand your mother's choices over the last nineteen years."

"Well, it doesn't help me. I'm more confused than ever, and I don't know what to do or how to feel. I hate Darion! My hatred towards him grows stronger with each thought of the suffering he brought upon my mother and Selkie. For all I know, he even killed our father. But he's also a part of my mother. There has to be some of her good in him somewhere."

"I understand your feelings." Felix patted my hand. "I think you should speak with Darion and ask him directly about Creagan's death. The spell on his bindings restricts his magic. He'll be incapable of masking any lies."

I cringed at the thought of being anywhere near Darion, but Felix was right. If Darion had answers, I needed to find out. I took a deep breath and pushed myself up from the step. Felix gave me a reassuring nod as my hand paused on the front-door handle.

Arden and Jasper were in the middle of interrogating Darion when I approached them. "I need a moment alone with Darion."

They both turned. Jasper stepped in front of me, blocking me from Darion's view. "I don't want to leave you alone with him."

I brushed away Jasper's concern. "I'll be fine, Jasp. If I need help, I'll call for you. He's bound in spelled bindings, remember?" I nodded toward a tied-up Darion sitting hunched in a chair in the middle of the living room. "He's harmless."

"I don't think he's ever truly harmless, but okay." He rubbed the tops of my shoulders. I looked up into his golden-amber eyes, and for a moment, I just wanted to bury my face in his chest and let him comfort me, but I remained resolute. As if reading my thoughts, he cupped my face in his hands and said, "I won't be far," and then left me alone with … my brother. I just couldn't get used to thinking of Darion as anything other than a monster, but for my mother's sake, I'd try.

Jasper joined Arden on the other side of the room, where they pretended not to monitor me. They moved far enough away to give me privacy, but close enough to interfere if the need arose.

"They're both in love with you, you know?" Darion said, as if we were having a casual sibling conversation. "Arden tries to deny his feelings for you, but it's a losing battle. I can't say I've ever known him to have such affection toward a woman back on our planet. And the boy is head-over-heels mad about you. You'll be the death of both of them."

His silvery eyes greedily watched for my reaction, but I didn't bite the bait.

"I didn't come over here to talk about Arden and Jasper. Did you kill Creagan?"

He flinched at my question. "You think I killed my father?"

I pulled a chair up and sat facing him. "Why wouldn't I? You've done nothing but act like an emotionless beast. You kidnapped my mother and held her against her will. You attacked Selkie and tried to kill her. You're evil, Darion. Why wouldn't I think you capable of killing our father?"

He sat silent, silver fury burning in his eyes. But then it faded, and something else replaced it. Sadness? Loneliness? Both. "I despised my father for the way he treated my mother. He always loved you and your mother more than us. My mother told me how he abandoned us repeatedly to escape to this disgusting planet to be with you. But no matter how much I wanted to hate him for never being there for us, he was still my father, and I loved him, even when I tried not to." His head bowed.

"You didn't answer my question," I said, undeflected.

Darion's head snapped back up. "I don't owe you any answers, sister," he hissed, "but no, I did not kill my father or have anything to do with his death. I don't know how it happened."

Darion looked away from me just as the pain showed in his eyes. I could sense that he was holding back his emotions, not wanting me to see them. He was telling me the truth. He loved Creagan. I *felt* it.

I wouldn't allow myself to feel sorry for him. "If you didn't do it, then Siobhan must have been involved in his death. She was jealous of his love for my mother."

"My mother would not have killed my father," Darion spat, but without his ability to mask his emotions, I sensed his own uncertainty behind his words.

"Siobhan may have raised you." I grabbed his face and made him look at me. "But she is not your biological mother."

Darion's sharp features twisted. "Your adulteress bitch of a mother lies."

Without thinking, I reached out and smacked him hard across the face, leaving a bright red handprint burning on his cheek. "Shut your mouth!" I snapped. "All you know are the lies you've been fed. My mom is not an adulteress. She and Creagan were in love long before he married Siobhan. Siobhan threatened Creagan into marrying her, and considering the timing of their marriage and our birth, I think you were a part of that threat."

Darion seethed, "It's not true. You and your mother both lie. I know who my mother is."

With a deep breath, I composed myself and spoke calmly. "I don't know how or what exactly happened, but you forget who you're talking to. I *felt* the truth in my mother's words. You are her son, whether or not you accept the truth. And believe me, I'm not any happier about it than you are. But by some twist of misfortune, you are my twin."

Darion shook his head in refusal, sending a lock of his raven hair into his eyes, and for the first time, I realized his hair was exactly the same shade and texture as mine … and my mom's. My gut twisted as I noticed other small similarities, but it didn't matter. Our difference in character outweighed any physical similarity. Darion and I shared the same blood, but he would never truly be my brother.

His silver eyes watched me as though he were noticing our indistinguishable similarities for the first time as well. Then he grimaced. "My mother will come for me, and she'll explain everything."

I sat back in my chair and lifted my lips into a taunting smile. "I hope she does come for you, Darion, but until then, let me ask you something. If Siobhan loves you so much, why didn't she offer to trade my mother for you? She must have known I would have traded you for her without a second thought, but she didn't do that. Why don't you think about why it was more important for her to recapture my mother than to let her enemies take her only son?"

Darion didn't respond, and I left him alone to think about my question, a question that also bothered me, and by the look on Darion's face, a question that he'd already been wondering. Siobhan had raised Darion. She might not be his biological mother, but she was his mother in all other aspects. She must care about him. He obviously cared for her, so there was some kind of bond between them. But why did she leave without even trying to get Darion back? Was revenge more important to her than protecting her son, or was there some other reason she hadn't offered a trade? She had made sure we wouldn't hurt Darion by threatening my mom. I couldn't shake the feeling that there was something more behind Siobhan's choice. From what I'd learned about her, she was smart and cunning and willing to do whatever it took to win, something we both had in common. Letting us take Darion would be a loss to her, unless she didn't see it that way. *What's her angle?*

Siobhan's intentions plagued my mind as I trudged my achy body to my room and lay on my bed. A knock on my bedroom door jolted me out of my thoughts. I hesitated before sliding my heavy legs off the edge of the bed, and as I stood, I noticed the blood spatters on my pants, a reminder of my failure tonight. I cracked the door open, and Arden stood in the doorframe, a question lingering in his eyes.

I swung the door further open. "Do you want to come in?"

His eyes lowered down to my lips. "I probably shouldn't." He pushed himself off the doorframe and moved a couple of inches closer. "Asking if you're okay would be a ridiculous question, but I wanted to check on you and let you know I'm here if you need to talk."

His breath brushed against my skin, creating a gentle and intimate caress. As I glanced at his hands, the sensation of their touch flooded back to me. My skin burned now for that sensation again, a feeling that would make me forget everything else. *I want to forget.* I moved closer to him and tilted my head up. The heat from his body wrapped around me, hugging me even closer. He reached his hand up, skimming my neck, and cupped the side of my face.

The sound of footsteps broke the spell, and we quickly separated just as Jasper came up behind Arden.

"I should go." Arden brushed by Jasper in his haste to get away.

Cold air now occupied the space where Arden's warm body had stood.

"What's his problem?" Jasper asked as he breezed straight into my room.

"I—" I cleared my throat, not really sure what to say. "I don't know. He's probably upset about me going after Darion alone."

"He's not the only one. What if I hadn't woken up to your alarm?" Jasper fumed.

All energy left me. I crashed onto the bed and leaned over my knees with my head in my hands. "I can't do this right now, Jasper. You're just going to have to deal with my choice."

The mattress sank as he sat next to me and scooted me sideways into him and the familiar comfort of his arms. I finally let it all out, and tears spilled from my eyes. Jasper held my shaking body for what felt like hours until I woke up to him sliding off my shoes and tucking me under the blanket.

❧

*T*he next morning rolled in, overcast and stormy. Calista's morning batch of veggie hash filled the cabin with the scent of herbs and garlic. I stood in front of the fireplace, watching the billowy fog that hovered outside the windows dissipate. The heat from the fire burned the backs of my legs, but I didn't care. The sound of raindrops pelting the windows and roof reminded me of happier days when I'd be curled up in an afghan with a good book, but those days were gone.

"Cozy little setup you have here," Darion commented as he shoved a mouthful of veggie hash into his mouth. He made eating in bound hands look easy, and I had to resist the urge to snatch the plate away from him.

I bit my tongue and watched him as he moved across the room. He was taller than me by several inches. His toned muscles shone through his clothing, and he moved confidently and fluidly. He emitted the dominant air of someone who strived for control. I couldn't help but wonder how different our relationship would have been if we had grown up together like a normal brother and sister. Would we have shared a special twin bond?

Jasper walked into the room, eyeing Darion coldly. He settled close to my side and wrapped his arm around me. I didn't resist, even though I was tired of being coddled and protected by everyone. My mood was as dark as the stormy clouds threatening to release their fury of rain and thunder on everything below, and I had to swallow hard to push back the burning anger that cinched tight inside my chest.

The stairs to the second floor creaked, and I glanced up just as Arden neared the bottom of the staircase. Our eyes locked for an instant before his gaze drifted to Jasper's arm draped across my shoulders, and he turned for the kitchen without saying a word.

Darion snickered as he observed us with a knowing grin. He winked at me when I threw him dagger eyes. His cavalier behavior was infuriating after everything he'd done. I could feel my temper boiling up, so I took a deep breath to regain control. Despite Darion's persistent attempts to provoke me, I had to remain composed in order to think clearly. I wouldn't give him the satisfaction of drawing me into one of his mind games.

"Where would Siobhan take my mother?" I asked him.

He gazed out the window he leaned against, and for a moment, I wasn't sure if he was going to respond to my question. "I don't know where my mother went." He pressed his palm against the glass and pulled it away, watching his imprint fade. "And even if I did, I wouldn't tell you."

I stormed at him. "How can you protect her when you know she had something to do with our father's death and she's holding our mother captive?"

"*Your* mother," he corrected, blowing his hot breath onto the glass and then tracing his fingers through the fog.

"You're a fool, Darion. Siobhan has twisted your mind. She's a witch, and she used some kind of dark magic to steal you from my mom. I don't know how she did it, and I don't care. What I do care about is finding my mom, and if I have to, I will kill Siobhan."

Darion shoved me back with his bound hands. My words bit at him and he wanted to hurt me.

Jasper came to my side in an instant and was in Darion's face.

Darion regained his composure. His glacial stare sent shivers down my spine. His lips peeled back into a snarl. "Aren't you a dutiful little puppy?" Darion mocked Jasper.

"Don't let him bait you, Jasp. He wants you to react. He's just deflecting from his own insecurities." I gave Darion a sharp look and put my hand on Jasper's shoulder, and his muscles relaxed. We both turned to walk away, but Darion wouldn't let up.

"That's right, little puppy. Follow your mistress and do as you're told. Has she told you about her feelings for Arden, and his for her?"

Jasper froze. My heart pounded, and for a moment, I

wasn't sure what he was going to do. Then he turned and charged toward Darion, but I moved in front of him. "Stop."

"What's he talking about?" Jasper's gaze bore into mine, intense and unwavering. An unfamiliar darkness filled his amber eyes.

"Nothing. He's just trying to create trouble." Jasper knew me better than anyone and could always tell when I was holding something back. The lines around his eyes tightened as he studied me, and I cast my gaze down. The lie hung heavy between us.

"You don't deserve her protection." He scowled at Darion and walked away.

"Jasp, hold on …" But he opened the front door and left the cabin without turning back.

I turned on Darion. "What's wrong with you? Why did you tell him that?"

He just smirked and shrugged his shoulders. "Someone needed to tell him, and it wasn't going to be you."

If looks could kill, Darion would be a pile of ash. It was all I could do to restrain myself. "You're a callous bastard."

He shrugged and shifted away from me to stare back out through the window.

"I know there's some part of my mom inside you. There has to be." *Or I can't live with myself for letting you survive.*

"I told you," he replied in barely a whisper. "Siobhan is my mother. Nothing you or your mother says will change that."

I stared at his reflection. Arguing with him was pointless. I left him standing there and hurried out of the cabin.

I found Jasper at the edge of the forest, heading toward a trail. "Jasper … wait—" I called out just as my foot hit a large rock, nearly making me fall face-first on the slippery ground. I regained my balance and continued toward him. "We need to talk." The storm hadn't completely let up, and my wet hair whipped across my face as I ran to close the distance between us.

Jasper finally stopped and turned to face me. Raindrops dripped from his hair and down his face. "Is it true?" he asked. "Do you and Arden have feelings for each other?"

"Jasp, it's complicated."

"Not really," he said, running his hand through his hair to smooth it back out of his face. "It's a yes-or-no answer, Ev."

"Jasp ... I ... yes ... it's true, I have feelings for him ... I'm so sorry." I wished my answer could be different for Jasper's sake, but I couldn't control how I felt for Arden.

"How did this even happen? Has anything happened between you two?"

I stared at the ground. I could taste my own salty tears as they ran down my cheeks and washed over my lips, along with the rain.

"It has, hasn't it?"

I met his eyes. "We only kissed." The words *we only kissed* sounded so innocent, but it had meant more than that, and by the way Jasper was looking at me, I knew he sensed it meant more to me than just a kiss. My heart ached seeing the pain I caused him. I reached out for his hand, but he snatched it back, and moved away.

"I need to be alone, Ev. Please—just go back inside."

Tears and rain blurred my vision. "Jasp, please. I love you. You're my best friend. I have feelings for you too. They're just different from my feelings for Arden."

"Thanks, Ev. That's supposed to make me feel better? Just go. I can't even stand to look at you right now."

I heard a crunching sound behind me, and then Jasper knocked me to the ground and released his energy shield. A sword crashed down into the invisible shield. I jumped to my feet just as more soldiers, men and women dressed and armed for battle, stormed out of a portal and swarmed the forest. Jasper grabbed my hand, and we both ran back toward the cabin.

Something must have alerted the others inside to our intruders, because Arden and Rheya came running out armed with their own weapons. A body flew into Jasper, knocking him away from me and causing me to slip in the mud. I pulled myself up to my knees and found that the entire field was filling with armed men and women. Arden and Rheya cut them down one by one. Before now I hadn't seen Rhal use his magic, but he used it now as he projected multiple shadow forms of himself that fought side by side. The apparitions were both eerie and magnificent.

A snapping sound hissed from behind me. Before I could react, something lashed my back, sending a searing pain through my body and causing me to stumble forward. As I rolled myself over, my heart raced at the sight of a figure coming closer, wielding a menacing blade. In a swift motion, I evaded the blade as it sliced through the air and struck the ground. With a forceful kick, I struck the assailant right in the kneecap. The sound of her cry echoed through the air as she crumpled to the ground in her red leather attire. I didn't hesitate to grab her fallen sword and use the handle to hit her in the temple, knocking her out.

I turned, searching for the one who had lashed my back. The wind and rain made it impossible to see clearly. I spotted her coming at me, swirling her whip, but it was too late to react. Her whip snaked around my ankle and yanked me off my feet. I hit the ground hard, my face smashing into mud and gravel. I knew I was injured, but there was no time to evaluate. With a grunt, I rolled over and propped myself up, feeling a surge of panic as I fought against the relentless grip of the rain-slicked whip, which stubbornly tightened with every futile attempt to break free. I twisted my body around to grab for the sword I'd dropped when I hit the ground, but it was just out of reach. My fingernails clawed at the mud, trying to inch closer to the sword, but it was no use. I shook rain and mud from my eyes and squinted through the chaos. Jasper battled soldiers as he tried to close the distance between us. My body burned with frustration as a pair of heavy black boots crunched near my face.

"Well, aren't you a pretty little thing?" said a haughty voice.

I projected an agonizing ball of pain toward her as she bent to mock me, but nothing happened. Her blond hair blew across her face as she stood and withdrew another whip. It cracked in the air as it lashed out and then furrowed around my neck, cutting off my windpipe.

"The whip is spelled. Your powers can't help you now. The queen will be very pleased when we bring her your head."

I clawed at the whip and gasped for air as the blond-haired woman laughed. Suddenly, a blade shot through her abdomen. Her laugh turned to a gurgle as blood bubbled out of her mouth, and she dropped to her knees and then fell forward onto her face in the mud. Darion stood behind the woman, holding a bloody dagger, looking surprised that he'd just killed one of his own to save me. He thrust out his hand. I swiftly unbound my ankles and tentatively placed my hand in his, and he hefted me to my feet.

"You … saved my life. But how did you get free?" Just as the words left my mouth, Darion flipped my palm and slit it open and then his own. He smashed our bleeding hands together and recited some words in Vitarian.

"NO!" I heard Jasper yell as he pushed me away from Darion, and then Darion had his arm around Jasper's neck, with the dagger to his throat.

"Let him go!" I demanded.

Out of nowhere, a portal materialized beside Darion. I took a step closer.

"Ah-ah-ah, I think Lover Boy will come along with me. I warned you that my mother would come for me."

"Please, Darion. Take me instead. Let Jasper go and take me—"

Darion studied my face with an emotionless expression. Then he loosened his grip on Jasper as he motioned for me to take his place.

"No!" Jasper croaked against the knife at his throat and propelled himself and Darion backward through the portal just before I reached him.

The portal vanished just as quickly as it appeared, along with Darion and Jasper. Another portal opened up at the edge of the forest, and the remaining soldiers that could flee jumped through as it was shrinking in size and closing.

My vision hazed over in a fog of red as shock reverberated throughout my body. An earsplitting wail filled my ears. I pressed my hands to my head to block out the noise, and I realized the sound was coming from me. A fiery sensation coursed through my arms, awakening my skin with an electrifying surge of energy. My arms moved out in front of me of their own accord. Through the red haze, I saw the bodies of those remaining in the field drop to their knees and cry out as they covered their own ears. Wind swirled around me in a rush, carrying with it twigs, rocks, and leaves from the ground. The trees swayed back and forth until their trunks bent in an unnatural form toward me.

"Everly." A hand clasped my shoulder. "You must regain control of your emotions before you harm those around you, including those you care about."

Felix moved to stand in front of me and gently squeezed my other shoulder. He released a healing energy, but I refused to allow myself to be freed from the pain. The wind gathered around us and whipped fiercely against our bodies.

"It's not your fault." Felix spoke over the noise of the howling wind. "You must let go of the rage and the guilt you feel. It will do you no good."

"Then what will do me good? These powers are useless when I need them. I keep losing the ones I love and am powerless to do anything about it."

"You are still learning to use your gifts, but allowing them to control you in this way will only cause harm to yourself and others." Felix swept his hand out.

When I looked around, I saw soldiers sent by Siobhan, both dead and alive. The living ones bent over and wailed in pain, and I felt vindicated for causing their suffering. Then I saw Rheya on her knees, screaming and holding her ears, as well as Rhal, Malakai, and Arden. They had done nothing to deserve the agony I was causing them. I let down my guard and allowed Felix's healing touch to calm me. His gaze penetrated the red fog clouding my vision and guided me back from the depths of despair.

The wind calmed, and the trees lifted back up to their normal stature as the remaining enemies scurried on their hands and knees into the forest.

"Let them go," I called to Rhal as he reached for a weapon.

My stomach wrenched with guilt as soon as the rage subsided, and I fell to the ground and threw up. From my hunched-over position, I glanced around at everyone, taking in their expressions. "I … I'm sorry." I dropped my face in my hands. There was shuffling around me as the others regained their composure, retrieved weapons from the deceased, and gathered the bodies.

They barely looked at me, and I didn't blame them. Mortification for what I'd done to them trickled through my veins.

Rheya charged toward me just as I'd gotten to my feet. Her expression was both livid and a little fearful. "How did she bend the will of nature? Only the original family had that kind of power." She was pointing a shaky finger at Felix while watching me with a cautious stare, like she was afraid that I was a rabid animal about to pounce. Maybe that was exactly what I was now.

She continued to shake her finger at Felix. "Her power did not affect you like the rest of us. You know something, Healer, and it's time you tell the rest of us the truth."

Felix looked at me for approval, and I nodded my consent to share the knowledge of my lineage. After what I'd done, they deserved to know the truth.

He turned his attention back to Rheya and the others. "Yes, I believe it is time. Cacsha and Everly," he said, pausing and glancing at me to make sure I hadn't changed my mind. I hadn't and motioned for him to continue. "Are the direct descendants of Oria and the last of the original royal bloodline. And they are the true heirs to the royal throne."

"What! How do you know this?" Rheya demanded. Her copper hair had tangled into a wild mess from the battle, and her energy teetered on explosive, but Felix remained calm as he explained.

"Oria entrusted my family to care for her daughter in secrecy when she made her choice to release her throne to the next in line. We honored our promise and looked after her daughter and each generation that has followed. And to answer your other question, Oria provided my family with a gift that she spelled with her own blood to protect her child's guardian from magic. The spelled item has been passed down to each designated member chosen to watch over Oria's descendant."

"What is this spelled item?" Rheya asked skeptically.

"I can't share that with you, my dear. A stipulation of Oria."

Rheya scoffed but said nothing more.

Felix glanced back at me, and his blue eyes held mine. "You asked me how their mother chose between the two. There's something I need to show you." Felix turned and walked toward the other side of the cabin. We all followed him until he stopped at the chicken coop. He disappeared inside and returned carrying a long rectangular box made of wood. He slid the top off the box, revealing a sheathed sword and a smaller, square box inside.

"You have Oria's sword," Rheya said, and then she gasped when Felix held the smaller box open. "The Ever ring." She pulled her eyes from the ring and glared at Felix. "You hid Oria's sword and ring in a chicken coop?" she asked incredulously.

Felix looked at her like she was daft. "Can you think of a more inconspicuous hiding place?"

She rolled her eyes. But I saw Felix's point. Who would go looking for royal treasures in an old, beat-up chicken coop?

Felix held the ring up for each to see. Everyone was still and quiet as they stared in a trance at the unique piece of jewelry, but they eventually turned away with squinted eyes, as if the sight of it pained them. I didn't understand their reactions. My eyes followed the swirls of color circling the ring. The colors radiated vibrant auras, pulsating with life and energy. This wasn't just your average energy, this was powerful and ancient energy. I inched closer, feeling drawn to it somehow. Felix held the ring out to me.

"Only a member of the Ever bloodline can tame the energy inside, and the magic within this ring will only respond to the one the ancestors deem worthy of ruling Aenoas-Vita," Felix explained. "This is the guidance their mother had. The ancestors sensed Orien's darkness, and when he put the ring on, they refused to respond to him. When Oria placed the ring on her finger, the ancestors welcomed her into their light, and their mother had the answer she sought."

I stared at the ring, mesmerized by the energy and magic flowing within it and outside it. The chickens in the coop clucked maddeningly as the wind rattled and whistled through the cracks of the old-rickety wooden structure.

"Oria Ever was the last to wear this ring. The spiritual energy inside has been dormant for too long. It recognizes the energy of its kin." He pushed the box holding the ring into my hand.

Its silver gleamed and sparkled like a shining diamond, and a small opalesque globe ornamented the top. It contained more auras of color, which stirred inside of their own accord. I tentatively lifted the ring from its box. The energy surrounding it was palpable, and my own connected to it instantly. I twisted and turned the ring, examining every inch. On the inside of the band, the engraving *Ever* caught my eye and another string of words that were in another language.

"What do these words mean?" I asked.

Felix answered without looking at the engraving. "Power is the heart of the people." He closed one fist over his heart. "The Ever family go back to the beginning of time on our planet, and they were the first and only ruling family for generations, and they ruled with the standard that to be Vitarian was to be one people and one heart, and that was the most powerful magic of all. The ring was designed to keep power from a ruler such as Orien, who would rule for the purpose of greed and control. One of my very own ancestors, a sorceress of great power who was a friend and adviser of the first family forged the ring with the blood of the first ruling Ever to bind the spell that would aid in the selection of future rulers and to carry with it, pertinent knowledge meant only for the next bearer. The ring holds a sliver of aura from each ruler before you. And like the royal staffs spelled to rule out those unworthy of guarding the royal family, the ring holds unique magic. It will not absorb any part of an aura from one who is not fit to rule. Should the ring choose you, it proves you are the individual from Oria's vision, and the ring will absorb a portion of you." Felix stated with finality.

My brows knitted tightly together as I thought of the ramification of Felix's words. "I don't want to be chosen. I don't want any of this." Filled with a mix of emotions, I quickly dropped the ring back into the box and shoved it into Felix's hand.

Rheya and the others watched my childish display without speaking a word.

"I understand," Felix responded. "We do not always have a choice over the events that occur, but we do have a choice as to how we react to them. You've inherited Oria's gifts, and I believe you are the one from her premonition. We won't know unless you put the ring on. That's all I ask, to at least try."

"Why does it even matter?" Rheya interrupted. "Oria relinquished her throne when she abandoned her people. Her brother nearly annihilated our race in his bloodthirsty craze for power. The Evers no longer rule, and even if the ring chooses her, she's no ruler. She's never even set foot on our planet. The Vitarian people will not follow this child."

"Rheya," Arden finally said. "Not one more word." His voice remained cold, and his glare even colder. I swallowed the lump forming in my throat.

"I can't do this. Rheya's right. It doesn't matter if the ring chooses me or not. I'm just a teenage girl who can't even keep the people I love safe and no ring or bloodline is going to change that." I walked away from them, embarrassed by my weakness.

I recognized Arden's energy as he came up behind me. "You're not *just* a girl, Everly. If you only knew how strong you really are."

I shook my head, and he placed both of his hands on my shoulders. "You mean so much to so many people: your mother and father, Calista, Selkie, Jasper, and … me. Turn around and look at me."

Reluctantly, I turned to face him. "I believe in you. You just have to believe in yourself." His hands fell from my shoulders and slid down my arms until his fingers laced with mine.

"I'm scared," I whispered and rested my forehead against his chest. The weight of failure settled heavily on my shoulders as I thought about my mom and Jasper. "What if I can't save them?"

"You can," Calista's voice came from behind us.

I lifted my head. "Calista!" I ran into her arms. "Are you okay?"

She rubbed the back of her head. "I'm fine. Darion caught me unawares. I'm afraid it's my fault he got loose. I'm sorry. If I'd kept a closer eye on him, he wouldn't have taken Jasper."

I squeezed her tighter. "It's not your fault. Jasper sacrificed himself for me. And now he's counting on me, and I won't let him down." I glanced at Arden, who gave me a reassuring smile.

I went back to Felix, resolved to overcome my fear and do whatever it took to rescue my mom and Jasper.

Felix nodded his approval and handed me back the ring. I

held out my right hand and slowly slid the ring onto my forefinger. I jumped when the ring reshaped itself to fit my finger as though the material itself were alive.

"Ouch." Something pricked my skin where I wore the ring. My eyes stretched wide as I watched a small amount of my blood fill the orb atop the ring. I felt a rush of panic as a bright light engulfed my vision and my heart pounded in my chest. Swirling auras enveloped me, pulsating with an electrifying energy and radiating vibrant hues that danced before my eyes in a wild frenzy.

"Everly," said a soothing female voice in the distant reaches of my mind.

Who's there? I called out to the essence of my subconscious.

"It is Oria, Queen of Aenoas-Vita. I've been waiting for you." Her voice echoed all around me. "I dreamed of you many lifetimes before you were born, when my spirit was still of the living realm. Do not turn from your fate. Wear this ring, and I will be with you, as all of us before you will be." The colors swarmed around me so quickly. My stomach churned. I spun around, searching in the light for someone, anyone, but there was nothing but bright light and dizzying colors. "Reunite the Vitarian people," she demanded, her voice growing stronger and louder, "and mend what has been broken. I was wrong to leave my people. I know that now. But you will take my place and remove the false queen." She was not asking, but ordering me.

The auras swirled around me, their restless energy filling the air with anticipation.

I'm no ruler, my mind called back furiously. *And I don't want to be. How can I lead a planet of people when I can't even control my own abilities and save the ones I love? I'm not the one from your vision.* All the energy left me, and I stood depleted.

"You are," her voice echoed, almost with a trace of anger.

"And you have the knowledge to save your loved ones. Wear the ring, and I will guide you. Refuse me, and you risk losing your mother forever."

A new dread filled me in the pit of my soul. My choice and free will became less my own every day. I ached to tear the ring from my finger and smash it, crushing the contents under my shoe, but if wearing it could help me save my mom and Jasper, then I'd do whatever I had to.

A small orb of light moved toward me and touched my forehead, and my mind filled with a vision from the paper mill. It showed my mother touching my temple, and I remembered the image I'd seen at her touch.

Suddenly the voice and the auras vanished, and I was once again standing in the forest, surrounded by Felix and the others, who watched me with bated breath.

It was Rheya who spoke first. "A cocoon of light surrounded you. What happened?"

"Oria spoke to me," I told them.

Felix nodded with a look of pride. "As I knew she would."

With a sigh, I shook my head. "I'll wear the ring for now, but I cannot and will not make any further commitment or claim beyond that." I intended my words for both Felix and the spirits of Oria and her ancestors within the ring.

Felix nodded and squeezed my shoulders. "That's a fair decision."

"Oria showed me something I had forgotten about." My mind buzzed with renewed hope, and I glanced at Arden, remembering the memory he'd shared with me during our training. "Felix." I directed my attention back to him. "Does my mother have the ability to share images or memories?"

He studied me thoughtfully. "Yes, one of Cacsha's unique gifts is her ability to show another past events."

Oria showed me that image for a reason. "There's somewhere I need to go. My mom showed me a memory at the paper mill just before Siobhan took her. So much was happening, and I didn't realize she'd done it intentionally, but now I know the vision had meaning."

A new energy filled me, and for the first time since Creagan's funeral, I felt sure of myself.

CHAPTER 12

The storm passed, and the sun broke through the clouds, clearing the way for cerulean skies. With a press of the button, the convertible top of Calista's Mustang smoothly retracted, preparing for the drive to the café. Arden sat next to me, his hair blowing wildly in the wind as we sped down the highway. He seemed like any normal guy in this moment, and it made me wonder what he was like outside of being the commander of a king's army. I was relieved that he and the others had unquestioningly followed my lead. It was a nice change of pace not to be questioned and treated like a child. I was sure the ring and the fact that I was Oria's heir had something to do with it, but I'd take the win.

We pulled up to the café. Seeing it closed and empty at this time of day filled me with a profound sadness, knowing that it should be bustling with the sounds of life. This was around the time my mom would set up for one of her DIY classes. My chest tightened as we removed the yellow police tape blocking the entrance to the front door and went inside.

Everything was exactly as it was the last time I'd been

here. The memory sent shivers down my spine. I hurried to the office, with Arden close behind. Glass crunched under my feet from the frame that had fallen and shattered the night I'd run out on my mom. Purposefully avoiding the bloodstain on the office floor, I made a beeline for the rolling plant stand. I moved it aside and threw back the throw rug, revealing the hidden floor safe. I spun the knob until it hit all the right clicks and lifted the heavy metal door. Leatherbound journals filled the safe, which had never been there before. I remembered how quickly my mom had closed the safe that night when I'd come in. She must have been stashing these.

I pulled out the first few journals and rubbed my hands over the smooth leather. Some had creases, worn with age, and others were still crisp with the scent of rawhide. The one on top had wider dimensions and was thicker than the rest. Someone had burned the word *Grimoire* into the leather cover. I flipped through the pages to find them filled with spells. I set the grimoire aside and picked up another from the top of the stack. It was titled with a year—the year I was born. I flipped it open to the first page with shaky hands. The sight of my mother's delicate handwriting brought tears to my eyes. I read the first entry.

Creagan was beyond-himself ecstatic when I told him of my pregnancy. I couldn't have been happier when I realized I was pregnant. I knew immediately twins grew inside me, for I could feel their tiny dual heartbeats. It should have been impossible to conceive twins, but when Felix revealed my relation to Oria, I knew it was the power inside my blood that made my pregnancy possible. If I'd only known this information sooner, maybe it could have saved us.

Our happiness was short-lived, because our children would never be safe if we did not flee. We had planned to leave Aenoas-Vita in secrecy the night Siobhan captured me. We were finally going to be free of all the secrecy and fear of being caught and of Siobhan's constant presence in our lives.

But once again, she snared Creagan in her web, taking from us something more precious than our freedom. How she accomplished siphoning my son from my womb into her own remains a mystery, but I will never give up searching for a spell to free my baby from the binding spell she has placed on him, linking his life to hers with dark magic and using him as a pawn to keep Creagan at her side.

My sweet boy was stolen from my womb before he had a chance to grow inside me, along with his sister, and bond, as a child should. Siobhan has ripped a part of my soul from me, and it will remain fractured until I get my son back.

I flipped through the journal before closing it. Just like the rest, every page was filled from front to back with my mother's handwriting, all of them labeled with the years they were written. A new sorrow filled me. And not just for my mother and father, but for Darion as well. He'd had no choice in his upbringing. A woman who cared only about using him as a means to get what she wanted had stolen and raised him, manipulating his emotions.

I brushed away the tear that escaped from the corner of my eye and then reached for the grimoire beside me. I assumed the spells were written in the Vitarian language, but as I turned the pages more slowly, I noticed each page had an English translation inscribed on the back side. If my mother took the precaution of adding the English transcriptions, she must have intended for me to read the grimoire someday.

A particular spell caught my eye: *To Merge One's Gift with*

Another. I read the English translation a second time as an idea sparked to life, then I pulled my cell phone from my back pocket and snapped a picture of the spell in both the Vitarian and English translation. After replacing the grimoire at the bottom of the safe, I topped it with the journals. They'd been safe here so far, but if anyone found the safe and figured out a way to open it, it would appear to just be a stack of personal journals.

"What are you doing?" Arden asked.

"I'm putting the journals back in the safe. They've been protected here so far, so it seems a good idea to lock them back up."

"What journals? All I see is you holding some old ledger."

"No. The safe is filled with leather-bound journals. Here's a stack of them right here, all dated by year, and there's also a grimoire filled with my mother's spells."

Arden grinned. "Clever. Your mother must have cast a cloaking spell that allows only you to see through. Did you find out anything useful?"

"I did indeed, and I know just where we need to go next."

~

*T*he club was alive with music and dancing bodies when we arrived. Neil wasn't posted at the front entrance, as he had been the last time. The girl who greeted us said he was in a meeting, but she would let him know we were waiting as soon as he finished.

We walked toward the bar. The bartender offered us shots of ever flower, but we both declined. I needed to keep a clear mind and didn't want a repeat of my last experience with the drink. Sultry music played over the sound system, and I wondered if all Vitarian music was this captivating or if

Neil just had good taste. Floating sconces of multiple colors lit the inner club tonight, a variation from the previous lighting I'd seen. The lighting, together with the sensual lyrics, created an alluring atmosphere. Bodies moved back and forth on the dance floor with abandon.

"Dance with us, darling." A tipsy group took my hands and tried to lure me onto the dance floor.

I gave Arden a pleading look, and he reached out and took my hand. "Sorry," he said to them. "She's spoken for."

Thankfully, the group moved on and disappeared into the crowd.

"Thanks for the save," I said. Heat tingled in my body from Arden's touch.

"No problem." He held onto my hand a moment longer; his thumb trailed the inside of my palm as he released his grasp.

"Hello—lovely," I heard a voice echo in my mind. I looked around to see Neil making his way through a boisterous crowd.

He made a beeline straight for us, his friendly face framed by the large black-rimmed retro eyeglasses that Jasper had told me Neil wore only as decoration for his attire. I found Neil to be an interesting character. He always said exactly what he meant, and his emotions matched his words and intentions, which gave him high marks in my book.

"Everly, darling. I'm pleased to see you again." Neil bowed his head and kissed the top of my hand.

"Commander," he said to Arden, and they clasped hands.

"And where's my favorite young Vitarian?"

"That's part of the reason we're here," I answered, wishing it weren't the case. "Darion and Siobhan have taken both Jasper and my mother, and I need your help, Neil."

"Oh dear, I am sorry to hear that. Of course, I will aid in

any way I can, but first—" he paused and carefully scanned the room— "follow me. Let's go somewhere more private."

We followed Neil back toward the main entrance. He pulled open a thick red velvet curtain that hung behind the front desk to reveal a staircase leading up to the second floor. "After you." He lifted his arm to usher us through.

The staircase led to an open and spacious flat. The sleek and slender furnishings that decorated the space were modern and sparse. Besides the books littered throughout the room, it was clean and orderly.

"Welcome to my home."

"Wow, you live above the club," I mused. "I suppose the noise isn't a problem, since you can block it out at will."

"Exactamundo, darling." He winked.

A glowing light caught my eye from across the room. My breath paused. A glass case housed a small garden of miniature ever flowers.

"Are those what I think they are?" I asked Neil.

I made my way to the glass case. The flowers leaned in my direction as if they were reaching out to me. They were so beautiful and delicate. An aura of colors surrounded the flower tops. I trailed my finger along the glass tank, and the flowers twisted and turned to follow my lead.

"I've been trying for years to grow the ever flower on Earth successfully, but it never survives much past this stage."

Neil peeked sideways at Arden. "I know it is forbidden, Commander, but perhaps in light of current events, you'd be willing to overlook this minor transgression."

"This is more than a minor transgression," Arden scowled. "You could unintentionally alter Earth's natural ecosystem if it were exposed to the ever flower, and I presume that is also soil from Aenoas-Vita. The ever flower would need the soil of its own planet to have even a remote chance of survival. Smuggling in the dried flower petals for your cocktails is one thing, but this is altogether a different matter. We'll deal with this later. We have more important issues at hand."

Neil's eyes widened. "I … Of course, Commander."

Neil glanced at me, and my heart went out to him. He was a good guy and not intentionally trying to do harm. He had brought us up here in good faith.

"Arden," I said. When he looked at me, the fire in his eyes cooled a degree. "We need Neil's help, and as payment, you'll overlook what we've seen in his apartment."

Arden stood somewhat shocked at my demand, but a crease formed as he fought a restrained smile. "I see you're a natural at giving orders already." He turned back to Neil, the scowl returning to his features. "These flowers and any other supplies you have to grow more will be transported back to Aenoas-vita under my supervision."

Neil beamed at me. "How may I be of service?"

I opened the photo app on my phone. "I found a spell written by my mother. If it works the way I think it will, I can use it to merge my gifts temporarily with the gifts of another Vitarian. I have the ability of sight. There's something important I need to convey to Darion. I should be able to enter his mind and see through his eyes, but I can't project thought, and that's where you come in. If we merge our gifts, I'll be able to communicate with Darion telepathically."

"May I see the spell?" Neil held his hand out, and I handed him my phone.

"Brilliant!" He swiped the screen to view both translations. "Yes, this will work. I must say, your mother has always had a special talent for crafting unique spells."

I stiffened slightly. "You know my mother?"

"I do. Cacsha and I go way back on Aenoas-Vita. In fact, she helped me craft some of my cocktail recipes served here at the club when I first got started. I'll do whatever is required to help both her and my young friend Jasper."

"Thank you, Neil." My relief was short-lived. "We have one problem."

Neil raised an eyebrow.

I chewed at my lower lip. "Well. I don't exactly know how to make it work. I've never intentionally used my ability for sight before. It has only happened to me on two occasions. Once here at the club when Darion arrived, and another time during my training. I don't even know how it happened, and when I tried to do it again, I couldn't."

"Why didn't you tell me?" Arden asked.

"I'm sorry, but when I learned only the original family could see through the eyes of other Vitarians, I just wasn't ready for anyone to know about my—" I glanced over at Neil, who was curiously watching the flowers follow my movements. Before I could finish my sentence, Neil was already connecting the dots.

His eyes lingered on my hand with Oria's ring. "I always knew there was something special about your mother, and I sensed it in you too the night Jasper brought you here."

I dreaded having to explain that I hadn't accepted the role Oria had vacated, but Neil, being an intuitive guy, saved me the trouble.

He smiled widely. "Back to your little issue. Don't worry, darling, I can help guide you once we merge." He took a seat and patted the spot next to him.

I sat next to Neil on the sofa and peered nervously at Arden, who took the armchair adjacent. "You've got this," he said.

"Take my hand," Neil instructed. "We must have physical contact for the spell to work."

I slipped my hand into his. His palm was soft and warm

against mine. Our conjoined energies buzzed, sending a spark vibrating up my arm.

"Everly." I met Neil's dark brown eyes. "Darion is quite powerful. Once he knows you're in his mind, he'll have the ability to repel you out. You'll need to convince him to hear you out before he does so. Are you ready?"

"Yes."

Neil gave my hand a gentle squeeze. "Okay. We'll recite the spell together. Focus your mind only on Darion. Envision a specific detail about him and let your defenses fade away. Allow your magic to flow freely and without restraint."

Neil began reciting the spell, and I followed his lead. He chose the Vitarian, while I spoke the English version. I manifested an image of the wall I'd conjured as a child to guard my magic and had continued to rely on. I saw it melting and crumbling into nothing. A powerful current burst inside me, and a rush of air whirled around us as our energies linked.

The spell is working.

I squeezed my eyes tightly shut and conjured an image of Darion. His liquid-silver eyes floated into existence. My mind called out to him: *Darion.*

The feeling of leaving my body made my head spin. When I opened my eyes, everything came across dark and uncertain at first, like ripples in water. As my vision cleared, Darion's reflection stared up from dark, murky water. He was bent over and staring into a river. Next to his own reflection, an image of a lighthouse rippled in the current.

I focused my thoughts.

Darion.

Startled, he staggered slightly backwards from the edge, his eyes opening wide in surprise.

"I see you've learned some new tricks, sister."

Darion, please hear me out. I have something important to tell you.

"Speak quickly, for I do not appreciate the violation of my mind."

The visions Darion had inflicted on me flashed in my mind, and I fought back a snarky retort. I bit my tongue and told him everything I'd read in my mom's journal.

"More lies," he hissed. "My mother loves me. She explained everything. Your mother didn't want me. It's her who has never cared for me," he argued.

I detected a faint trace of an emotion in his voice that betrayed his words, so I pushed on.

Darion. Listen to me. My mom can prove what I say is true. She can show you the memories of the events as they took place. It's one of her gifts. Please, just allow her to show you the truth. She's never stopped looking for a way to break the spell Siobhan has on you. She loves you, Darion. You are her son, and losing you broke her heart. Siobhan used dark magic to steal you and link you to her in some way. I don't know how, but she used you to force Creagan to stay with her. She doesn't care about you, Darion. You're just a pawn in her pursuit to remain queen.

"I—" Darion's voice broke off as someone approached him from behind.

"Darion. Are you speaking to someone?" said a wickedly silken voice.

"No, Mother. I'm just going over our preparations."

He turned, and there stood the woman who had taken everything from my mother. She wore a gown that reminded me of ancient Greeks, accentuating her long and slender figure. A gold belt encased her waist, decorated on the front with a sparkling black gem that matched the soft onyx fabric. My mind filled with Darion's apprehension as she closed the distance between them.

Siobhan studied him, her eyes two dark pits of a bottomless well. She reached up and brushed a lock of hair out of his face. There was the slightest hint of affection in her touch, but she hardened her heart against him. She obliterated the emotion as quickly as it emerged. The son her husband had created with the woman he truly loved. The resentment was not only evident in her restrained touch but also brimming in the cool colors of her aura. Watching her mechanical interactions with Darion, I wondered if she'd ever felt any genuine tenderness toward him. Or had it always been an act?

"Is everything okay, darling?" she asked with false concern, even creasing her brow as she did so.

How could Darion not see through her? And then I knew. Being in his mind, his unrestrained emotions gave him away. He was desperate for her love and affection. He felt abandoned by Creagan, and Siobhan had been the only steady presence in his life. And seeing her now, I knew she used Darion's insecurities to her full advantage.

"Of course, Mother. I'm fine," he said without showing a hint of his inner turmoil.

"Good." Her mouth turned up in a smile, but there was no emotion in her expression. "We must prepare the portal. We take the prisoners home tonight."

What! Darion, no. Please don't let her take them. Go to our mother and let her show you how Siobhan has lied and twisted you to her will. She killed our father, Darion, and she plans to do the same to our mother. Don't let her do it.

My body jerked with a jolt. Everything went black and fuzzy again, and then I was back in Neil's apartment. My head pounded, making it hard for me to get my bearings.

Neil seemed to suffer the same side effects as I was. He removed his glasses and rubbed his temples. "I could see and hear everything that was happening, but it felt like my mind was submerged underwater. It was like I was a barnacle on your subconscious." He shook his head as if trying to discharge water from his ears.

"A barnacle?" Arden asked, amused by Neil's reference to being a crustacean.

Neil lifted his shoulders. "I like fish, and it was all I could think to compare it to." He looked over at me with a crumpled frown. "Do you think Darion will listen to you?" he asked, his voice groggy.

"I don't know." My head was still spinning as I pushed up from the couch. "I sensed something in him when Siobhan approached, a feeling of mistrust that he denies. I hope it's enough to convince him to let my mom show him the truth. But we can't rely on Darion's help. Siobhan plans to transport my mom and Jasper back to Aenoas-Vita tonight through a portal. Darion rejected me from his mind as soon as Siobhan began discussing their plans for preparation."

Arden moved toward me. "Let's get back to the others and find a way to locate them."

"That's unnecessary," I told him. "I know where they are. When I was in Darion's head, I saw a reflection of a lighthouse in the water he was peering over. It was the lighthouse at Warrior Rock."

"Are you sure?" Arden asked.

"I've hiked that island dozens of times. I'm positive that's where they are."

"I have a friend who can portal you there," Neil offered.

"Constructing a portal will take too long; we need a quicker way. Everly—how far is this Warrior Rock?" Arden asked.

"It's east, down the river. We can get there by boat in thirty minutes, and I know where we can get one fast enough to get us there."

Arden grabbed a piece of paper and a pen from Neil's table. His hand moved quickly as the pen scrawled across the paper. He handed the note to Neil. "I need you to send this message to the people on this list right away."

"Yes, Commander." Neil took the sheet of paper and held his fist to his heart.

Neil grasped my hand. "I would offer to come with you, but I'm useless in battle."

"You've helped me tremendously, Neil." I gave him a hug. "I plan to return the favor someday."

"No need. I'm honored to offer my services, even if you weren't the true queen of Aenoas-Vita." He bowed his head.

"You're a loyal friend. Thank you."

He said something in Vitarian that I didn't understand.

"What does that mean?"

"You are fearless, and may the spirit of Oria and her predecessors be with you."

I smiled at him and followed Arden down the stairs. My heart quickened with each step. We finally knew where Darion and Siobhan held my mom and Jasper, and we were going to save them, at *any cost*.

~

*W*e ran down the marina ramp. The sun was setting, and the dark lavender sky reminded me that time was running out. It would be night soon. I picked up the pace, with Arden easily keeping stride.

I lifted the horseshoe knocker and knocked on the door of the boathouse, hopeful that Ty would be home. His dad worked nights, so Ty usually had the place to himself. If he wasn't working at the café, then he normally spent his time building worlds in one of his video games.

The door opened, and relief flooded my body. Ty stood on the other side of the door, video game controller in one hand, and a slice of pizza hanging from his mouth. He pulled the pizza free and beamed at me. The sight of Ty reminded me of normality and brought a smile to my face. He wore his trademark bandanna, tied around his forehead to keep his dark hair from falling in his face, and a tie-dyed T-shirt.

"Hey, Ev. What's going on? Everything okay? Did they find your mom?"

He looked at Arden as if noticing him for the first time. His eyes grew wide as he took in Arden's full frame. "Hey, man. I'm Ty." He stuck the pizza back in his mouth and shot out his hand.

Arden grinned in response. "Arden. Nice to meet you, Ty." He shook Ty's hand.

Thankfully, Rheya wasn't here to mock Ty's gesture.

Ty gave a curious grin. He was about to say something when a buzz came from his pants pocket. His expression became more serious. "Molly's been texting me like mad. She's been crazy worried about you. We haven't heard anything for days. I went by the café earlier, and it's still taped off."

Guilt washed over me, causing a sharp pang in my chest. I hadn't been a good friend lately. "Ty, I'm sorry I've been out of touch. I … I'm just so worried about my mom. Everything is so messed up."

"Hey, Ev. Say no more. I can't imagine what you're going through right now. We're all worried about your mom and want to help if we can. What can I do?"

"Well, there is something. I was hoping I could borrow your dad's fishing boat. It's an emergency." I knew it would be too much to hope that Ty would just give us the boat, no questions asked.

His eyes narrowed. "What kind of emergency? Does this have to do with your mom?"

If Ty thought I was lying, he'd refuse to give me the keys to the boat. "Yes, it does. But I can't tell you more than that right now. We're running out of time, and I just need you to trust me."

He reached up and grabbed a set of keys hanging on the wall beside him. "Let's go." He slipped his bare brown feet into the flip-flops on the floor near the door.

"Well—actually, it would be better if just Arden and I went alone." My eyes pleaded with Ty, hoping he would understand.

Ty's face fell, and I wished I could tell him more.

"I'm sorry, Ty. It's not that I don't want you to come, but it could be dangerous."

"We should call Sheriff Baze," he said.

"No. I can't explain now, but I promise I'll tell you as much as I can later. Right now, time is running out, and we need to leave. Promise me you won't call the sheriff, and please don't tell Molly about this." I was really pushing Ty to his limits.

His brows knitted together as he contemplated what to do. "Okay, but only if you promise to call me if you get into trouble, and swear to tell me what's going on when you're back."

"I promise that I'll do my best on both accounts."

"Okay, then. Good luck, Ev." He hesitantly handed me the keys.

Ty's dad had parked his boat in a boat slip just around the corner from his boathouse. He'd taken Ty, Molly, and me out on many fishing trips over the years, letting us take the wheel, so I was familiar with operating the boat. I started the engine and slowly backed out of the boat slip, being careful not to hit the sides of the dock.

"Are you sure you know how to drive this thing?" Arden asked, his face a shade paler than a moment ago.

"You see that row of sailboats over there?" I pointed, and his gaze followed the direction of my finger. "The one parked in the third slip over to the right belongs to me and my mom. We've been sailing since I was a kid. My mom loves the river.

I'd take our boat, but the engine's smaller and slower. This fishing boat has a bigger engine that's made for speed, and we'll get there a lot quicker. Plus, this isn't my first time behind the wheel of this boat. So rest easy, Commander. I know how to handle this bad boy."

His tightened expression relaxed a little as I continued to make my way out of the marina and into the larger body of water.

I stood behind the glass windshield and accelerated the engine. The tide was up, and the wind and current rolled in strong. Water sprayed over us as we ripped through the small waves.

"What was the message you asked Neil to deliver?" I called out over the wind.

"Reinforcements." Arden kept his gaze straight ahead. His hands gripped the top of the windshield, and I wondered if Arden had ever been on a boat before, or maybe he wasn't a fan of water. My phone buzzed, and I slid it out of my back pocket. The screen lit up with a text message from Calista:

Got Arden's message. Meet us on the back side of the island. Not far behind.

"The others are on their way." I slipped my phone back in my pocket.

As the sun set behind the mountain, the sky transformed into a canvas of darkness. The silhouette of Warrior Rock appeared in the distance. A forest and numerous wild animals inhabited the island. Shadows of treetops created a mirage of shapes in the night sky. The lighthouse stood on the east-facing side of the island. It hadn't been an active lighthouse in some time and functioned now as a tourist hiking attraction. A light coming from the top illuminated the darkened sky. I turned and headed for the west-facing side of the island. It was completely dark, but I knew where all the pilings would be, and took the water slowly as I crept in toward the visitors' dock, near the shore. I wrapped a rope on the front and back cleats of the boat and held onto it as I jumped onto the dock and secured the rope around a beam, keeping the boat from drifting away with the current.

Arden leaped onto the dock and grabbed the rest of the rope, helping secure it to the other end of the beam.

The low hum of an engine came from nearby, and Calista's red speedboat, her second baby and the only other flashy item she had splurged on, came into view as she cruised toward the dock. She tossed me a rope, and I tied her up. Standing bodies wobbled inside her small boat as Rheya pushed her way through.

"Watch out," Rheya called as she tossed a stuffed bag of weapons onto the dock and jumped out of the boat.

"Ugh ... I thought we'd never get out of that thing."

"Don't like boats, do you?" I teased.

"Not my first choice of travel." She pushed past me and moved to stand next to Arden.

My eyes shifted back to the boat, and to my astonishment, Jasper's parents were standing there. Calista must have contacted them.

"Mr. and Mrs. Shade. I'm so sorry I haven't called you," I blurted out. Jasper's mom climbed onto the dock and wrapped her arms around me and gave me a motherly squeeze. She pulled back and smoothed the black wisps of hair that blew into my face.

"Calista explained everything. We were already on our way home to help find your mom after we received Jasper's message about what happened. And now that witch has our son. If she's hurt one hair on my boy's head, I'll—"

"Jocelyn." A large hand rested on Mrs. Shade's shoulder. "We'll get both Jasper and Cacsha back, but we need to keep our wits about us. This is Siobhan we're dealing with."

"I know," she choked out as she held her husband's hand. "I'm worried sick about them both."

"It's all my fault," I said to them. "I never meant for Jasper to get involved. If I could trade places with him, I would."

Jasper's mom placed her finger under my chin. "It's not your fault, dear. Please don't blame yourself. You couldn't have kept Jasper from your side if you tried. And, Everly." She reached for my hand. "I want you to know that Jasper has wanted to tell you the truth since you were children. He never wanted to keep secrets from you. We forbade him to tell you. It wasn't his or our place. That decision belonged to your parents alone. I hope you can forgive him and us."

Jocelyn stared into my eyes with a pleading look. She shared the same golden-amber eye color as her son, and looking into those familiar eyes now, I knew in my heart that I had already forgiven Jasper.

"I was angry when I first learned that Jasper knew the truth, but I know why he kept it from me, and I understand. There's nothing to forgive. Jasper has always been there for me, and now I'm going to be there for him. I'll do whatever it takes to save him and my mom."

She reached out and clenched my hand. "Let's go get them back."

Jasper's mom released me and crossed the dock onto the island. She began reciting words in Vitarian and moving her hands in circular motions. Swirls of light emerged as if she were holding sparklers and swishing them through the air.

"Jocelyn, are you able to detect their portal?" Felix asked.

"It's nearly finished but not complete," Jocelyn answered, using her ability to detect portal magic. Her worried expression relaxed slightly.

We crept as a group through the sand and circled the edge of the forest until we came within view of the lighthouse. The full moon beamed brightly over the octagonal white tower, offering a natural glow of light. A handful of guards stood surveying the area from the top of the flat roof, and more circled the bottom.

We backed up around the other side of a sand dune and prepared to split off into groups to cover more ground and maintain the element of surprise.

Calista hugged me and then moved off with Selkie. I could sense their fear, even though they tried desperately to keep it bottled up tight.

Felix stood before me, his blue eyes a deep well of timeless knowledge. The first time I'd looked into them, I'd found them dizzying, but now they grounded me. "Allow your power to aid you, not control you. And you have the ring to call on the magic of your ancestors."

I nodded, even though the last thing I wanted to do was to call on Oria. If I did, she would never let me refuse her. She wanted her bloodline back on the throne of Aenoas-Vita, and that was the last place I ever intended to be.

A darkness that had nothing to do with the rotation of Earth hovered in the night. Each gust of wind seemed to cry out, hauntingly reminding us of the forthcoming loss, as if it had already been written in the fate of blood. As I watched Felix, Calista, and Selkie disappear into the black forest, I knew that this other darkness threatened to swallow us all.

Rhal, Malakai, and Jasper's parents went in the same direction as Felix and the others, while Arden and Rheya followed me. The two flanked my sides as we continued along the beach. Rheya's energy buzzed with the excitement of battle, while Arden maintained the calm of a commander. My adrenaline pumped loud and fast. I breathed deeply and released all mental shields, allowing my magic to flow freely, as I had earlier with Neil. My abilities were becoming stronger in ways I'd never known before.

Two guards stood at their post on the side of a boulder up ahead. Arden motioned to Rheya, and she crept from the fallen tree trunk that hid our shadows. She moved like a cat in the night and pounced on one guard before he even realized she was on him. Before the second guard could call out, she had her legs twisted around his neck, cutting off his windpipe.

Arden and I hurried our way to Rheya's side. A swirl of fluorescent colors lit up the air on the other side of the massive rock formation.

"Is it nearly finished?"

The energy pulses moved up and down my arms like electrical shock waves at the sound of her slithery voice.

"Not much longer, my queen."

Crouching against the boulder, I peeked around to the other side. Four guards stood around Siobhan as she glowered at a man who stood hunched in her presence. His milky-white dreadlocks stood in stark contrast to his dark attire. He looked down as the queen berated him.

"It better not be. It's taken you long enough. Your inadequacy tests my patience, Bracken. Your predecessor's fate may soon be your own."

"Yes, my queen." Bracken's voice rattled. He lifted long, slender arms, the same milky white as his hair, and continued working his spell. The fluorescent opening forming in the air grew wider as he chanted.

Siobhan directed her attention to one guard, a woman who had rubbed some kind of gold dust on her dark skin, which sparkled under the moonlight. She stood alert, awaiting her orders. "Salandra. Go see what takes my son so long. He should have been down here with the prisoners by now."

Mom ... Jasper.

Salandra turned to leave and then stopped. "He comes

now, my queen, but I do not see the woman. He brings the boy alone."

My heartbeat quickened, and I stepped out from our hiding place. Arden and Rheya followed my lead. "Sorry, Bracken, but I think you'll be disappointing your queen."

Bracken's eyes widened as he shifted his gaze from his queen to me and then to Arden and Rheya, whose deadly smile made me glad that the look wasn't aimed at me.

"You little witch. You think you can stop me with an army of three?"

Soldiers appeared from the darkness and encased their queen.

I looked toward the lighthouse, and it was true. Darion moved down the beach with only one captive. *Where is my mom?*

Jasper fell forward in the sand. "Jasp," I called out to him. His shirt showed torn lash marks and was stained with blood.

Darion looked up at me, and our eyes met. There was something in them that hadn't been there before: sorrow, regret, confusion, but not the hate I'd seen the last time he looked at me. He picked Jasper up and forced him forward.

"Where is the other prisoner, Darion?" Siobhan asked.

Darion avoided eye contact with Siobhan. "I released her, Mother."

My stomach tightened as Siobhan regarded Darion with a menacing glare.

"You released her?" Her bitter tone sent a chill down my spine. "You're proving to be more like your father every day."

Darion continued to stare down into the sand.

Siobhan nodded to Salandra. "Find the other prisoner and bring her to me." She turned back to Darion. "Look at me."

When Darion lifted his face, he looked at Siobhan differently than he had before. The desperation for her approval was gone and replaced with something else. Darion had so many emotions running through him it was hard to focus on just one, but one thing was for certain: he feared Siobhan.

She considered Darion for a moment. Her voice softened slightly when she said, "We'll deal with your insolence when we return home."

Two female guards came forward from the trees, hauling my mother, who was once again bound in chains, chains that I now knew suppressed her magic.

The guards holding my mother stopped near Darion. Even through the dirt and grime and bruises, her resemblance to Darion was apparent. Darion winced apologetically, and she stretched a chained hand out toward him. "It's okay," she whispered.

Siobhan watched their interaction with narrowed eyes. I expected her to feel anger, and she did, but there was another emotion that consumed her more than anything: jealousy. Her body shook when she said to my mom, "What is it about you that inspires such loyalty?" When she asked this, just for a moment, her aura showed a vulnerability that I hadn't seen in her before, and a sudden realization hit me. There may have been one thing she wanted more than being queen: unconditional love. But that desire was gone now. The darkness in her aura quickly snuffed out the light, and she turned her building wrath on me.

"And you." She lifted a gold-dusted arm in the air and pointed a slender finger at me. "You think you can turn my son against me? I'd sooner he be dead than allow you to warp his mind."

"Warp him against you!" I countered. "You're delusional. He's not your son. You stole him from my mother and used him against us. You killed our father—you're going to pay for everything you've done." My blood boiled with rage.

"You think I killed Creagan?" she scoffed. Her kohl-lined eyes narrowed.

"I know you did. You have nothing to lose by admitting it. Your reign is over."

The wind lifted her flaxen hair. "You are a naive child." Her voice echoed all around. "I did not kill my husband." Her words were forceful and true.

I faltered at the absolute truth in them. If Siobhan hadn't killed Creagan, who had?

She smiled at my confusion. "But I am going to kill you and your bitch mother, as I should have done all along."

Low growls came from all directions. The glowing eyes of cougars and wolves emerged from the forest, hungry for prey. My breath caught, and I took a reflexive step back as the dangerous animals encroached on us. But they were moving only toward Siobhan's people.

Malakai.

I smiled at Siobhan.

Her eyes blazed. "Kill those beasts," she commanded.

The animals leaped through the air, tearing into Siobhan's guards. Rhal's shadow forms twisted and turned as he sprang from the forest, fighting side by side with the wild animals.

"Finish the portal!" Siobhan commanded of Bracken, who had frozen with fright. He shook himself from his stupor and followed Siobhan's order.

She looked up toward the trees and chanted in Vitarian.

"She's using dark magic," Jocelyn shouted as several guards closed in on her. Wolves leaped from the ground, tearing at the guards' throats. Just as Jocelyn had a clear path to escape, a sword slashed from the side, cutting down her arm. Jasper called out to his mom as she fell to her knees. "Don't let her finish the spell!" Jocelyn shouted, but it was too late.

Black crows came rushing from the treetops and

swarmed the sky in a thick black cloud of wings. My ears rang with the sounds of echoing roars and howls as the cougars and wolves fought off the crows pecking maddeningly at their eyes. The sand quickly turned from white to red as blood sprayed from man and beast. Malakai must have lost his hold on some animals, as they fled back into their natural habitat, becoming once again a part of the unseen background of the island.

Instinct kicked in, and I lifted my arms up toward the sky. Magic surged through me, searing the tips of my fingers. I called to the wind, and a pulse of energy released from me like a cannonball being fired. A loud humming filled the air. Wind gathered around in a tornado, its magnetic force sucking the birds into its midst. I called to the trees, and more energy surged from me. It was like I was tapping into a reservoir I'd never had access to before. Leaves bustled in the night as the trees bent their trunks in reply to my command and swatted the swarm of birds out into the sky, where they flew off in different directions. My fingers curled as I sent out the silent command, and tree roots stretched through the ground, wrapping around Siobhan and binding her arms and legs.

She threw her head back and laughed. The vines began to smoke and burst into flame, disintegrating off her. "I have tricks too," she said as she held her hands in a ball formation and a swirling mass of fire formed. The flames danced and stretched, responding to each of Siobhan's movements as though following an unspoken command. She thrust her arms out, and flame shot through the air. Arden met fire with sword, deflecting the flame from me, but Rheya had been caught by a second flame. The blaze encircled her in a heated prison, licking at her skin.

"Rheya," I called out as the flames wrapped around her long, red braid.

She shook her head and closed her eyes. When she opened them, they were no longer green but ice-blue, and the shade of her skin changed into the frosty color of Arctic ice. The flames froze into solid ice formations. Rheya pulled her sword free and cut into the frozen flames, shattering their hold on her. She didn't hesitate before jumping through the air and crashing into the guards that Arden fought back from me.

Siobhan conjured more flame until the sand was a prison of fire. Jasper's cries caught my attention. He struggled against his bindings to free himself from Darion. Darion unsheathed his dagger, and my chest filled with panic, but when he brought the blade down, it cut through Jasper's ropes. Jasper thrust out his invisible shield, pushing against the flames to get to his mother. When I looked back toward my mom, Darion was fighting Siobhan's guards to get to her, but the flames were cutting into his path, making it impossible for him to free her.

I reached out my mind. *Water.*

The sound of crashing waves filled the beach behind us. I lifted my arms as Siobhan lifted hers. Magic howled from behind, above, and around us. Just as Siobhan thrust a burning blaze toward me, water rushed over our heads and snuffed out her fire in midair. I twisted my arms around, and the water separated into ribbon formations as it circled Siobhan, putting out her fire as quickly as she conjured it.

Water dripped from her hair and clothing. She bent and brought her arms up in a circle over her head and threw them toward the ground as she spoke in Vitarian, and the water fell to the sand, receding back into the river.

She smirked as she undid the whip she had tied around her waist. A growling cougar and wolf approached her on either side. Their lips peeled back, revealing sharp, long fangs. The whip lashed out back and forth, biting into the animals' skin, but they were relentless in their task. They bit at her arms and clawed at her skin, causing blood to rain from her.

I moved through the sand, closing the distance between us. The animals moved aside, allowing me to pass unharmed. When I stood face-to-face with her, I thrust out my hand and clamped it around her throat. "Who killed my father?"

Her expression changed, and I caught a momentary glimpse of sadness, but it vanished as quickly as it appeared. "I could tell you, but I'd rather you suffer with never knowing what really happened to him." She twisted her head. The guard holding my mother recognized some unspoken sign Siobhan gave her, and a golden dagger gleamed over my mother's chest. "With pleasure, my queen."

The guard's arm came down, with the point of the dagger heading directly toward my mother's heart.

"No!" I screamed as I released my hold on Siobhan and ran for my mom.

Darion spun on his heel and moved at an inhuman speed. He shoved our mother out of the way, and she fell to the ground as the dagger sank into Darion's side.

"No!" Siobhan gasped as she clutched her own side in the same place the dagger protruded from Darion.

I remembered the words from my mother's journal, about Siobhan linking herself to Darion, and I wondered if this was what she'd meant. Had she linked Darion's life to her own? Had that been how she'd forced Creagan to stay with her even after Darion was born? It was all making some kind of crazy sense. Was she so desperate to hold on to him she would put her own life in jeopardy for the sake of getting what she wanted? The answer was in front of me as blood oozed from her side, the same side where blood poured from Darion.

Rheya grabbed Siobhan by the hair and held her sword under her chin. The sharp blade cut into Siobhan's skin.

Darion yelled out and gripped his neck. His skin had turned sickeningly pale as he lost blood from his wound. I balked as a cut formed under his chin in the same place as Siobhan's.

"Stop!" I ordered.

"Why should I?" Rheya argued. "We can take care of them both once and for all."

"Not my son," my mother cried as she moved his body over hers to cradle him. "Everly, stop this madness," she commanded. "If Siobhan dies, so does my son. I can't lose him. Not again. Please do something before it's too late!"

"Let him die," Rheya called to me. "They both deserve to."

Tears flooded my mother's face as she clutched Darion's limp body.

If I let Siobhan live, then she would only wreak more havoc. But could I let Darion die with her? He'd committed unforgivable acts, but under the manipulation of Siobhan. I needed to break the link that Siobhan had with Darion. But how?

I touched Oria's ring, and a bright white light blinded my vision.

"Everly," the voice of Oria echoed in my mind. "I have the answer you seek."

How do I break the link?

"You know my terms. I will give you the spell you require only if you agree."

If I agreed to Oria's terms, then I would sacrifice myself for Darion. But after seeing my mom's response, I knew she'd never recover from his death.

"You will sacrifice more than you think if you save your brother, but you must decide now. Darion's spirit begins the transition from the living life to the next. He is running out of time."

What do you mean? How are you reading my thoughts?

"You are in the spirit realm. Your thoughts are not your own here. Dark magic makes up the curse that binds Darion to the false queen. The only way to undo it is to take the curse into yourself."

My breath caught.

Are you saying that to save Darion, I have to link my life to his?

"It's the only way I know of, and you don't have time to find another. What is your choice?" Oria's question rang in my ears.

Did I really have a choice? With a heavy heart, I agreed.

A floating ball of light moved toward my eye and touched my forehead, vanishing into my flesh, showing me a vision of what I needed to know.

I saw the scene reappear before me, with my mother arching over Darion, sobbing in misery as his body convulsed with his last breaths.

"Take the sword from her throat," I ordered Rheya.

Felix and Malakai rushed out from the trees, accompanied by Jasper's father, who had blood covering him that didn't seem to be from any injury of his own. "Felix," I called to him, and he met my stare and responded to my unspoken command. He took in the scene and hurried toward Darion as healing light emerged from his palms.

"You can't let her live." Rheya refused to budge. "She will only come back for revenge." She pressed the blade deeper into Siobhan's flesh.

"Stop her." My mom's strangled plea shook me to the core.

Without hesitating, I sent out an energy pulse that caused Rheya to double over in pain and drop her sword. She scooted away from Siobhan's convulsing body and snatched her sword. As she lifted herself back to her feet, she said, "Don't say I didn't warn you." She slammed her sword into its sheath and stalked off. There was more to her anger than wounded pride, but I didn't have time to worry about what it was.

I pointed to Siobhan. "Bind her and bring her to me." Arden and Rhal moved without question and bound Siobhan in the chains they removed from my mother.

Arden lifted Siobhan and carried her weak form, then laid her at my feet, next to Darion.

Felix removed the dagger from Darion's side and continued to work his healing magic. As Darion's color improved, so did Siobhan's.

I placed one hand on Darion's heart, and one on Siobhan's, as Oria had shown me in the vision. *I'm ready.* When the white light appeared before me, I stood in its clouded mist. The auras of my ancestors emerged from the ether and disappeared inside me. One by one, the auras entered me, filling me temporarily with their knowledge and power. Their words flowed from me in Vitarian as though my tongue had always known the language. The spell linking Siobhan and Darion unraveled as the dark magic moved out of Siobhan and into me. I felt the weight of the spell as soon as it finished.

"What have you done?" Jasper fell before me, grabbing both of my shoulders. "He'll use this against you the second he gets the chance. You can't do this, Ev."

"It's done, Jasp." I held my hand over my heart, its beat now weighted with the curse.

"Why? He doesn't deserve your mercy."

I met Jasper's amber eyes with stern resolve. "He cut you loose, Jasper. He was willing to sacrifice his life to save our mother. I'm giving him back what Siobhan took from him:

his life and a second chance." I meant this as a final statement to all surrounding me.

A pressure tightened around my hand. I looked down to find Darion's hand wrapped atop mine.

"Everly." My mother held my other hand. "I'm so sorry."

"Darion is free of her now, Mom."

Tears ran down her cheeks, and I knew she struggled between feeling sad about the responsibility I had taken upon myself and feeling relieved that her son was finally free from the woman who had stolen him.

∾

*F*elix made rounds, healing the most pressing wounds of our group. I urged him to rest when I noticed the healing taking a toll on him.

Once Jocelyn's arm was healed, he agreed and asked her to finish the portal that Bracken had abandoned. He'd sent a message to Torin, who was waiting to come through with reinforcements.

When Jocelyn finished, she made the portal large enough to walk through. The black hole swirled in the air, surrounded by a golden ring of stars. Its center had a watery appearance. Light flickered throughout, and a form materialized within the watery substance. Like walking through water, Torin emerged from the portal, followed by several guards. His long silver hair, intricately twisted into sections and braided together, cascaded down his back. He held the same tall staff, its polished wood gleaming in the moonlight.

The guards acknowledged Arden and greeted him in their customary fashion, speaking to him in their native language. They began culling Siobhan's defeated ensemble.

Torin joined Felix. "I received your message," he said in a deep and authoritative voice.

"I do not wish to delay my departure. Two trips in such a short time. I am too old to endure the effects of this planet for long." He looked around our group, his eyes settling on my mother momentarily and then finding my own.

"This is to be our young queen." His eyes swept me from head to toe, probably searching for queenly characteristics that I didn't possess. "The council is now aware of your rightful place and the unimaginable suffering your mother endured. You can be confident that we will take care of the situation."

"I am your queen. Torin, you will follow my orders or I will remove you from your seat in the council," Siobhan declared.

His gaze moved to Siobhan, raking over her. And I wouldn't have believed it myself if I hadn't just seen her recoil with fear.

He turned back to my mother. "You will oversee the execution of this woman." He glanced back at Siobhan. "You have no more power over the council. Your family will not aid you. They received an ultimatum and, unsurprisingly, chose themselves, as your clan tends to do." Siobhan struggled with her bindings, to no avail.

My mom stood and smoothed her rumpled clothing. "You honor me, Councilman Torin, but with deepest sadness, I will not return to Aenoas-Vita without my beloved Creagan. I shall remain on this planet with my children, but I have one request."

He nodded for my mother to continue.

"This woman took everything from me: my home, my son, and my love. Death would be too good a punishment for her. I ask that she be stripped of all of her magic and confined to the royal dungeon, where she will spend the rest of her days knowing we have overcome all she has done to us."

Torin paused, considering the request put to him. "You show too much mercy," he said dispassionately. "Her fate is yours to decide." He looked at me, offering me an opportunity to prove myself worthy of his respect.

My mom was right. Death was too good a punishment for Siobhan. She deserved to suffer for the pain she had caused. "I agree with my mother. Stripping Siobhan of her magic and imprisoning her is the only solution."

"You little witch. I'll kill you." Siobhan scrambled up and attempted to run at me.

The councilman lifted his hand, and Siobhan sprang up into the air, grasping at her throat for breath. Her flaxen hair flailed around her head as she struggled. He closed his hand, and she fell back to the ground.

"We will return home," Torin said, "where we will publicly strip Siobhan of her powers." Then he turned his attention to Arden, giving him instructions I couldn't understand.

"Everly." My mother's agonized expression tore at me.

"It's okay, Mom. I'm not going anywhere."

Torin faced me. The gold thread decorating his silver-hooded robe shimmered under the swirl of light he cast from his staff.

A commotion near the trees drew our attention. Two wolves had crept out of the forest, trying to make away with one of Siobhan's fallen soldiers. They growled when anyone attempted to take their prize.

Malakai approached the animals. He paused, and after a few moments, the wolves dropped the body and turned back into the forest.

"You were saying?" Torin asked.

I straightened my back. "I will not return with you. Not until I'm ready."

He nodded. "If that is your decision, but before I depart

with the prisoner, you must perform the extraction ritual of absorbing Siobhan's powers from her."

"What?" I cried. "Why me?" I knew that to take another's powers, you had to drink their blood, and the idea of drinking Siobhan's or anyone else's blood was appalling. "I will not drink her blood. Someone else has to perform this ritual."

His mouth twitched in a half grin as though I amused him. "Felix tells me you can siphon magic as Oria could. While you wear your ancestors' ring"—he glanced down at my hand—"you have access to their powers if they grant it from the other side, as I presume they did to aid you in taking the curse Siobhan cast on your brother. Their power combined with your own will give you enough to take another's magic without the vile act of drinking blood. Oria performed this very act on her brother, Orien, as a punishment for his crimes, before she left us."

I stiffened as Torin moved closer to me. His aura was a mirage of color. "You are not familiar with our ways," he said patiently, easing my tension slightly. "As the next queen, it is your duty to perform this task you have commanded. Would you like to reconsider the execution?"

I dreaded calling on Oria again, but if it meant avoiding drinking blood, I'd do it.

"Wait." My eyebrows shot up. "If I absorb her magic, then it becomes my own. I don't want any part of Siobhan inside me." Dark energy consumed Siobhan, and I wanted no part of that.

A wave crashed onto the beach, spraying a soft mist of water onto my skin.

"I can't hold the portal open much longer," Jocelyn informed us. Her energy was weak, and I knew I had to act quickly.

Torin's forehead furrowed and his jaw clenched. He

didn't enjoy prolonging his departure. "If you don't wish to return to Aenoas-Vita at this time, you must perform the ritual here and now. As first councilman, it's my duty to stand as witness, but I grow impatient." His ancient features creased into a slight scowl.

I looked at my mother and Darion, and then over to Jasper and the others. *My life is slipping farther away.*

"Let's get this over with."

Siobhan recoiled at my approach. "I can help you find who killed Creagan. If you let me keep my magic, I swear I'll help you."

"Who killed my father?" It was Darion who spoke. He scowled down at Siobhan with a twisted mixture of hate and love.

"Darion. Son. Please don't let them do this to me." Siobhan clasped her hands together, pleading.

"I'm not your son." His words were cold and final.

"If you know who killed our father," I said to her, "tell me now, and I'll reconsider your punishment."

She backed up in the sand. "I ... I don't know who did it, but Creagan was meeting someone at that club run by that little weasel, Neil. He'd been searching for a way to break the linking spell. That's all I know."

She was telling the truth. But it wasn't enough to save her from her fate.

I knelt down over her and stared into dark eyes. "This is for everything you did to my family." I grabbed hold of her arm.

She tried to pull away. "Darion, please. I'm your mother. Who took care of you when Creagan wasn't there? It was always me."

Darion turned from Siobhan, and she shouted after him. "You were never my son. I never loved you. How could I when all I saw was *her* every time I looked at you?" Darion kept walking without turning back and went to stand next to our mother, helping hold her steady from exhaustion.

"I hope whoever killed Creagan comes for you next," Siobhan hissed, and spit on me.

I wiped her spit from my cheek and took hold of her other arm as she continued to struggle. I didn't have to call out to Oria for help. The magic of the ancestors flowed through me unbidden. By taking Siobhan's magic, I fulfilled part of my promise to Oria by removing the woman she referred to as the false queen from power. My body buzzed as Siobhan's magic transferred from her to me. It slithered in my veins like a serpent on the hunt for its next meal. Siobhan finally stopped struggling as her power left her, and her dark eyes lost their vitality. Her hair dulled as her skin turned ashen. She stared at nothing as her body went limp on the ground. Depleted of her magic, she had no fight left in her.

I had no idea what it would mean, having Siobhan's powers, but her magic was a foreign entity writhing within me. I stood and left her in the sand without a glance back.

When I got to my mom, I fell into her arms, finally able to appreciate that I had her back.

"Commander, if you will," the councilman said to Arden, who picked a defeated Siobhan up and carried her to the portal behind the councilman, followed by Malakai, Rhal, and Rheya. The guards Torin had brought through had already cleaned up the fallen bodies and taken any survivors back through the portal.

Arden stopped for a moment at the edge of the portal, his eyes locking with mine. The green in his eyes burned through the blue. I wanted to run to him and feel his arms wrap around me, but this wasn't the time. I smiled and mouthed, "Thank you," and then he followed the others into the portal, where they all disappeared to an unseen world, a place that I would one day also depart this world, *my home,* for.

～

he door clicked softly behind me as I pressed it closed. My mom's face was so peaceful as she lay sleeping on the bed in Felix's spare room that, since our arrival, had become the official room for the wounded. She'd slept through the night and the next day. I breathed a sigh of relief now that the color of her skin was once again vibrant and had lost the sickly ashen hue it'd taken on.

Sitting carefully on the bed, I slid my hand under hers. I'd come too close to losing her. My fingers stroked her thick raven hair, and the scent of lavender filled the air. Calista had brought my mom's favorite shampoo when we'd gotten back to the cabin for Felix to heal her, and she'd helped wash my mom's hair while she'd soaked in a much-needed hot bath.

My mom stirred, and her eyes fluttered as my hand smoothed her hair over the pillow. "Hey, sweetie." She smiled her motherly smile.

"Hi, Mom. How are you feeling?"

"My body is as good as new, but so much sadness fills my heart. If it weren't for you and the return of your brother, I wouldn't be able to bear the loss of your father. It breaks my heart that he never got the chance to see your brother freed from that woman. I miss him so much." She pushed herself up against the pillows.

"I'm going to find out what happened to him, Mom, and I'm going to make whoever took his life pay for what they did."

She inhaled sharply and adjusted herself. "Everly, please don't put yourself in any more danger. Creagan wouldn't want that, and I need you to stay safe. Please," she pleaded, and shook her head.

I didn't want to argue or worry her further, so I kept quiet. She didn't need to know my plans.

She exhaled. "I'm so sorry I never told you the truth while your father was alive. You had the right to know, and I'll never be able to forgive myself for taking away your time with him. I deeply regret my choices. I'm so grateful to you for everything you've done." She lifted my hand and smoothed it against her cheek. "You are a remarkable person and have sacrificed so much. Your father would be so proud of you." She kissed the back of my hand. "I finally have both of my children. It will take time with Darion, but thanks to you, I now have the chance to be his mother."

It was hard enough to think about Darion as anything other than a threat, and even harder to think of him as a part of our family. "Mom. After everything Darion did to you, Selkie, and Jasper, how can you just forgive him? I mean, I know Siobhan was using him, but he still committed those acts."

She sat up further and leaned her back against the wall, then indicated for me to do the same.

"Your brother—" She paused when she saw me scrunch up my face.

"I'm sorry, Mom, but I'm just not ready to refer to Darion as my brother. It's going to take me a lot longer to forgive him. Maybe forever."

She put her arm behind my head and lowered it to her shoulder the way she'd done since I was little.

"I understand," she said, brushing her fingers through my hair. "Darion made terrible choices, but he wants to atone for them. He's my son, and I want to help him change, if he'll let me."

Her hopeful expression made it impossible for me to disagree with her.

"Where will Darion stay? On Earth?"

Her energy jittered. "If it's okay with you, I'd like Darion to remain on this planet, and I want to offer him one of the apartments above the café. I haven't had time to rent out the one Stephanie moved out of when she relocated to Portland. He'll be right above the café, and I'll get to see him every day, and I was thinking …" She paused and looked down at me cautiously.

"What is it, Mom?"

"I was thinking of offering him a job at the café. I could teach him everything I know about herbs and show him how gratifying it is to help people with our magic instead of using it to harm them."

I barked out a laugh at the thought of Darion in an apron, waiting on customers, but the laughter died on my lips as I felt my mom's energy plummet. Her face fell at my reaction, and her eyes lost their excited glow.

"I'm sorry, Mom. I just have a hard time imagining Darion waiting tables. Plus, I don't know if I'd trust him around our customers."

My mom sat silent. My heart twisted seeing her so downcast when she'd been so excited just moments ago. I quickly tried to repair the damage I'd caused. "But—if it means that much to you—ask him. If it will make you happy, then I'm good with it."

Going along with my mom's plan would serve multiple purposes, but I didn't need to mention that part. Since my life was now linked to Darion's, having him nearby would allow me to monitor him closely, which made my mom's plan the ideal choice. And I could question him about Siobhan's magic and find out if he knew anything useful that could help me.

Her eyes filled with tears. "You truly are an amazing daughter. I'm the luckiest mom of all the planets, you know." She squeezed my shoulders. "I love you infinity times infinity infinities."

I smiled brightly at her. Her odd comment about being the luckiest mom of all the planets finally made sense.

"I love you infinity times infinity infinities too, Mom. And I'm the luckiest daughter of all the planets," I replied, wondering just how many other planets out there had life like ours.

She wiped away the tear that had escaped and beamed at me.

I took a deep breath. "Mom, there's something I need to talk to you about."

"What is it, honey?" Her head rested against mine.

"I've made a deal with Oria."

CHAPTER 13

I packed my car with the necessities. Darion stood waiting for me in the carport. There was a noticeable vulnerability emanating from him as he stood with his hands in the back pockets of his jeans. He was unsure of himself and his place on this planet and in his new life. He'd been in the apartment above the café for a few weeks now, and helping at the café, but the change of lifestyle had been difficult for him, though I had to admit, he really was trying.

"I should go with you," he said, handing me my bag.

"No," I replied, tossing my bag into the trunk of my car. "I'll only be gone a few days, and I need you here to cover my shifts at the café. If we both take off, Mom will get suspicious, and I don't want her to know that I'm following another lead. She's worried I'll get hurt, but I can't just stop looking." Taking a cautious look at the house, I scanned the back door, ensuring my mom wasn't on the verge of stepping outside. I shifted my attention to Darion, speaking in a low, confidential voice. "I need to know what happened to Creagan. We all do. Now, do you remember the story?"

Darion rolled his eyes and waved his arms as he said,

"You're going to some energy mumbo jumbo seminar run by humans who know nothing about real magic or energy healing. And"—he widened his silver-gray eyes—"you know she's going to see right through me. She's the only person I've never been able to lie to successfully."

I huffed at his dramatic flair. "It's not mumbo jumbo, Darion. It's called Pranic Healing. And you're not technically going to be lying to her. I am going to the seminar, just not until after I follow up on a lead I got from Neil."

Darion narrowed his eyes. "Can you really trust him? After all, his club was where our father was last seen alive."

"Are you seriously questioning me about trust?" I shook my head. "And yes, I trust Neil. He's been doing everything he can to help figure out what Creagan was doing there that night and who he was meeting."

The sound of a motorcycle revved up the driveway.

"Looks like one of your suitors has arrived," Darion teased with a grin.

"Darion! I told you before that my personal life is not up for discussion."

"I know, I know. I'm sorry, but I couldn't resist," Darion said when I glared at him. "Well ..." He stepped forward, and I took a quick step back, instinctively.

He tried to hide the disappointment he felt by drawing up his wall, but his face betrayed his feelings. In the last few weeks since Darion had been unlinked from Siobhan, the mask he had constructed to show no emotion had cracked and kept peeling away. Spending time with our mother had brought out another side of him that I didn't think even he knew was there.

"Look, Darion, I'm sorry, but it's going to take time for me after everything."

He stared down at his feet, kicking at a pebble.

"You have my cell number. Call me if anything comes up. I'll be back by Monday."

He nodded, and we looked at each other with an unspoken understanding before he walked back into the house, the back-porch door swinging shut behind him.

I turned and met Jasper in the driveway. His dark-cocoa locks spilled out of his helmet as he pulled it off. "Hey, Ev."

My stomach tightened. Things had been awkward between us since we'd had "the talk."

"Hey, Jasp." He climbed off his bike, then closed the distance between us in two quick strides and wrapped me in his arms.

"Are you sure you don't want me to come with you?"

My heartbeat sped up with the familiar anxiety I'd been getting every time Jasper brought up spending any alone time together. He still felt hurt over my feelings for Arden. We'd both forgiven each other, but things still hadn't gotten back to normal between us.

"Jasper …" I pulled back. "As much as I would love your company, I need you here keeping an eye on things."

He glanced away, out toward the cluster of trees. Unlike Darion, Jasper had never been good at masking his emotions, and I knew he sensed my recent avoidance. "Don't worry. I'll stay in your apartment, as promised, and stick to your mom like glue. But she's going to know something is up."

Retrieving a pamphlet from my trunk, I offered it to him. "I told her I'm going to this seminar, which I am on my way home. I'm sure she'll guess that I asked you to stay here to monitor Darion when he's around, and I'm fine with that, because that's exactly my intention."

Jasper took the pamphlet and set it back in the trunk. "I don't like you chasing down these leads alone. You're putting yourself in danger."

With a deep breath, I reminded myself that Jasper was my

shield. He was overprotective by nature, and magic had etched it into his DNA. "I'll be fine. I rested my hand on his shoulder. It'll probably be another bust, anyway, just like every other lead I've found so far. But I'm not giving up until I find out what happened to Creagan."

His jaw tightened in the stubborn way that it did when he didn't want to accept something. "I guess some things haven't changed." He walked away.

My chest ached, and I fought back a hot tear. Jasper was struggling with my decision about our relationship. He still wanted more than I could give him. But deep down, I knew it wouldn't be fair to either of us or our friendship when my heart yearned for someone else.

I closed the trunk and followed Jasper to the wooden bench that looked out over the garden and forest. He ran his hand over the worn carvings of our names that we'd cut into the wood so many years ago.

"It seems like so long ago that we engraved our names here, and yet it also feels like just yesterday. Things were so much simpler then, huh?"

"Yeah. In a way, it seems like someone else's life." I tore my gaze from the faded letters and turned my head into the breeze. The tops of the trees lining the property swayed and rustled as a gust of wind swept through. I shivered and zipped my sweater up and tucked my hands into the sleeves. The clouds were darkening, and a thick moisture was building in the air. A storm was moving in.

Jasper looked up at the stirring clouds and then closed his eyes. When he glanced back at me, it was with a saddened acceptance. He smiled half-heartedly. "I wish you'd let me help you."

I smiled. "You've always been here for me, Jasp. And you're helping me by staying here while I'm gone."

"Don't worry." His expression darkened. "I'll keep a

watchful eye on Darion. He may be your twin brother, but he's a completely different pedigree, and I don't trust him, no matter how much he convinces anyone else that he's changing."

I squeezed his hand. It was understandable that Jasper was taking a tough stance with Darion, given the circumstances. I felt the same way about him, which was why I wasn't leaving my mom alone with him, even for a couple of days.

"Walk me to my car?"

Jasper closed my driver's side door and pressed his hand against the glass. I touched the other side, then watched our handprints fade as I put my car in gear, and turned out of the driveway.

While I was driving towards the highway, I saw someone I would recognize anywhere coming out from the side of the road lined with trees. I slowed my speed and pulled over, then got out of my car. I'd asked Neil to get a message to Arden for me, and he'd come through like always.

My stomach sat heavy with knots as he moved toward me. I hadn't seen him since the night he'd left in the portal, and all I could think of was the feeling of his lips on mine.

"Thanks for coming."

"You asked for my help, and I told you I'd always give it." His eyes studied my lips as we instinctively moved closer together.

"I know—" was all I got out before his lips were on mine. His kiss was hot and full of passion. His tongue found mine, and our mouths moved together hungrily. My body melted into his, and a feverish heat moved through me. I wrapped my arms around him, and he lifted my legs up around his waist and pressed me into him. I ran my hands through his soft hair as his kiss moved from my mouth, down my neck, and he backed us up toward the trees.

"Arden," I uttered. I knew if I didn't stop now, I never would. As good as it felt being in his arms, it wasn't the time.

"Hmm." His tongue traveled up my breastbone, neck, and chin. "You're all I've thought about for weeks. The sweet smell of your skin. The soft touch of your lips on mine. I can't get you out of my head, no matter how hard I try."

His kiss was eager for more, but he sensed my hesitation and immediately pulled back. The familiar green of his eyes had nearly shaded over the blue. "I didn't intend to do that. I'm sorry."

I shuffled my feet as I caught my breath. "I want to be with you. But with everything …" I ran my hand through my hair, fumbling to find the right words. "With my mom, Darion, and searching for Creagan's killer. The timing's just not right. Your life and duty are on Aenoas-Vita, and mine is here. At least for now."

The heat of Arden's desire cooled, leaving behind a distant look of yearning in his eyes. "I understand. Take all the time you need. I'll be here when you're ready." He placed a soft kiss on my lips that made me reconsider everything I'd just said. With a knowing grin, his mouth curled up at the corners. "So …"

"Right." I shook myself from the daze of his kiss, then took the key out of my back pocket and handed it to him. "It's unit A, and it's just down the hall from Darion's apartment. Someone has rented it, but the new tenants don't move in until next month. The painters and cleaners have already finished their work, so no one will come in." I chewed on my lower lip.

Arden took the key and slid it into his pocket as he climbed into the passenger seat.

The tension eased as we drove down the highway.

"I'm sorry to ask you to play private detective, but I need as many sets of eyes on Darion as I can get while I'm gone.

Neil will send in some friends to the café to pose as customers over the next few days."

Arden peered over at me with approval. "You've thought of everything. You're strategic, just as a queen should be. And you have nothing to apologize for. If Darion steps out of line, I'll be there."

~

*A*fter I dropped Arden off at the apartment above the café, I headed to my last stop.

"Everly," Neil greeted me at the entrance of his club. "Your presence always brightens my day." His smile was warm and genuine, easing some of my tension.

Music filled the building as usual, and I realized I'd never seen the club closed, no matter the time of day.

"Hi, Neil." My lips lifted into an easy smile. My body naturally relaxed around Neil's easygoing nature and calm energy.

"Live band tonight? They sound amazing."

"Oh, yes. One of my favorites. Cost me an arm and a leg, though, to get them to portal to this planet. They don't like to leave their own galaxy."

Laughter echoed on the other side of the curtain, and I peeked my head through to check out the scene. My eyes widened when they landed on the musicians.

"Those people look nothing like Vitarians."

Neil smiled wickedly. "Nope, not Vitarian. They're from an entirely different planet. So much for you to learn, my dear." He looped his arm through mine and walked me over to the front desk. "I have everything you asked for." He retrieved a packet from behind the desk and handed it to me. "Just ask for Lucas when you get there. We have everything lined up."

"I can't thank you enough. You've been such a major help in more ways than one."

His face filled with a radiant smile. "It has been my great honor to be of service to you. I look forward to your return, but in the meantime, have safe travels, and I hope this helps find the answer to who Creagan met with. He went through a lot of trouble to keep the identity of this mysterious person a secret. I worry about your safety."

"You're not the first person to tell me that, but I promise I'll be fine, Neil. Besides—you've already insisted on this Lucas chaperoning me the entire time."

Neil's mouth quirked mischievously. "He knows the town well. I think you'll find him good company."

His eyes widened in surprise as I pulled him into a hug. "You're a good friend." I squeezed him tightly.

"Thank you." His cheeks brightened at my gesture.

I tucked the yellow envelope under my arm and headed for the exit.

"Oh—and one more thing."

I stopped and turned back at Neil's words.

"Lucas is currently single and quite the catch." He winked.

"Oh, hilarious." I pushed open the door and called over my shoulder, "I don't need any more of that in my life right now."

When I got inside my car, I dumped the contents of the envelope on my lap. Neil had included a passport with a fake name and birth date so I could investigate without giving anyone my real name. I stuffed the passport back in the envelope and flipped through the names of locations and pictures taken from security cameras from places where Creagan had met with a hooded figure. The mysterious figure always kept their face aimed away from any camera in the room.

"Who are you?" My finger slid across the hidden face in

the photo. "What am I missing? And why was Creagan secretly meeting with you?"

I placed the envelope and its contents on the passenger seat and drove into the mounting storm.

Creagan's killer is out there, and I will not rest until I find him.

THANK YOU

Thank you for reading Fate of Blood. I hope you enjoyed it. Help other people find this book by visiting S.L.'s website and writing a review at slwatsonauthor.com.

While you're there, check out some of S.L.'s hand crafted book inspired goodies like fabric book covers, book marks and bundle deals available for purchase and sign up for her newsletter to receive great discounts and special offers. Have a great day!

Everly's journey continues in Last Descendants (Vitarian Chronicles Volume 2)
Read on for more …

I post occasional exclusive updates on:
Facebook: https://www.facebook.com/slwatsonauthor/
Instagram: https://instagram.com/slwatsonauthor/

LAST DESCENDANTS SAMPLE
CHAPTER 1

As the students settled into their Nadi Shodhana, I held the burning sage high while I circled the room, contacting each unique energy field. The pungent smoke filled my nostrils and clung to my skin as sweat trickled down my body. Deep exhalations of expelled energy whirled, forming into dark shapes. The more toxic the energy, the more hostile it became once outside the body. The energy hovered above, struggling to reconnect with its hosts, but its attempts were useless now that it was trapped in my protected space.

I continued to circle the room, weaving the earthy smoke into the air. There were always one or two students in every class who couldn't release the soul-draining energy that leeched off them, and they needed extra assistance. I sensed this resistance now as I stopped in front of a shaking young woman. Her aura was dim and webbed with black tendrils. A whimper escaped her lips as she sat in her pose, unable to free herself. Heat burned in my stomach. This darkness had leeched off the poor girl for so long that it'd tangled her aura into a knotted mess.

"Very good," I called out to the class. "Continue to let the energy flow through you with each exhalation." I bent down near the shaking student and placed my hand on her back and corrected her spine upright from her hunched position. "It's okay," I told her. "Just let it out." I closed my eyes and drew the heavy darkness from her as I stood. It resisted, but its fight was futile against my power.

The young woman stopped shaking as her body relaxed into the pose, and her aura immediately brightened. Silent tears slid down her cheeks as I moved away to give her space. It was time to cleanse the rest of the room of the hot energy soaring above the group.

"Now, on your next exhalation, allow any remaining toxic or negative feelings to flow away from you. Feel the energy traveling down your arms and flowing out through your fingertips. Once you've done this, place your palms flat against your heart and imagine a bright protective light shielding you."

I set the burning sage onto a plate and headed to the back of the room. The air became dense and nearly tangible with dark, menacing tendrils that swarmed together to resist my power. One by one, I drew each tendril from the swarm and into my own biofield, where the energy dissipated upon contact.

Exhaustion settled over me as relieved sighs mingled with tears spread across the room. The group had no idea what I'd just done; they only sensed they'd suddenly been released from the burden of something toxic and heavy weighing on them. It was normal for pent-up emotions to follow the expulsion of dark energy.

"Now, gently lower your hands and elbows onto the mat, and push back into Child's Pose, stretching your arms and fingertips out in front of you, and resting your forehead on the floor. As your hips relax down toward the—"

Before I could finish, the door to the studio swung open,

and a blast of cold air hit the room. I glanced to see who'd ignored the Hot Yoga in Session sign hanging on the door.

"Oh, wow! Did I interrupt? Phew! The smell in here could rival a boys' sweaty gym locker room." The intruder waved her hand across her nose.

I swallowed my irritation and pasted a friendly smile on my face. "We're just finishing up our session. I'll be right with you."

She quirked her eyebrow like she wasn't used to being dismissed, and smoothed her flat-ironed platinum hair. The humidity in the room was causing it to frizz.

That's what she gets for ignoring the sign.

My gaze landed on the basket dangling at her side. I recognized it as the one I'd packed with my homemade candles, tea, and honey, and left with the front-desk attendant of the new yoga studio across the street. Was this the new owner of the studio? And why was she carrying the gift I'd left her?

I shrugged away my curiosity for now and turned my attention back to the class. "On your next inhalation, slowly push yourself up and come to standing. Take a deep breath as you lift your arms over your head and release into prayer. Namaste."

"Thank you, Everly," said the students in unison.

The haughty girl stood giving me dagger eyes as I walked around the room answering individual questions. She definitely wasn't used to being made to wait.

I smiled inwardly at her obvious annoyance as I meandered my way toward her.

Molly marched to my side, flicking her sweaty ponytail just as we reached the girl.

"You didn't see the Do Not Disturb sign before you barged in, interrupting our class?" Molly demanded before I could get out a word.

"I must have missed it." The girl brushed at her arm as if wiping away something offensive.

"Mm—hmm," Molly hummed.

I gave Molly an appreciative wink and interjected before any claws were bared. "I'm sorry. Is there something I can help you with?"

Her green eyes raked me over. "You're Everly?" The girl lifted the basket and set it on the front desk, next to us.

I nodded. "You must be Bree. I see you got my welcome package." I smiled.

She didn't return the gesture. "I won't be using these things, so I'm returning them."

"Oh, okay," I responded, taken aback. *How odd.*

"See you tomorrow, Everly." Some of the students waved as they stacked their yoga mats and headed out of the front door.

I waved back, then turned my attention back to Bree, giving her a more thorough look-over. Her clothes were likely designer by the look of the finely tailored threads, and the glossy, pointed red stilettos she wore begged to catch an eye. I wondered what had brought someone like her to our rural town of St. Helens, Oregon. She looked to be in her early twenties, maybe a year or two older than Molly and me. But where we preferred hanging out at my mom's café, drinking tea and chatting about books and recipes, Bree had the air of someone who preferred big-city life and night-clubs. Yet she had opened a yoga studio here. Why?

"You're returning a gift?" Molly stepped in, her tone peeved.

"Who's returning a gift?" Darion asked, coming up behind Bree and positioning himself next to Molly.

Bree's eyes widened and then turned calculating as she took Darion in. "I'm Bree." She extended her hand. Her tone flipped a complete one-eighty when she addressed Darion.

"Pleasure." Darion gently took her hand and then released it quickly. He'd been trying hard this last year to get past his distaste of common human gestures. Handshaking was one of them. Most Vitarians weren't fond of the hand-to-hand greeting.

Molly narrowed her eyes at Bree. "Bree here is returning the welcome gift that Everly gave her."

Darion glanced at the basket. He reached in and pulled out the candle I'd made, and popped the lid off. "Hmm …" He breathed in deeply. "Patchouli and lavender. My sister makes the finest candles in town." He peered into the basket. "And is that your baby's breath honey?" He plucked the jar out.

Bree watched Darion hungrily. "There must have been a misunderstanding. I was actually bringing the basket over to thank Everly," Bree backstepped. "I love candles and honey." She smiled only at Darion.

Molly huffed. "You said you weren't going to be using them and were returning them." She stomped her foot.

"Back off," Bree hissed at Molly, edging closer to Darion and slipping the candle and jar of honey out of his hands and into hers. "Maybe you'd like to come over to my studio and share the basket with me?" Her teeth grazed her bottom lip. "I'll put together a cheese plate to pair with the honey." Her unnaturally long lashes fluttered as her eyelids drooped with hidden meaning.

"Studio?" Darion's brow quirked with curiosity.

Molly's face fell when Darion didn't move away from Bree, but he seemed entertained by her invitation. Unable to resist an opening for a snarky retort, Molly added, "Bree's the owner of the new yoga studio across the street, Bree's Yoga. You know, like the smelly cheese."

I stifled a giggle while Bree rolled her eyes.

"Actually," Bree said. Her tone had pitched up an octave.

"It's B-r-e-e, as in a hot summer breeze." She trailed her finger across Darion's arm.

He watched her hand skim his skin without a hint of emotion, while Molly's face flushed the color of a fire truck.

Heat flared inside me, and before I could rein it in, the jar of honey cracked open, and honey oozed out all over Bree's hand and dripped down onto the hardwood floor.

Bree screeched and dropped the jar and candle to the floor. Shards of glass and globs of honey scattered at our feet. "What did you put in that honey?" Bree demanded.

"We'll grab some towels," said a student who'd been locking up her equipment in one of the personal lockers I had for rent. Another student came running over with the broom and started sweeping the glass into a pile.

I folded my arms to hide the tremble that had taken hold. I couldn't think of what to say and just stared at the broken glass on the floor. Luckily, Molly was quick to reply to Bree's accusation. "You probably cracked the glass, the way you swung the basket up on the counter."

"Whatever," Bree snapped. "Just fetch me something to get this sticky mess off."

"I'm so sorry," I muttered. "I'll grab you some wet towels." I spun away and ran to grab some fresh towels from the supplies shelf.

Darion followed me to the sink. "I saw the look in your eye," he whispered in my ear. "It's Siobhan's magic. You need to learn to use it instead of stuffing it away. You could've injured her."

"Oh, look who's talking," I whispered back. "I have it under control, Darion."

"I can see that," he taunted. "And all this dark energy you're siphoning from your students every day isn't doing you any favors."

I turned on the faucet and stuffed the towels under the

tepid water. "Drop it, Darion. It won't happen again. And I'm helping people with what I do here."

His mouth quirked up into his usual sly grin. "Okay, sister, but don't say I didn't warn you."

Fire burned in my chest, and water sprayed upward from the faucet unnaturally. I huffed in exasperation.

Darion didn't say a word, but the look on his face gave away his thoughts. He raised an eyebrow and strolled away as though nothing out of the ordinary had just happened.

"Here." I handed Bree the warm towels.

She didn't say thanks.

"So, what's the name of your studio mean?" she asked as she wiped at her hands and eyed the students who'd helped clean up the broken glass and spilled honey.

The unfriendly glares she was giving people weren't going to help her business. If she planned to have anyone signing up for her classes in this town, she'd need a warmer approach, but I doubted any advice from me would be welcome, or from anyone else she considered gum under her heel.

I kept my other thoughts to myself and just answered her question. "Pranayama," I said. "It means 'extension of life force.'"

Molly clicked her tongue. "Pranayama is a type of yoga that focuses on breath work. How can you not know that if you're a yoga instructor?"

Molly made a good point. I let my guard down and scanned Bree's energy as she answered.

Bree glared at Molly. "My studio is a more modern version of today's yoga."

Her responses were snotty, and her vibes capricious, and without a doubt volatile. But I didn't pick up any indicator she wasn't telling the truth.

Molly placed her hand on her hip. "*Modern*? Have you ever even practiced yoga?"

"Okay." Darion stepped in. "Molls, let's go get that breakfast we talked about." He pulled Molly in by the waist, and she gave Bree a hot smile as she sauntered off with Darion.

"So, are those two, like, a thing or something?" Bree asked me, glancing one last time at Darion.

I watched Molly and Darion make their way out to the street, arm in arm, and wondered the same question.

"Or something," I mumbled, not sure myself what was going on between Darion and Molly these days. They'd been spending more and more time together over the last year and seemed to have grown close, but neither one would admit to being more than friends.

A familiar bark drew my attention back toward the door, which had been left propped open. Luna came catapulting in and slid across the floor. She barely came to a halt as she jumped up and licked my face. I laughed and held her paws as I guided her back down onto all fours. My entire body relaxed in Luna's presence.

"Oh my God!" Bree stumbled back. "Where did that beast come from?"

I struggled to keep a straight face, looking at the expression Bree had plastered on hers. You'd think a dragon had just burst into the room spitting fire, instead of a boisterous dog.

"Bree, this is my German shepherd, Luna."

Luna regarded Bree skeptically but offered her a warm welcome by bouncing over and licking Bree's hand. She must have smelled the scent of sweet honey on Bree's fingers. She sat and looked up at Bree with her big brown eyes and goofy dog smile.

For a flicker of a second, it looked like Bree might reach out and pet Luna, but then she seemed to rein in her softening expression and returned to her cool countenance with a tone to match.

"You let animals in your studio?" She scrunched up her face at Luna and took a step back, folding her arms across her chest.

Luna ignored Bree's unfriendly demeanor as she pranced back toward the door and cheerfully yelped.

"Luna isn't just any animal. Are you, girl?" Jasper walked into view and bent down, giving Luna a good full-body scratching while Luna's leash dangled over his shoulder.

Bree's eyes trailed over his long body as he stood and ran his hand through his dark-cocoa waves.

I didn't miss the way her eyes lingered on his biceps before she finally drew her attention upward.

Luna licked Jasper's hand and darted toward the few remaining students, who always stayed after class to help clean up the supplies for the next class.

"I haven't seen you before," Jasper said to Bree. "Are you a new student?"

Bree's cheeks brightened with a hint of crimson. "I'm Bree" was all she said, and she coughed to clear her throat. Her aura turned a shade of red to match her cheeks. She was nervous. A feeling she probably wasn't used to experiencing.

I jumped in before Bree's silence could get any more awkward. "Bree, this is my best friend, Jasper." I turned my attention to Jasper. "Jasp, this is Bree. She just opened the new yoga studio across the street."

The anxious energy surrounding Bree relaxed a bit, and for the first time since she'd walked into my studio, her expression softened with gratitude. *Maybe there's more behind that snobbish exterior after all.*

"You don't look small-town. Are you a transplant?" Bree asked Jasper.

Okay, I guess I'm wrong. Maybe she's just as vain as she seems.

Jasper's expression twisted with confusion. "Transplant?" He glanced my way, and I shrugged.

"You know," Bree said. "Did you move here from California or something?"

Jasper's amber eyes met mine for an instant, and we shared a hidden smile. If Bree had known where we were both really from, she'd have run screaming from the building.

Jasper winked at me before answering Bree's question. "Not a transplant. Born and raised in our beautiful small town." His answer was a part truth.

"Not to be rude," he continued, appraising Bree's haughty posture, "but why would you open a yoga studio across from an existing one? Everyone who takes yoga in this town already comes to Ev's studio."

Bree recovered from her bout of nervousness, and without missing a beat, she flipped her hair and answered, "Well, I'm sure Ev won't mind if people want to try something a little less ... traditional." She flicked her hand around the room and batted her eyelashes at Jasper. She huffed when she didn't get the reaction she was hoping for.

Bree was definitely not Jasper's type although, based on my brief interactions with her, I guessed she'd find it hard to believe she wasn't anyone's type.

"Bree's right," I offered. "There's nothing wrong with some friendly competition."

Jasper edged closer to my side as he studied Bree. "I don't think *friendly* is in her vocabulary," he whispered in my ear, earning himself a green-eyed dagger glare from Bree.

I nudged him in the ribs with my elbow and added, "Besides, my wait list is always full." I smiled at Bree. "There's more than enough business to go around."

"Great!" Bree announced. "Then I think it's time I go open my doors. May the best studio win." She spun, her heels clicking against the wood floor as she whisked out the door, and left the gift basket and its remaining contents behind.

Luna moved between Jasper and me, and watched Bree go. She glanced up at us like she was thinking the same thing we were: What was that all about?

"Is it just me, or did she seem overly enthusiastic about taking your clients?" Jasper wondered, concern etched upon his brow.

I leaned my head on his shoulder. "Don't worry about her. I won't."

"That girl is trouble," Jasper mused.

I laughed. "You would know. You dated enough like her in high school."

Jasper placed his hand on his heart. "Oh, ouch. Don't remind me. Those days are long past."

"Hi, Jasper," chirped the remaining students in unison as they passed to leave the classroom. They couldn't resist glancing back at Jasper several times before finally turning out of the door.

The laugh I'd held in burst free once the room was clear. "Those days might be long past for you, but you're still the heartthrob you've always been. Why don't you ask one of those nice girls out on a date?" I suggested. "Who knows? Maybe it'll turn into something special."

The smile faded from Jasper's face. "You know why."

A knot formed in my stomach.

I glanced around the studio at everything I'd worked hard to build over the last year, and a crushing weight settled over me.

"Yeah, I know."

ALSO BY S. L. WATSON

Fate of Fury: Vitarian Chronicles Free Short Story
Felix: Vitarian Chronicles Free Short Story
Fate of Blood: Vitarian Chronicles Volume 1
Last Descendants: Vitarian Chronicles Volume 2
Stone of Fire: Vitarian Chronicles Volume 3

Book 4 coming soon